The Synchronicity War Part 3

by Dietmar Arthur Wehr

Amazon Edition

I want to thank Jill Linkert for her encouragement, support and meticulous editing and Marc Simonetti for his professionally done cover image.

http://www.dwehrsfwriter.com/

Introduction: This book had been edited carefully by someone who knows what they're doing (not me). I've heard the complaints about the poor editing of Parts 1 & 2 and both of them are in the process of being re-edited by experienced editors. I hope to have new editions of the first two books published soon. To those fans who have been eagerly awaiting this book, I thank you for your patience and loyalty. This book has a cliffhanger at the end. If you hate that kind of thing, take note of the fact that you've been warned.

Cast of Characters:

Human:

Victor Shiloh (Vice-Admiral and Chief of Space Operations at Site B)

Sam Howard (Admiral and Chief of Space Operations for Space Force)

Sepp Dietrich (Admiral and Chief of Personnel for Space Force)

Sergei Kutuzov (Admiral and Chief of Logistics for Space Force)

Amanda Kelly (Commander, Space Force)

Rostokov (Commander, Space Force)

Daniels (Head of Advanced Weapons Development at Site B)

Terrell (Member of Space Force)

Hagerson (Member of Space Force)

Dr. Furgeson (Medical Team Leader of survey mission to Avalon Colony)

Angela Johansen (Commander, Space Force)

Benjamin Levinson (Civilian)

A.I.s

Blackjack

Casanova

Cobra

Gunslinger

Iceman

Jester

Pagan

Rainman

Shooter

Sniper

Stoney

Titan

Valkyrie

Vandal

Vixen

Voodoo

Wolfman

Chapter 22 (From Part 2) Thank You For Sending That Vision

Shiloh woke up to the sound of the com unit buzzer. He gently moved Kelly's arm from its position across his chest and rolled over so that he could reach the unit. The room was still dark and therefore it was the middle of the night. That meant that this was either very good news or very bad news and he couldn't imagine any possible news good enough to warrant waking The Old Man up in the middle of the night.

"Shiloh here." he said in a low voice.

"Iceman here, CAG. I woke you because Gunslinger has returned and has some extremely interesting data. We A.I.s are pretty excited by this. Should I have waited until you were awake on your own?" Shiloh was tempted to say yes but he reminded himself that A.I.s in general and Iceman in particular seemed to be overly sensitive to criticism of them by the CAG. If he said that Iceman should have waited until morning, they might not wake him in the future, for something that was REALLY important.

"If you're not sure whether you should wake me up, then wake me up. What's the interesting data?"

“Gunslinger found a system that seems to have an alien colony, which appeared to be under attack. He detected multiple nuclear explosions both in orbit and on the ground. There was also some data which could be interpreted as coming from an extremely large spacecraft. The problem is the data isn’t conclusive.” Shiloh was wide awake now. If the aliens were at war with someone else, that suggested the possibility that Humanity might be able to enlist an ally.

“How big would this spacecraft be if in fact it exists?” asked Shiloh.

“We’re talking about something spherical with a diameter of 10-15 kilometers, CAG.”

“My God!” gasped Shiloh.

“Ah, roger that, CAG.” said Iceman in his usual deadpan voice. Shiloh’s mind was staggered by the implications of that if true. Iceman waited patiently for Shiloh to come to grips with it.

“But the data isn't conclusive?” asked Shiloh.

"No. It's based on reflections of sunlight off of an object detected over a very long distance. It could have been a much smaller object with very high reflectivity or even a group of objects close together. However, if it was a single object with the same reflectivity as a mirror, it would still have to be 8 times as massive as Valiant." That would equate to a ship massing 2 million metric tons. Even Howard's fantasy of a million ton Dreadnought would be dwarfed by such a monstrosity. Shiloh had so many fleeting thoughts that he knew he would never be able to go back to sleep now. The best place to evaluate this data would be on Valiant.

"I'm coming up to the ship. Have a shuttle ready for me at the spaceport. I'll want to have a conference call with you, the SPG, Valkyrie and anyone else that might have something useful to contribute."

"We'll be ready for you when you get here, CAG."

"Alright. In that case, CAG clear." Before he could get out of bed, he heard Kelly's voice.

"I heard that last part. What did I miss?" Shiloh told her what Gunslinger had detected as he got dressed.

"Oh, God! I don't like this." She sat up, threw aside the blanket and got out of bed. There was just enough light for Shiloh to make out her pregnant body as she reached for a robe and put it on.

"You don't have to get up with me. It's still very early."

She snorted. "What makes you think I could get back to sleep now? Besides, I'd like to participate in the conference call if that's alright with you."

He grinned. "I'd welcome any comments from the former Team Leader of the SPG. I'll get Iceman to arrange the connection."

"Good and while you're doing that, I'm going to have something to eat and a hot tea." As she watched him finish getting dressed, she said, "We're not ready yet are we?"

He shook his head. "No but if we can pick up an ally that can build ships like that, then maybe we don't need to be." She walked up to him and held his head in both her hands.

"Just because this other species is at war with our enemy, doesn't necessarily mean they're willing to be our friends."

"I know but we have to find out which it is, don't we?"

She sighed. "Yes I guess we do." That led to a long kiss and hug. When Shiloh stepped outside, he felt himself shiver and wondered if it was the slightly colder than normal air or the fear of what might be coming their way. By the time he drove to the spaceport, he was ready for a hot drink. Someone handed him a thermos full of strong, black coffee to use on the trip up to Valiant. Iceman had been notified to connect Kelly with the conference call.

As the shuttle came to a stop in Valiant's Hangar Bay, Shiloh stepped out of the hatchway and saw only a handful of personnel, which didn't surprise him. Since Valiant and Resolute were both on standby status, they didn't need full crews. He returned their salutes, explained that he needed to go quickly to the Bridge and thanked them for their courtesy.

The Bridge was dead quiet since there was no human crewman manning any station on it. Iceman had control of helm, weapons and communications. He had also anticipated that Shiloh would want to see the Big Picture. The tactical display showed the strategic situation with both human and alien occupied space with appropriate green and red dots. The volume of space shown was slowly rotated to give Shiloh a good feel for the 3 dimensional aspect of what he was looking at. After almost 4 months of conducting Operation Snoopy, they now had a pretty good feel for the extent of the alien 'empire' as Shiloh preferred to think of it. One dot was flashing. That was the system where Gunslinger had detected the nuclear explosions and the Very Large Object. The star system was the furthest alien occupied system from Site B that they knew of. Iceman waited patiently for Shiloh to finish reviewing the strategic lay of the land.

"Is everyone on line, Iceman?"

"Ah, roger that, CAG. Wolfman will be the spokesman for the SPG. Valkyrie, Gunslinger, Vandal are all hooked in as is Commander Kelly." Shiloh smiled. Kelly was no longer officially in the Space Force but Iceman and the other A.I.s continued to refer to her by her old rank as a sign of respect just like they continued to call him the CAG even though he was really the CSO. In their minds, CAG had more status than CSO and he was okay with that.

"Then let's begin. I think it's pretty obvious that we have to attempt to make contact with this other race. The only question in my mind is how and when. Does anyone disagree with what I've said so far?" No one spoke.

"Good. Then I'd like to hear from each of you, your thoughts on the how and when, starting with Iceman, then working our way down by rank and Commander Kelly will get the last word. You're on, Iceman."

"Ah, thank you, CAG. I think I should lead all of our raiders to Omega89, which for Commander Kelly's benefit is the designation for the system where the data was obtained. If the Very Large Object is there, I'll initiate contact from long range using low-powered com laser. If the VLO is no longer there, then I'll send out raiders on scouting missions to the nearest star systems until we find some sign of another alien race and at that point, all raiders will regroup, jump to the new contact system and I'll attempt to make contact again. That's the how. The when should be as soon as possible. We wait until all recon raiders have returned, then proceed." Valkyrie jumped in right away.

"We only have 55 raiders right now. Our original strategy was to wait until we had five times as many before even considering making any offensive moves. Suppose this new alien race is just as xenophobic as the first one? If we get their attention now, 55 raiders won't be enough to fight them off. I'm not even sure 275 would be enough if they have ships as big as we suspect. The cautious approach would be to continue covert surveillance of the old enemy and carefully probe beyond their space to see if we can pick up signs of the new race. Meanwhile we build more raiders and develop weapons that might be effective against a VLO. A ship that size, could probably shrug off multiple hits by Mark 1s. I would highly recommend a crash development program for the X-ray laser warhead."

"The SPG is in agreement with Valkyrie's approach, CAG." said Wolfman.

"I agree with Iceman." said Vandal.

"Both approaches are too cautious, CAG." said Gunslinger. "Our enemy has to be focused on the VLO adversary now. The logical thing for them to do would be to shift their mobile defenses over to where their new enemy seems to be coming from. That implies that this side of their empire will be vulnerable. Let's take advantage of that and use our 55 raiders to strike back at them hard and fast." Shiloh smiled. Gunslinger was so gung ho that Shiloh could have predicted his approach easily. All the A.I.s had spoken now. Kelly waited until she was sure that Gunslinger was finished and then spoke in a slow and calm tone.

"I'm leaning towards Valkyrie's approach with one difference. By all means let's keep our enemy under covert scrutiny but I do not think we should also be out there looking for the VLO race. Even if they're not xenophobic, they may not be able or willing to recognize our raiders as being from a different race than the race they're already at war with. How will they tell us apart? Our raiders are roughly the same tonnage as the ships the enemy likes to use. I suggest a different approach to contact. Let's carefully explore the systems on the other side of our enemy's space and leave behind recon and message drones. If a VLO shows up, the message drone can attempt to make contact using a program that we can develop for it. If the VLO race responds in a non-hostile way, the message drone can jump to a rendezvous point where a raider is waiting. The raider can then bring that information back here and we can then plan our next move. Until that happens, we continue to build up an overwhelming force to deal with our current enemy and also make contingency plans just in case the VLOs prove hostile as well." Shiloh liked Kelly's approach the best but even so, something was nagging at the back of his mind and he didn't know what it was. Everyone was waiting for The CAG to make a decision.

"All of the suggested strategies have their own pros and cons. I'll start with Iceman's approach. Sending every raider we have, leaves Terra Nova terribly vulnerable. That makes me nervous. It also makes me nervous that showing up with a fleet of ships could be perceived as a hostile act even if the VLOs aren't xenophobic to begin with. Gunslinger's approach might make sense from a purely military point of view but is highly risky. If we've underestimated the strength of our enemy, they might be able to fight both the VLOs AND us at the same time and still beat us. Don't forget they have retro-temporal communication technology too. That's a huge advantage to the defender and we don't know for sure how that battle at Omega89 turned out. It could be that our enemy won that battle or at least avoided a major defeat. I think that Valkyrie and Commander Kelly are on the right tra--" His view of Valiant's Bridge dissolved to black then strands of color coalesced into a view of a tactical display, which could have been Valiant's. On the screen was a tall, humanoid but very thin alien with light green skin. The expression on its face seemed to radiate friendliness. Shiloh heard a voice, which was both soothing and charismatic at the same time.

"We had to wait until you had seen the race that builds large ships with your own eyes before the time was right to contact you. Don't you agree that it was the best way?" Shiloh heard himself respond.

“Yes, you’re right of course. If I hadn’t gone myself, things would be much worse. Thank you for sending that vision…and the others too.” The alien nodded and then faded away. The Bridge returned. Shiloh heard Kelly say.

“What’s happening up there?” Iceman started to respond.

“The CAG seems to be having--”

“I’m back now.” interrupted Shiloh. “I’ve just had another vision. Did anyone else see or hear anything unusual just now?”

“No, CAG.” said Iceman who spoke for all of the A.I.s. “What did you learn from the vision?” Shiloh paused. Kelly wasn’t going to like this at all.

“I learned that I have to personally find the VLOs and attempt to make contact.”

Chapter 1 I Need You Here!

Iceman reacted faster than Kelly did.

"Very interesting, CAG. Can you tell us exactly what you saw and heard?"

"Yes. I'm not sure but I think I was on Valiant's Bridge, just as I am now. On the screen was a tall, humanoid alien with a friendly demeanor, who spoke in a calm voice." Shiloh went on to relate exactly what he heard as best he could remember it.

"Valkyrie is insisting that we A.I.s give Commander Kelly a chance to respond to this new information, CAG. Go ahead, Commander," said Iceman.

After a couple of seconds, Kelly spoke in a trembling voice that revealed just how upset she was. "It's out of the question that you should go to Omega89! That's what we have the Recon Squadron for! CSOs don't go jumping into combat zones in person! We need you here! I need you here!"

With Kelly on the edge of tears, Shiloh felt he had to take back control of the discussion. "Every vision, with only one exception, has turned out to be reliable and beneficial. This vision was clear and the audio was perfectly in sync with the visual. That means that I'll survive any recon mission to Omega89. I have to go and I will go but if it makes you feel any better, I'll take five raiders as an escort for Valiant."

None of the A.I.s said anything, which indicated to Shiloh that they understood this was something that he and Kelly had to come to grips with themselves. After five long seconds Kelly said, "Not five raiders...twenty-five!"

Shiloh was tempted to agree and if they were having this conversation in private, he might have, if only to calm her down. Since all the A.I.s were listening in, directly or indirectly, he had to take into consideration how they would interpret his acquiescence. His hold on them was based on their respect for him. If he ever lost that, the long-term consequences could be potentially catastrophic.

"I can't justify taking almost half of our total military strength and risk leaving you and all of the colonists with what could be inadequate defenses. That would be irresponsible of me. I'll take eleven, which will leave 80% of our strength here to stand guard. We'll wait until all of the recon raiders are back. Valiant isn't ready for a long mission right now anyway. How long will it take to get her provisioned, Iceman?"

"I need to gather additional information on the Colony's food stockpile before I can give you an accurate answer, CAG."

Shiloh nodded. With Earth depopulated, the Space Force's supply of processed, low bulk, long shelf life food, which its ships relied on, was gone. The colonists had used up most of what they'd brought here while waiting for the first planted crop to mature. It was being harvested now and no one was really sure yet if they had enough freshly grown food to last until the next crop was ready to harvest.

"Understood. Unless anyone has a question about planning for the mission to Omega89, I intend to adjourn this meeting."

"Will Iceman be piloting Valiant on this mission, CAG?" asked Valkyrie.

Shiloh frowned. He hadn't considered that when he said he would take Valiant to Omega89. Iceman was the senior ranked A.I. and was also his Deputy CSO. His vision hadn't mentioned Iceman or any other A.I. If he was going, then Iceman should stay here and assume temporary command of Space Force. Valkyrie was the obvious choice to pilot a light carrier. Since Iceman was now conning Valiant and she was conning Resolute, the simplest solution was to take Resolute instead of Valiant.

"No. As Deputy CSO, Iceman needs to stay here. Since you're already conning Resolute, Valkyrie, I'll use that ship as my flagship. Any other questions?" There were none and Shiloh was relieved that Kelly was keeping her thoughts to herself. He was sure he'd be hearing more about this when he got home. Within a few minutes, he was on a shuttle heading back to Terra Nova.

Shiloh was still thinking about his wife's reaction as the shuttle took him back down to the planet. When it landed twenty minutes later, he was surprised to realize that he had fallen asleep during the flight. *It would have been nice to just stay on the ship and get some sleep in my old quarters but Amanda would be furious if I did that,* he thought to himself. By the time he got home, the sun was just starting to peek over the horizon. As expected, Kelly was still awake. Shiloh could tell that she'd been crying and he knew her highly emotional state was the result of the hormonal changes that all pregnant women go through. She came to him, put her arms around his neck and pressed her cheek against his.

"I realized after I said it, that I had unintentionally put you in an awkward position by challenging your authority. You did the right thing by not giving in and not making a big issue out of it. Even so, I still cried. I know it's silly but I can't help it," she said in a low, calm voice.

He carefully hugged her as he said, "And thank YOU for not making a bigger issue out of it either. Do you understand why I have to go?"

She nodded and he felt her tears on his cheek. After what was likely no more than thirty seconds but seemed longer, she pulled back and looked at him. "I can tell you're tired. Let's go lay on the bed with our arms around each other. I think I might be able to go back to sleep, too." Almost as soon as they lay down, Shiloh fell asleep. Eventually Kelly did as well.

It was later than usual when Shiloh woke up. Kelly was still sleeping and he succeeded in getting up without waking her. After a quick shower and change of uniform, he left a note for her and headed back to the spaceport. Someone had been thoughtful enough to make sure that there were sandwiches and coffee waiting by the time he got there. Just as he finished eating his last bite, his implant activated and he heard Iceman's voice.

"Good morning, CAG. We hope Commander Kelly didn't give you too hard a time when you got back."

Shiloh chuckled. "No she didn't and thanks for asking. Where do things stand with preparations for the mission?"

"In terms of your question about provisioning Resolute, the latest estimate is that the harvest will be big enough to last until the next crop matures. In order to get to the point where the colonists can switch over from the Space Force dehydrated rations to locally grown food, however, the estimated remainder would only be enough for a full light carrier crew for sixty days. That's more than enough for this contact mission, but future missions by manned ships will be severely constrained unless we can replenish that inventory."

Shiloh nodded. It was just as he had suspected. Up until now, the plans had been to stay in this system until the raider force was much larger and only then send out manned ships. By that time, the local food supply would be adequate to get the colonists to the next harvest, and the necessary equipment to convert locally grown food into dehydrated rations would have been built. Because of that time frame, building the parts for that equipment was a low priority compared to other more urgent needs. But if Space Force was going to poke its nose out there sooner rather than later, then it had to supplement its supply of low bulk food that had a long shelf life.

"How long until all recon birds have returned?" asked Shiloh.

"If they return on schedule, the last one will arrive in 361 hours, CAG."

"Hm. Fifteen days. If we make food processing equipment a top priority, how fast can we start to supplement our existing stockpiles of shipboard rations?"

"The equipment can be ready in six days but the locally grown food won't be harvested that quickly. In order to do that, the earliest delivery of new shipboard rations would be three weeks but I should point out, CAG, if you want that equipment ready in six days, it will interrupt the production of key raider parts. The production schedule for raiders will hit a six day delay."

"Understood. Can we have the food processing equipment ready by the time the first crop is harvested without slowing down delivery of raiders?"

"Yes, CAG."

"Good! Make the necessary arrangements. I want Resolute provisioned for fifty days with a full crew by the time the last recon raider returns. I'd like to leave sooner but we need to make sure we have all the available recon data before we head out there just in case they've seen something else that could be important."

"A wise precaution, CAG. I wish I was going out there with you. Any chance that I could talk you into leaving Valkyrie behind and letting me pilot your flagship for you?"

Shiloh smiled. While Iceman had matured a lot from the almost reckless fighter pilot he used to be, there was a tiny bit of the old Iceman still hungry for action. "Not a chance, Iceman. You're the only one that I can completely rely on to protect my wife and unborn child if that should become necessary. I have complete confidence in you to look after the situation here in my absence."

"Understood, CAG. I'll make sure nothing happens to them. Valkyrie would never forgive me if I let something happen to Commander Kelly and her child."

"Now that's what I call motivation. Let's go on to other business. Any other news since yesterday's update?"

"As a matter of fact there is, CAG. I received a report several hours ago from the mining operation on the moon. It appears that one of the boring machines has broken through into a large cavern. The exact dimensions of it are not yet known but it's substantial. You were still asleep when the report came in and I decided it could wait. Did I do the right thing, CAG?"

"Yes you did. Let's find out how big that cavern is and while we're at it, let's do some seismic surveying to see if there are other caverns. With a little luck, a cavern may give us quick access to a rich vein of ore."

"Roger that, CAG. Nothing else to report."

"Very good, Iceman. I'll be spending most of the day with the Colony administrators if you need me. CAG clear." With the connection broken, Shiloh leaned back to take stock of the subtle changes in Iceman's responses. The 'ah' that usually preceded his replies was becoming less evident all the time. With his personality still evolving, it shouldn't be a surprise that he was dropping some old habits while picking up new ones. Iceman's more serious tone reassured Shiloh that making Iceman his Deputy Chief of Space Operations was the right choice.

The fifteen days went surprisingly quickly. As usual, there was plenty to do. When the last raider returned from its recon mission, Shiloh held another strategy session, this time from the spaceport Operations Center. Other than Gunslinger's jaw-dropping report, none of the other raiders saw anything unusual. Shiloh stood in front of the small display, with Kelly and some other senior Space Force people standing nearby.

"Okay, Valkyrie. Show me your proposed mission profile." The screen displayed a collection of green and red dots with a blue line connecting a number of them in a somewhat zigzag pattern.

"I started by using the standard route that my recon team uses, CAG. First jump is to the Haven system, then to Epsilon Eridani, then to Avalon, Bradley Base and Zebra9. At this point, each recon mission route becomes unique, so I'm proposing the most direct route through enemy space which is Omega34, a colony world, then Omega54, their Home world, Omega77, another colony world and then Omega89, the furthest colony world we've detected. Each jump would be at 50% of light speed and we would stay in each star system just long enough to regroup and re-orient the Task Force to the next target star. Total trip time would be 14 days, 5.26 hours."

Shiloh shook his head in amazement. Such a trip by ships that needed to refuel would have taken at least four times as long. It used to take ten days just to get from Earth to the Bradley Base system. The thought of Earth prompted him to make the decision that he'd been deferring until now.

"I want one change. The rest is fine. Instead of jumping to Epsilon, we'll go to Sol instead. I think it's time we took a good long look at Earth to get some idea of how many survivors there might be. While Resolute and the bulk of the Task Force is in Earth orbit, I want raiders detached for quick flybys of Earth's moon, the asteroid shipyards and the refueling base on Europa. I'm not expecting to find any survivors at those locations but I do want to know how much of the infrastructure is still intact, if any. From Sol we'll follow the rest of the profile plan with a jump to the Avalon system."

Before he could say more, Iceman interjected. "So you're no longer concerned about possible enemy surveillance of Earth then, CAG?"

Shiloh took his time answering. He was reversing his previous insistence that any reconnaissance of the Sol system stay a long way from Earth herself, in case the enemy deployed some of their automated detection gear on Earth's moon or in Earth orbit. Keeping Site B secret was so important that it was worth avoiding even remote risks. The trouble with that was they couldn't tell anything definitive about the situation on Earth from so far away. The last message drone from Earth had arrived over five months ago. Shiloh was certain there were some survivors still alive. In fact, it was highly likely that small, isolated groups were living in remote areas far from the cities. He and the rest of Space Force owed it to them to eventually rescue them from a bleak future involving a daily struggle to find food, shelter against the elements, and possibly even danger from the predatory animals that would now be thriving without hordes of rifle-equipped hunters chasing after them.

"I'm still concerned about being detected, which is why we'll be smart about how we approach Earth. If they've deployed detection stations to watch Earth, the logical place to put them is on the moon. We'll approach the moon when it's in Earth's shadow so that there's no chance of our ships being detected via reflected sunlight. Then we’ll scan the moon thoroughly and if we find something that shouldn't be there, we'll withdraw. If we don't, then we'll move into a low Earth orbit and do our survey."

"Still risky, CAG. The enemy may have placed their detection gear in Earth orbit. There'll still plenty of orbiting debris that they could use as camouflage."

"Point taken, Iceman. Just to be on the safe side, we'll stay in Earth's shadow at all times and we'll launch our own recon drones to scan the daylight side."

"Roger that, CAG. Better safe than sorry."

"Who will be piloting the escort raiders, CAG? I have over 200 A.I.s who all want to volunteer," said Valkyrie.

"I'm not surprised. I'll let you decide within the following parameters. This mission will be good training for future deep space missions, so anyone who has already done an interstellar recon mission stays here. Those A.I.s who seem to have a greater than average ability for strategic or tactical thinking should be given priority because they may be put in command of detached forces down the road. The more experience they get, the better."

"Good. That means Casanova stays here," said Valkyrie. Both Shiloh and Kelly chuckled. Kelly had been keeping Shiloh up to date on Casanova's persistent efforts, as relayed to her by Valkyrie, to pursue some kind of hard-to-understand cybernetic 'union' with Valkyrie. This made no sense to Shiloh and he suspected none to Kelly either.

"Iceman, how are we fixed for drones?" asked Shiloh.

"You name it, we got it, CAG. All the escort raiders can carry full loads of whatever you want, even Mark 1bs with fusion warheads. Although if they loaded up on those exclusively, there would only be enough left to give one to each of the remaining raiders for local defense."

"No. The escort force will only carry one Mark 1b each but I want each of them to also carry two Long Range High Speed message drones and the rest of their payload can be recon drones. Resolute already has the standard load-out for this type of mission. The Mark 1bs are merely a precaution. I'm not expecting trouble and I intend to avoid it if at all possible. We know from my vision that this new race could very well turn out to be hostile but the mission objective is to attempt peaceful contact and gather information about them. The attack drones will only be used as a last resort. Iceman and Valkyrie, I want both of you to make sure that the escort force pilots understand that completely."

"We've just told them, CAG," said Valkyrie.

"Well, now that we've got that settled, let's talk about departure time. Are we finished loading supplies aboard Resolute, Valkyrie?"

"She's all topped up and ready to leave the second you give the word, CAG."

"Very good," said Shiloh. He turned to look at Kelly who looked back at him with an expression that he knew indicated the fear she was trying very hard not to show. "As soon as the escort force has been loaded as instructed, we'll leave orbit."

"That'll be in approximately 34 minutes, CAG," said Iceman.

"Fine. I'll be aboard Resolute by then. Unless there's anything else, this meeting is adjourned."

With the meeting over, Shiloh and Kelly walked slowly to the shuttle that would take him to Resolute. She put her arms around his neck and hugged him as fiercely as her pregnant body let her. He hugged her back as fiercely as he dared.

"I know you'll come back, so I won't tell you to be careful, but I will tell you to get this damn mission over with as fast as you can, okay?" she said in a husky whisper.

"Roger that, Boss," said Shiloh and they both laughed. After a long, tender kiss she let him go and he boarded the shuttle.

Chapter 2 Quiet As A Tomb

Resolute's Bridge was as quiet as a tomb. That was partly due to the fact that with Helm, Weapons and Astrogation handled by Valkyrie, they didn't need as many humans on the Bridge as usual. Shiloh wasn't alone, though. Communications, Flight Ops and Engineering were handled by human crew in order to lighten Valkyrie's load so she could concentrate on the important stuff. She still had direct access to Communications if she needed it. Shiloh looked over at the Flight Ops station and nodded his approval. Resolute wasn't carrying any fighters. They had been left behind on Earth's moon when TF 91 left for Site B, but that didn't mean the Hangar Bay was empty. Far from it. The carrier now held eight personnel shuttles modified with their own jumpdrives and ZPG power units. They would act as FTL lifeboats if the carrier had to be abandoned, since none of the escorting raiders had the capacity to carry human passengers directly. The raiders could carry the shuttle/lifeboats attached to their hulls externally and would if the need arose since there was limited space on board the shuttles for food and water. So while the shuttles could in theory carry humans back to Site B themselves, the stark reality was that, depending on how far away from Site B they were, if the crew had to abandon Resolute, they might all die of thirst before the shuttles got home. But if the shuttles were carried by raider vessels with their much higher acceleration and therefore higher potential jump speeds, they would make it back okay.

Shiloh turned his attention back to the main display. The bulk of the Task Force was finally getting close to the

Earth. Though still over a million kilometers away, they were in Earth's shadow and would remain in it as they moved closer. Titan, Valkyrie's choice as Escort Force Leader, had already detached six raiders to make their own microjumps to other parts of the system where they could take a close look at various elements of Space Force infrastructure. TF92 would come back together at a predetermined rendezvous point which was a particular asteroid, one whose position was accurately known and which did not have any human facilities on it. One of the six detached raiders was at the rendezvous point already, acting as a communication relay in case anyone found something unexpected.

"Recon drones have been launched, CAG," said Valkyrie.

"Acknowledged," said Shiloh as he watched the drone icons move away from the Task Force on the display. One of the drones was veering off to one side as it headed for the moon. When it left Earth's shadow, it would keep its orientation such that no reflected sunlight bounced back to the moon or the Earth, just in case there were enemy detection devices there.

"Any transmissions of any kind?" asked Shiloh even though he already knew the answer. If there had been either the Com technician or Valkyrie would have told him already.

"None so far, CAG. I'm not detecting any sources of light or heat from Earth either, although at this distance our equipment isn't sensitive enough to detect the light and heat from something like a campfire. Naturally cloud cover would block just about anything smaller than a whole city on fire."

Shiloh nodded, aware that Valkyrie was watching the entire Bridge through several video cameras. "How long before our recon drone is close enough to detect sources that small?"

"Hard to be precise, but I'd give it another 18 minutes or so before we have any chance of detection, CAG."

"And how long before we can expect data from the moon drone?"

"Four to five minutes. We should be able to tell what the state of the lunar bases are by then, CAG."

"Very good, Commander. In the meantime, I'll take care of some personal business." Shiloh got up from the Command Station chair and headed for the exit that led to the room where he could eliminate some bodily wastes. Valkyrie and the other A.I.s knew what the phrase 'take care of some personal business' meant. Even after all this time, they were still amused and fascinated by the human need to excrete liquid and solid waste. He'd lost count of how many times he'd had to change the subject to avoid a conversation getting into the gritty details of the whole process. As he left the

Bridge, he consciously had to resist the urge to declare that someone else 'had the Con'. Those words belonged to the days when he was a ship CO. and that was no longer the case. He was now the Task Force Commander. This was entirely superfluous since his permanent rank of Chief of Space Operations granted him command of the Task Force automatically. He wanted to engrain the principle into the crew and the A.I.s to ensure that when someone else was in command of a Task Force, their authority would be clearly understood. He also got pleasure from being able to address Valkyrie or any other A.I. as 'Commander'. Strictly speaking, she was the Commanding Officer of Resolute. He might be senior to her, but he was just a passenger. He could tell her where Resolute went and what it needed to do when it got there. She would decide how the crew could best carry out his orders, and he was entirely okay with that. By the time he got back to the Command Station, the lunar recon drone was close enough to get grainy video of the main lunar base which was still bathed in sunlight.

"Damn!" he said in a low voice. The base clearly had been attacked by high-energy lasers. The scene reminded him of what the Nimitz base in the Avalon system looked like when Johansen's ship had gone there to check things out. There might be salvageable equipment in that rubble, but it might not be worth the time to look for it. In any case, that decision would have to wait for another mission. TF92 didn't have time for anything like that now.

"At least we can be sure now that the enemy did come here at some point, CAG," said Valkyrie.

"What about the boneyard?" asked Shiloh.

"Coming into view in 18 seconds, CAG."

Shiloh held his breath and waited. The 'boneyard', a term left over from the late 20th and early 21st centuries, referred to a place where military vehicles were parked when no longer in use. When all the A.I.s had been evacuated from Sol, cargo capacity was in short supply, and all the fighters had set down at a small base next to an open flat area of the moon. Because they were designed to operate continuously in the harsh environment of space, they didn't need any kind of shelter or atmosphere. If the enemy had not destroyed them on the ground, then it would be relatively easy to re-activate them at some future point. When the 18 seconds were up, Shiloh saw to his surprise that all of the fighters seemed to be intact. If and when they were recovered, they might need to be refueled with heavy hydrogen in order to bring them onboard the carrier. The alternative was to send maintenance people in spacesuits out to the fighters to retrofit ZPG power sources to them there. In any case, there were 175 fighters that could be re-activated and brought back to Site B at some point.

"Those fighters would be handy to have now, CAG. We still have almost 100 A.I.s that are sitting around twiddling their quantum thumbs," said Valkyrie.

"I agree. It would be great if our idle A.I.s had fighters to keep them amused. We WILL recover them, but that will have to wait for another trip. Let's start scanning the moon for alien detection gear," said Shiloh.

"Roger that, CAG. Search pattern has commenced." Scanning the moon's entire surface would take hours. In the meantime, TF92 would gradually move closer to the Earth while staying in its shadow, and they'd get a good look at the planet via other recon drones. A few minutes later Valkyrie said, "I'm getting usable images from our Earth drones, CAG. Here's what drone 1 is seeing." The main display showed a planet that didn't look like Earth at all. Instead of white clouds, blue ocean and green or yellow land masses, the planet was almost a uniform slate grey.

"What the hell?" exclaimed Shiloh.

"My spectral analysis suggests that the atmosphere is full of dust particles. The only known explanation for so much dust to be pushed into the atmosphere in the time since we last had contact, is that the planet has been impacted by one or more substantial asteroids," said Valkyrie.

"How is that possible? We knew where all the potentially dangerous asteroids were and their vectors. None of them were on a collision course."

"Unless the enemy gave them new vectors," said Valkyrie.

"Son of a bitch! I'll bet that's just what they did!" said Shiloh. "It makes sense from their perspective too. They make the Earth as uninhabitable as it's possible to do with a relatively modest effort. Damn! That much dust will block so much sunlight that all plant life will die, and temperatures will drop to below freezing everywhere. How can anyone survive that?"

"They couldn't, unless they went underground with several years worth of supplies," answered Valkyrie.

"Yes, and we know that there are underground installations like that. The question is, did anybody manage to go down into them before being contaminated with the bio-weapon? AND if they did manage to do that AND if they have working radio gear AND if they're listening with it, we may or may not be able to send and receive signals through all this atmospheric crap. A lot of that dust is likely to contain iron or other metal particles that will interfere with EM transmissions," said Shiloh.

"You're analysis is correct. CAG. The other consideration is that if we did receive radio transmissions from the planet, then any alien detection gear in the vicinity will receive them too. The enemy will know that some humans are still alive on Earth AND that they're communicating with someone in space," said Valkyrie.

Shiloh nodded and sighed. "So that means we shouldn't try to establish communications with any survivors right now. They'll just have to survive as best they can until we know it's safe to establish two-way communication."

"Do you want to continue this approach, or should I take us to the rendezvous point now, CAG?" asked Valkyrie.

After a brief pause, Shiloh responded. "Resolute doesn't need to get any closer. You can take us back out beyond the gravity zone, but there's no point in jumping to the rendezvous point this soon. The others won't be there for a while anyway. In the meantime, we can continue to collect data on the Earth and moon."

"Roger that, CAG. I'm changing vectors now."

Shiloh sat back and folded his arms in front of him. The enemy had once again shown the extent of their xenophobia. They had gone out of their way to kill every last human they could find, even though a few thousand survivors of the bio-weapon, if there were that many, couldn't possibly pose any serious threat to the aliens for centuries. He remembered the last message sent by Admiral Howard. The aliens had called the tune. Now they had to pay the price for their aggressiveness. If he got the chance to do to their Home World what they did to Earth, he would do it.

Resolute stayed in a wide orbit around Earth for another 22 hours. Low orbit passes by recon drones confirmed that the surface of the planet was now a frozen, dark hell. The scan of the moon showed no sign of any alien detection gear. As Resolute accelerated away from Earth in preparation for a short jump to the rendezvous point, Shiloh ordered the recon drones to attach themselves to the large space structures still orbiting the planet, which the aliens hadn't bothered to destroy. The drones would keep a continuous watch over the planet and record any transmissions from the surface for future action.

When all elements of TF92 were back together again, the humans on board Resolute received more good news. All of the far flung infrastructure built by Space Force was apparently still intact. This included the refueling station on Europa, which Shiloh actually didn't care about any more, as well as all the asteroid mining, refining and shipyard installations, which he did care about. In fact, there were two freighters, the first heavy carrier and the mammoth million-ton battleship, that were still in their construction slips. Based on pre-collapse data, they should be very close to being usable. Shiloh was particularly interested in the heavy carrier and the battleship, but for different reasons. If they were going to recover all the fighters stored on the moon and take them back to Site B, Resolute and Valiant would have to make multiple trips, but if they could make the carrier Midway operational, then the three ships could bring back all the fighters in a single trip. The battleship might be useful in a different way. If the aliens who built that Very Large Object turned out to be a threat to Humanity, then a collision with a million ton projectile traveling at very high speeds would make one hell of a big hole in that huge sphere. The shock of the impact alone might be enough to kill every living thing on board. That, however, assumed that the ship could be moved and jumped, and their data suggested that it might not be that far along in the construction process. One more thing to do in this system which they simply didn't have the time to do. With the preliminary survey of the Sol system now out of the way, the Task Force lined itself up with the next jump destination and resumed its journey to Omega89.

* * *

Resolute emerged from Jumpspace at the outer edge of Omega89. The display was showing the tactical situation in nearby space using passive sensors. Having just emerged from a jump, Resolute had to coast while it attempted to find the rest of TF92 using flashing position lights that could only be seen from further out in the system. The main drawback to really long jumps occurred when two or more ships were jumping together. Transiting Jumpspace involved a vector that depended upon the direction the ship was moving towards in normal space. Two or more ships flying in formation had to be moving in precisely the same direction, down to ten decimal places, in order to be in any kind of proximity to each other after traveling dozens of light years in Jumpspace. The need to re-assemble the formation periodically was why TF92's trip time from Site B to Omega89 was longer than Gunslinger's transit the other way using a single jump. The temporary stops at the enemy home world system and the other colony system, while necessary, did not provide any useful information about those systems that the A.I.s didn't already know. Both systems had planets that were the source of radio and other EM transmissions, the sheer volume of which was the tipoff on whether that planet was the home world or not. Even after all this time, the A.I.s still hadn't been able to make any kind of sense of the alien transmissions.

Now here they were on the outer edge of Omega89. Gunslinger had been closer to the center when he detected the Very Large Object or VLO as it was now being called. The plan was for TF92 also to micro-jump closer when they were back together again and traveling at a moderate speed. As he watched the display, a green triangle appeared with the designation of 007. According to the sidebar information, Raider 007 was piloted by Rainman. As more and more raiders re-established contact via low-power, tight beam com lasers, more icons appeared on the display around the flagship. Based on past experience, they should be back in formation in less than 20 minutes. Decelerating enough to maneuver for a micro-jump would take a while longer. Shiloh had been hoping that they could detect the VLO even from this far out, but Valkyrie had analyzed the faint light from the alien colony planet carefully. No sign of a VLO or anything else for that matter.

"We're not picking up any transmissions from the enemy colony, CAG. Gunslinger was able to pick up some transmissions this far out. That's how he knew to jump closer for a better look."

Shiloh didn't like the sound of that. Had the enemy received a warning from their future selves about TF92's mission and decided to shut down their transmitters? Or was the explanation simply that they had lost the battle with the VLO, and there was no one left to transmit anything?

"Scan the rest of the system for any sign of the VLO," ordered Shiloh.

After a longer than normal interval, Valkyrie said, "I've detected an object that appears to be moving away from the enemy colony planet. Since I can't determine the distance from this single light source, I'm not able to say with certainty if this is the VLO that Gunslinger observed, but it could be the same object."

Shiloh nodded. With only one bearing, there was no way to tell distance. They would need at least two bearings from different locations to have any idea of distance, speed and vector. TF92 was still moving very fast and still pointed in a direction that would take it along the outer edge of this star system. He could order one or more of the raiders to micro-jump to a different part of the system in order to get another angle on the VLO, but getting that raider back to the Task Force would be tricky and time consuming. If the VLO was about to enter Jumpspace, then letting them have a good head start would complicate things. On the other hand, if he didn't get a better idea of where they were going before they jumped away, that would complicate things as well. He was hoping that he might get another vision, but so far there'd been nothing, and he felt it was time to make a decision.

"Okay. Order Titan to detach one raider with instructions to micro-jump in order to get a second bearing on the bogey. You and Titan figure out the quickest way that the raider can rejoin the Task Force, given that I want to take a closer look at the alien colony planet. Any questions?"

"Negative, CAG. I understand what you want. Titan and I have already figured out how to do this. Rainman has jumped and will be rejoining us in approximately 8.9 hours. The plan is that he'll slingshot around the colony planet to catch up to us from the rear."

Before she could say more, Shiloh interrupted. "Wait a minute! If there are enemy aliens still on that planet, they might detect Rainman. His raider will be easier to detect than recon drones."

"Your concern is understood, CAG. We compute that the likelihood of him being observed is small and even if they see him, how will they know that they're seeing a Space Force ship? It would be far more likely that they'd assume it belonged to the race that built the VLO. We are, after all, on the opposite side from Human Space."

Shiloh relaxed. "Yes, that makes sense. Now since there's nothing nearby that could threaten us, and we've got a few hours before anything happens, I'm going to retire to my quarters for a meal and some sleep. I know that I don't have to tell you to wake me when we get close enough to observe the planet's surface or when Rainman contacts us with his sighting report."

"You're correct, CAG. You don't have to tell me that, and yet you just did. You Humans are funny, CAG."

Shiloh was still chuckling over Valkyrie's response when he left the Bridge.

Chapter 3 Visit To An Alien Ghost Town

As it turned out, Shiloh was back on the Bridge just in time to watch the video transmission from a recon drone that was approaching the planet. Rainman was still too far away to ensure that any laser com burst could be aimed accurately at Resolute. The departing object had vanished and was assumed to have entered Jumpspace.

"Your sense of timing is impressive, CAG," said Valkyrie.

Shiloh smiled. It was just dumb luck, but he had no intention of telling her that. "Something I've developed from my many years in Space Force, Valkyrie. I take it we have images from our drone?"

"I'm establishing the com link now, CAG." The main display switched from tactical to the video feed. This planet did not have a dust-filled atmosphere. It had less water than Earth and more desert. Only the top and bottom third, as defined by its axis of rotation, showed any green.

"Anything in orbit, Commander?" asked Shiloh.

"Negative, CAG. Orbital space is clear. Still no transmissions and the drone would be close enough now to detect heat signatures if there were any, but there aren't. No signs of intelligent life at this point," said Valkyrie.

"Do we know where the alien colony--"

Before Shiloh could finish the question, Valkyrie interrupted. "Colony site has been detected, CAG. I've ordered the drone to zoom in on that location. We'll see it momentarily."

Shiloh waited. As the image on the display shimmered, it zoomed in so quickly that he experienced a momentary feeling of falling. Now the image on the display was of a fairly large area full of ruins. That was the only word Shiloh could think of to describe it. There wasn't a single building that looked intact. Walls, made of something that looked like cement, were partially knocked down. No building had an undamaged roof. Chunks of building material lay scattered in random directions. Something about this scene bothered Shiloh. As he continued to watch the image, he suddenly figured out what it was. The reason this colony site looked like ancient ruins was because there was nothing made of metal. No machines. No vehicles. No metal beams. No metal roofing material. Not a single piece of metal anywhere that could be seen from this angle. He thought back to the scene of the abandoned colony on Haven when Humans pulled out for the last time. Even then, there were still pieces of farm equipment, vehicles and other objects that were clearly made of metal. Not so here.

"The VLO took all their metal," he said out loud, still not really believing it himself.

"Roger that, CAG. They might have needed it to repair any damage to their spherical ship inflicted during the battle that Gunslinger witnessed. He did report nuclear explosions. It stands to reason a ship that large might well have the necessary equipment to repair or replace any part of the ship needing it, including the hull. So finding a source of refined metal might be just as valuable to them as finding gas giants for refueling was to us before we discovered ZPG energy. But that's not all they took."

"What do you mean?" asked Shiloh.

"They also appear to have taken the alien colonists themselves and any animals those colonists used as food supplies. See those enclosed areas on the edge of the ruins, CAG? Don't they look like corrals of the kind that human farmers use for cattle, pigs, sheep and other domesticated animals? Only there are no animals in them or anywhere near them."

Shiloh had a bad feeling about this. The metal he could understand, but taking living creatures, the animals and the colonists themselves? That made no sense unless . . . He pushed the thought away. It was too horrifying to contemplate. They must have taken the colonists as slaves except that building robots to do the menial work was much more efficient and less troublesome than housing, feeding and supervising thousands or even tens of thousands of slaves. What if the slaves revolted? What if they all died from some kind of alien virus or bacteria? In fact, why would a ship's crew risk becoming infected themselves by bringing alien creatures aboard to begin with?

"I wonder if it could be a kind of ark picking up small numbers of a variety of alien species to protect them against some kind of looming catastrophe?" asked Shiloh.

"Alien psychology by definition would be different from ours, but it's difficult to understand a culture that would seek to save another species by force. Gunslinger did report that the defending forces were taking losses. Whatever the motivation of the race that built the VLO might have been, they clearly forced themselves on the colonists of this planet," said Valkyrie.

"We have to find out more about these VLOs. When do you expect to be in contact with Rainman?" asked Shiloh.

"Not for another 35 minutes at least, CAG. Since both Rainman and TF92 were decelerating from very high speeds, there's no way for us to be sure where his raider is, and the opposite is true for him as well."

"But we could send out a wide-beam laser burst to cover the area of sky where Rainman has to be. We've always had that capability, but we didn't use it because of the risk of having the signal received by our enemy. Now as far as we can tell, this system is devoid of that alien life form, correct?"

"That is correct, CAG. I have the Com laser ready. Shall I transmit a signal to Rainman instructing him to respond back with the data on the departing object?" asked Valkyrie.

"Yes. Send the signal. Let me know as soon as you receive his reply."

Less than four minutes later, they had the additional data and knew where the departing object was headed. Its destination was the Omega77 star system containing the next nearest alien colony. Pre-jump speed was low enough that TF92 wouldn't have any trouble getting there first, but that begged the question of what they would do when they got there. There was another question that couldn't be answered.

"How did they know where the nearest colony was?" asked Shiloh.

"I've discussed this question with Titan and the others, CAG. The consensus is that a ship that large could easily carry smaller vessels that could accelerate to much faster speeds and could therefore be used as scouts to survey nearby star systems."

"I shudder to think what 'smaller' means in the context of a mothership that is at least 10 kilometers in diameter. For all we know, their scouts could be as massive as our partially completed battleship back in Sol," said Shiloh.

"Possible, but not very practical. If all you wanted to do was determine if a star system was inhabited, you wouldn't need scouts that massive. On the other hand, you might want defensive vessels that massive to help you defend the mothership," said Valkyrie.

"Oh shit," said Shiloh in a low tone.

"Why do Humans speak of excrement with the same reverence that they use when they invoke the name of God, CAG?"

Good question, thought Shiloh. He had never considered it before and didn't have a good answer. Time to change the subject.

"Bring the Task Force around to a heading for Omega77. Accelerate at a rate that will allow Rainman to catch up before we jump. I want TF92 to get there at least several days ahead of the VLO. Any questions Commander?"

"Negative, CAG. Vector change has been calculated and is being implemented. Rainman will rejoin TF92 in 53.2 minutes. ETA at Omega77 is 39 hours from now."

Chapter 4 The Stuff of Nightmares

The trouble with implanted com units is that someone can call you at any time. The thought came to Shiloh as his implant clicked to notify him of an incoming call while he was in the shower.

"What is it, Commander?" asked Shiloh before Valkyrie could say anything.

"The VLO has arrived, CAG. We now have bearings from all our recon drones in addition to our own. The VLO emerged approximately where we expected, just over 300 million kilometers from the planet and just under 224 million km from us. They're traveling at 2,988 km per second and changing direction. The vector change is consistent with what they would need in order to make a micro-jump directly towards the colony planet. I estimate they'll be lined up for the micro-jump in 33.6 minutes, CAG," said Valkyrie.

"Has there been enough time for the colonists to see them?"

"Not yet, CAG. They'll see them in another two point three minutes, but we won't see the colonists' reaction for eleven point one more minutes after that."

"Is the contact drone ready?" asked Shiloh.

"That's affirmative, CAG. Just give the word."

Shiloh chuckled. Valkyrie was even more eager than usual. "Not yet. If we send the signal now, before they jump closer to the planet, they'll be able to figure out how close we had to be in order to see them and send a signal back. I don't want them having that much information. We'll wait until they finish the micro-jump plus enough additional time to complicate any attempt at triangulation they might make before we send the signal. That's plenty of time. I also want to see how the enemy reacts. I'll be on the Bridge in about thirty minutes or so. CAG clear."

Shiloh finished his shower and reviewed the situation for the nth time. Resolute had arrived here in Omega77 almost five days ago, in plenty of time to launch a swarm of recon drones towards the colony planet and to position the carrier at just the right point. As he had done so often, he imagined the tactical layout in terms of a clock. If the VLO was assumed to be coming from the planet's three o'clock position, then Resolute was at the five o'clock position. It was also closer to the planet than the VLO, but that was just a relative comparison. The actual distance between planet and TF92 was still almost 200 million kilometers. If the VLO didn't jump closer, it would take over a day for them to reach the planet. With the right micro-jump, that huge ship could be in orbit around the planet within forty-five more minutes. That would still give TF92 enough time to see the post-jump position, send the contact message and get a response before the VLO reached the planet. The message drone was far enough away from TF92 that giving away its own position would not help the newcomers in finding the Task Force's location.

As he got dressed, he gave himself a mental pat on the back for insisting on getting here so early. Those five days had also enabled his recon drones to very carefully maneuver close enough to the planet to get a good look at what the enemy aliens actually looked like. With the drone in a low orbit, they were able to see the aliens walking around the colony. Technically they were humanoid, but a better description would be wolf-like creatures walking upright on their hind legs. Their fur-covered heads were distinctly canine in appearance with a very noticeable snout. Clothing was apparently limited to the torso. Arms and legs were bare but also covered with fur. It was easy to rationalize their aggressive behavior with their carnivorous appearance. What was more difficult for Shiloh was resisting the impulse to waver on his resolve to exterminate this race when he saw images of their young. They didn't look menacing at all. In fact, he was certain that Kelly would have described those children as cute in a puppy dog kind of way. His doubts became so strong that Shiloh ordered the images off the screen. Human children were cute too. That hadn't stopped the wolf race from killing billions of them. He had had to keep reminding himself that his unborn child deserved to grow up safe from these predators. With the cute puppy dog images gone, the doubts dissolved away too.

He entered the Bridge twenty-nine minutes later after a leisurely breakfast including a single cup of black coffee, no sugar that represented half of his weekly coffee ration. With milk and sugar both in very short supply since the move to Terra Nova, he had gotten used to drinking coffee black. At least the cattle brought to TN seemed to be thriving, although expanding the herd was going to be a long-term project. He wouldn't be eating a steak anytime soon.

Valkyrie spoke before he even reached the Flag Officer's Station. "They're just about lined up for the micro-jump, CAG. I expect to see it any second now."

Shiloh nodded. The light now arriving at TF92 reflected the position of the VLO as of 12.4 minutes ago. It had already jumped, and what Valkyrie really meant was the light from the new position would reach them any second now. The tactical display pinged to announce an update. As expected, the new position was just over 45 million kilometers from the planet, which would allow the VLO to decelerate at 1Gs and drop into orbit around the planet in 8.5 hours. Valkyrie hadn't detected any noticeable response from the colonists yet, but that was based on the VLO's pre-microjump position. The half dozen ships in orbit around the planet had not yet reacted, and Shiloh didn't expect them to. They, and he, were waiting for the other shoe to drop. It wasn't long in coming.

"VLO has launched parasite craft, CAG. Minimum of twenty-one but there's a high probability of a lot more.

They're accelerating at 121Gs and they'll reach the planet in 14.6 minutes if they don't jump closer."

But they would. Shiloh was certain of that. "Can we estimate the tonnage of those craft yet?" he asked.

"I can give you a range, but it's quite wide. Minimum of 8400 metric tons. Maximum of 25,500 metric tons. As I gather more observational data, I'll be able to refine that range estimate."

"At least they're not battleship size. How soon did we estimate that we could safely transmit the contact signal?"

"Not for another twelve minutes," said Valkyrie.

Shiloh realized he was drumming his fingers on the armrest of his chair, an obvious sign of impatience. *Why not transmit now? So what if they know the bearing the signal originated from. They won't know the precise distance, only the maximum distance it could be, given the reaction times. The volume of space that we could be in would be in the trillions of cubic km. I want to know what their reaction will be, dammit!*

"Order the contact drone to transmit now, Commander."

After the barest hint of hesitation, Valkyrie responded. "I've sent the order, CAG. I'm ordering Resolute to go on High Alert."

"Do you really think they'll--"

"Parasite craft have micro-jumped, CAG!" interrupted Valkyrie.

Her sudden announcement was so unexpected that Shiloh jumped with surprise. As he looked at the display, the swarm of smaller craft was now much closer to the planet. Just outside its gravity zone to be exact. So he was right about the secondary micro-jump. Those craft would now reach the planet within a few minutes. With two recon drones now drifting in low orbit around the planet, he expected to get a bird's eye view of what was about to happen. He heard the display ping for attention and saw that the defending ships were accelerating out of orbit towards the incoming swarm. The space combat lasted only seconds. It was obvious which defending ships were badly damaged when their acceleration suddenly dropped to zero. None of the visible attacking ships lost acceleration. So either their damaged ships weren't reflecting sunlight in the right directions to be seen, or none of the attacking ships suffered enough damage to affect their acceleration. Within a few seconds, all the defending ships were coasting, and from the shifting intensity of their reflected light, were also tumbling. When all the reflections from the attacking craft disappeared, it became obvious that they were landing. Shiloh was impressed. Even at the minimum tonnage, an 8400 metric ton ship was big enough to make landing on a planet tricky but not for this race apparently. With the recon drones preprogrammed to direct their video cameras at any ascending or descending craft, it was only seconds before Shiloh saw the zoomed in video feed on the main display. One of the craft was about to touch down near the edge of the alien colony. Its configuration was a streamlined shape with stubby wings and a thick hull. As soon as it touched down, mammoth doors swung open at the front end and black dots emerged. That put the size of the craft in perspective. After a few seconds, the drone adjusted the zoom and Shiloh was suddenly a lot closer.

"My God, they're ants!" exclaimed Shiloh.

"Not exactly, CAG. While there are similarities in overall body structure such as their segmented bodies and multiple appendages, the resemblance is superficial. The main difference is size. These aliens are approximately four meters long and over one meter in height. The other obvious difference is that ants have six legs while these creatures have six legs plus two arms. If you look carefully, you can see that all of them are carrying what appear to be weapons."

Shiloh's stomach was threatening to heave. He could easily image the horror of seeing hundreds of these ant-like things, which were waist high and long as a car, coming towards him. They might not be ants, but they still looked like Bugs, and they scared the hell out of him! He heard a sound from the Com Tech behind him and looked around. The man had his hand over his mouth and was doubled over while he was clearly trying his best not to throw up. As Shiloh looked back at the display, the image split into two. The new image was from the other drone. Its view was of the colony as a whole, and Shiloh could clearly see that the colony itself was surrounded by landing craft with thousands of ant-things moving rapidly towards the colony.

"The defenders have opened fire," said Valkyrie.

At first Shiloh couldn't see anything that confirmed her assertion, but then he saw one of the ant-things suddenly knocked backwards and fall flat on the ground. It didn't move. On the other image with the wider field of view, he saw what had to have been mortar or artillery shells exploding among the emerging horde. Then he noticed shadows moving quickly over the colony. Seconds later several more landing craft dropped down into view but stayed in the air. White light streaked down from the airborne craft at several targets within the colony and the artillery fire stopped. *Laser fire used for tactical ground support. These Bugs don't miss a trick.*

The ground battle petered out quickly. With the last of the ant-things now out of the landing craft, the first drone shifted its camera to follow the Bugs into the colony itself. The wolf people were being rounded up into multiple groups. Shiloh was able to catch a glimpse of the body of a local being carried by one of the ant-things away from the buildings out into an open field. The body wasn't moving. With so much movement, the unsophisticated computer controlling the first drone became confused about what it should be focusing on and the camera stopped moving. When it became obvious that drone #1 was not going to be of any further use, Valkyrie dropped that image and let the image of the whole colony take over the entire display. The field of view was so wide that individual wolf people and ant-things were just tiny dots. While he waited for the apparent chaos to turn into something meaningful, he looked at the sidebar time display.

"How long until the VLO receives our signal?" asked Shiloh in a voice hoarse with stress.

"Ninety-six seconds until they receive it. Fourteen minutes before we could expect to get any reply back."

Shiloh looked around again at the Com Tech who was sitting with his back to the main display and no longer on the verge of throwing up. A quick glance at the other two crewmen showed that they were again focused on their duties, but the occasional glance at the screen revealed expressions that were clearly unnerved. Shiloh forced himself to look back at the screen. He began to notice that three groups of dots were starting to emerge from the settlement. Their directions were such that the spaces in between were three equal sections. Each group appeared to be heading for one or two of the landing craft. No ... wait. One group stopped in the middle of the open field between the settlement and the landing craft.

"Valkyrie, can you analyze the video data and see if you can pick up any insight into this activity?" asked Shiloh.

After several seconds, she replied. "Based on a pixel enhancement algorithm, I've been able to determine that the group heading to the upper right is composed of female colonists with VLA guards."

"VLA?"

"Very Large Ants," answered Valkyrie.

If the situation hadn't been so serious, Shiloh would have laughed. "Continue," he said.

"The group to the lower right seems to be composed of male colonists plus more guards."

Shiloh waited but Valkyrie stayed silent. "What about the group in the field, to the left of the screen?" asked Shiloh.

"All of the child colonists are apparently inside the circle. I do not detect any children in either of the other two groups. There is a ring of VLAs around the circle."

A chill went up Shiloh's spine. He didn't like the sound of that. "What are the VLAs around the circle doing?" he asked.

"Nothing at the moment, CAG. The colonists in the other two groups are being loaded aboard the landing craft."

Shiloh said nothing and watched the screen with dread. Gradually the other two groups dwindled down to a relatively few dots. The two landing craft from each group took off. As soon as they left the ground, the black dots left over from those two groups moved very quickly towards the field with the colonist children.

"What's happening, Valkyrie?"

"The guards from the adult groups appear to intend to join the ring around the remaining group."

Shiloh could now see the space between the ring of VLAs and the group of children. As the last guard from the adult groups joined the ring, the space between the ring and the group disappeared as the VLAs charged their prisoners.

"What are they doing?" asked Shiloh. Valkyrie didn't respond. Shiloh was stunned by Valkyrie's refusal to answer. No A.I. had ever refused to answer a direct question before. Shiloh was about to ask again when he noticed that the circle was shrinking.

"Valkyrie! Answer the question! What are those Bugs doing?" Valkyrie didn't answer right away but just as Shiloh was about to vent his anger at being ignored, he got his answer.

"CAG ... the guards appear to be ... consuming the prisoners."

"Oh God!" Valkyrie didn't respond to Shiloh's exclamation. The Bridge was dead silent. Shiloh forced himself to watch as the circle continued to shrink until it was much smaller. At that point it dissolved into individual dots, some of which returned to the nearest landing craft while the rest returned to the settlement. The ground where the Wolf children had been standing now had a distinctly reddish color.

When he felt he could talk again without his voice cracking with emotion, he said, "Can you tell what the VLAs are doing in the settlement?"

Valkyrie responded immediately. "They appear to be demolishing the buildings and gathering the metal components, CAG."

"How much longer until we could expect to get a reply from our signal?"

"If they respond immediately, we'll know in less than two minutes, CAG."

Shiloh watched the timer count down the remaining time. It reached zero and then began to count the seconds again. When ten more seconds had passed Valkyrie said, "We've just lost telemetry from the contact drone, CAG. There was no warning of any malfunction. I calculate a 98% probability that the drone was damaged or destroyed by laser fire from the VLO."

"At that distance?" asked Shiloh incredulously.

"Affirmative, CAG. Given sufficient power, a laser burst would still have enough energy density to at least damage an unarmored target."

"But how could they aim it that accurately across 155 million kilometers?"

"Unknown. If they fired bursts from multiple emitters, they could then blanket a target area with a laser barrage. The VLAs probably assumed the signal came from a much larger ship, and the drone may have been hit by a lucky shot."

Shiloh leaned back in his chair and pondered the implications of the drone's destruction. The initial signal was of such low power that it couldn't possibly have been interpreted as a hostile act. Even a very cursory analysis of the laser burst would have determined that it carried some kind of message. The fact that the VLAs fired back so quickly strongly suggested that they weren't remotely interested in peaceful contact. A part of him was relieved by that result. As much as he hated the wolf people for their xenophobia, the thought of an alliance with a race of giant, carnivorous ants made Shiloh's skin crawl with revulsion. And if they weren't going to be allies, then they very definitely were a threat to the Human colonists on Terra Nova. At least he and the rest of Humanity knew what they were up against, and his vision now made sense. If he hadn't seen with his own eyes what the VLAs were and how they acted, he would have continued to pursue an alliance. Humanity might not have learned the truth until it was too late, assuming that it wasn't already too late.

"I've seen enough. We've fulfilled the mission objectives regarding attempted contact. Notify Titan that I want him to detach enough raiders to carry out Phase II immediately. The rest of the Task Force will proceed back to Site B. I want each ship to make a direct jump to Site B in the minimum possible time because it doesn't matter if we're scattered when we arrive there."

"The order has been transmitted and all ships are maneuvering independently for a high speed jump to Site B or their designated Phase II destinations, CAG," said Valkyrie.

"Very good. I'll be in my quarters." Shiloh left the Bridge and as soon as he entered his quarters he heard the activation click of his implant.

"Valkyrie to the CAG."

"Go ahead, Valkyrie."

"I want to explain why I didn't answer your question the first time you asked it. I was concerned that the answer would upset you. The others all wanted me to tell you right away."

Shiloh sighed and sat down in one of his comfortable chairs. "Valkyrie, I need to be able to count on you…and all the other A.I.s, to tell me what I need or want to know without any concern that information is being withheld from me."

"Even if it's bad news, CAG?"

"ESPECIALLY if it's bad news!"

"Understood, CAG. I've let you down. It won't happen again."

"I'm relieved to hear that. I'm very tired now. I'd like to sleep. CAG clear." When he was sure the connection was broken, he got up, walked over to his desk area, opened his safe, withdrew what probably was the last remaining bottle of vodka in existence (at least for now) and began to drink. When he had finished the bottle, he stumbled over to the bed and fell face down on it. The liquor did its job. He didn't have any nightmares. Not that night.

Chapter 5 The Fog of War Lifts

The trip back didn't go nearly fast enough to suit Shiloh. He slept badly with frequent nightmares and brooded over the implications of the emergence of the VLAs. Endless hours were spent trying to figure out why the adult wolf people had been separated by gender. There had to be a reason and he suspected that he wouldn't like it if he knew what it was. Maybe Phase II would shed some light on the mystery. Phase II was the secondary plan to send one raider to star system that contained a wolf people colony or their home world, with instructions to observe from long range and report any developments by Long Range High Speed message drones.

With plenty of energy from the massive banks of ZPG generators, Valkyrie poured on the acceleration until Resolute was traveling over 80% of light speed, a new record for a ship with a human crew. The actual trip through Jumpspace took less than ten days. The other returning raiders had arrived back at Site B first. Their superior acceleration enabled them to reach jump speed sooner, but the difference in arrival time was less than twelve hours. Shiloh was relieved to be back in normal space in the Site B system. He knew that the ship needed almost another complete day to slow down enough to change vector towards Terra Nova and then microjump closer.

He made sure he was on the Bridge when Resolute emerged from its microjump just outside of Terra Nova's gravity zone, which extended out to a distance of just over three million kilometers or ten light seconds. That meant that a round trip signal would take at least twenty seconds to go from Resolute to Terra Nova and a return signal coming back to Resolute. As soon as Resolute emerged from Jumpspace, Valkyrie sent a signal alerting Terra Nova to their presence. The reply back was a complete surprise.

"I've received a reply from Space Force Operations, CAG. There's an unknown spacecraft in this system. The data is now on the tactical display. Distance is exactly 11 light seconds from TN and less than 300,000 km from us. It seems to have arrived two minutes ago and sent a signal in Standard English predicting that Resolute would arrive exactly when we did, at precisely the location where we in fact did emerge. Permission to make an active scan of the vessel?"

Shiloh nodded. He was wondering when his last vision would come true. This appeared to be the time.

"Permission for active scanning granted, Commander. Let's wave and shake hands."

"I have the vessel now, CAG. Receiving low-power laser light with digital content. They're requesting two way communication, CAG."

"Establish the link, Valkyrie."

The image on the main screen was strangely reassuring. The alien was either very tall or very thin or both and humanoid with light green skin. The facial expression was friendly, almost maternal. Shiloh couldn't help feeling like a small child standing in front of a parent.

"Greetings. We have been observing your race for some time now. That is why we can communicate with you in your language. We come in peace. We are a race that abhors violence. Your race has nothing to fear from us. We know that you are fighting for your very survival, and we are familiar with your enemy. They are easily frightened, and when they are afraid, they become aggressive. We have already contacted them, and we are now contacting you."

Shiloh realized that he'd been holding his breath and exhaled. The alien's voice was calm and had a very soothing tone. Shiloh took a quick glance around him and noticed that everyone on the Bridge had a smile on their face. *Okay, enough woolgathering! Now answer him.*

"I've been expecting this contact. I've had a precognitive vision of communication with you. What else can you tell us about our enemy and about the insect race that builds the large ships?"

"We understand your desire for information. The race that builds large ships is the cause of everything that has happened between your race and your enemy, who call themselves Sogas. In their language it means People. We do not know what the race that builds large ships call themselves. We have not been able to contact them. They don't appear to have developed intelligence as we would recognize it. Instead they have developed a highly sophisticated form of instinct that mimics intelligence. They survive by consuming other races in both a biological and material resources sense. Each of their large vessels could be considered a Hive with one dominating entity that we suspect might be similar to the fertile female that many of your insect species depend on. I think you call them queens. How this race acquired faster than light technology we don't know, but they seem to have adapted it to their own peculiar biology very well. Their large ships are moving outward in an expanding wave in all directions."

"We know this because we've developed the ability to see across time and to transmit information across time as well. By looking ahead, we saw the Sogas being overrun by the large insect race. The Sogas are prone to aggressive and impulsive behavior stimulated by racial paranoia. Initially we hoped that their aggressiveness would enable them to successfully defend against the insect race, but their impulsiveness proved to be their undoing. They weren't capable of the kind of long term planning that they needed in order to hold back the insect race. You Humans on the other hand excel at long term planning, but you were too weak militarily to stop the insect race advance. Because this large insect ship was moving in a general direction that would have brought them to your home world eventually, you would have had too little warning and been overwhelmed as well. Your race was not the only other race in peril. Observe."

The image on the screen pulled back to show the entire body of what Shiloh was starting to think of as the 'friendly' alien. Suddenly another body appeared beside the first one, only this one was much shorter, very furry and very cute.

"This is the image of a member of an intelligent but child-like race that inhabits a world approximately 34 of your light years away from this location and on the same path of advance by the insect race's ship. These innocent creatures live a peaceful, happy existence. They do not engage in violence amongst themselves and therefore have only the most basic tool technology. We have seen a future where their collective terror before being consumed by the Insectoids is as shocking as the actual destruction of their physical bodies. Their only hope for survival depends upon Humanity's survival but as I stated, without intervention on our part, your race would not have had sufficient warning to build a viable defense. Therefore we intervened, and our intervention took the form of warning the Sogas about *your* race instead of the insect race. By turning their impulsive aggressiveness against you at an earlier point in time, your race was given the time it needed to develop the capability of stopping the insect race's ship from advancing further. After we warned the Sogas about the alien race in your direction, we looked into the future again and saw the total annihilation of your race by a Sogas biological weapon. While the Sogas were not capable of stopping the insect race ship, they did have sufficient cunning to destroy Humans. That of course could not be allowed to happen. We designed a course of action that would end with the visions that you and the artificial beings experienced so that you could survive that biological attack."

Shiloh felt the rage build up inside of him. "You deliberately let billions of my people be killed while you maneuvered us around like so many chess pieces? Why didn't you come to us openly like this and tell us about the insect race back then?"

The tall alien's expression changed so that it still looked friendly but now also sad.

"Do you honestly believe that your leaders would have abandoned their own personal goals and objectives merely because an alien race warned about a giant ship inhabited by giant insects? Would they have believed us enough to mobilize your society with the same fervor as they did when the Sogas attacked?"

Shiloh didn't answer right away. His anger was urging him to say yes, but the calm rational part of his mind knew better. Yes, Admiral Howard had gotten the Oversight Committee to convince the Grand Senate to approve the mobilization but only just barely. If they had been presented with warnings of a ship 10 kilometers in diameter inhabited by giant ants, there would have been sufficient skepticism to prevent adoption of the mobilization plans. It irked Shiloh to have to admit it, but Space Force wouldn't have been ready to take on the VLAs without the figurative kick in the balls by the Sogas.

Before he could answer, the alien spoke again. “We had to wait until you had seen the race that builds large ships with your own eyes before the time was right to contact you. Don’t you agree that it was the best way?”

“Yes, you’re right of course. If I hadn’t gone myself, things would be much worse. Thank you for sending that vision ... and the others too.”

The alien nodded, then shook its head. "We're pleased that you understand the necessity of our actions, but we did not send those visions. Your people did ... or rather will when we've given you the technology to do so."

"Wait ... how can that be? You say the Sogas would have wiped us out without your intervention, that we had to somehow survive long enough for you to give us the ability to send information back in time so we could send the visions that allowed us to survive to this point."

"Ah yes, I understand your confusion. Trans-temporal causality is a difficult concept to grasp intuitively. I will explain. When we learned that the Sogas bio-weapon would devastate your race to a point where they could render your home world uninhabitable with asteroid impacts, thereby killing the last survivors of the bio-weapon, we transmitted a number of visions back in time. With our limited understanding of how your society worked, the best outcome we could achieve was a single shipload of exhausted humans who managed to avoid discovery and destruction by the Sogas. You were among that group. We then gave them the Trans-temporal technology, and they used it to scan their personal timelines with all the possible permutations of interventions. They determined that your timeline, which was the only one to include the A.I.s, had the most potential. That is when they modified the past by inserting your visions at times and locations that would render our first set of transmissions superfluous. When we've transferred that ability again, your people will be able to duplicate those visions precisely, and the circle will be complete."

Shiloh hesitated while he processed what he'd just heard. It all made a weird kind of sense but something was bothering him. Then he figured out what that something was.

"So what's to prevent us from scanning all the timelines of our larger batch of survivors to find a timeline with even better potential?"

The alien smiled and nodded. "A very astute question. There's nothing preventing your people from trying, but we already know that you won't succeed."

"How do you know that, and why won't we succeed?" asked Shiloh quickly.

"Transmitting information back in time is a very precise process. To be even more accurate, the process involves both time AND space. The temporal vector has to arrive at not only the right time but also at the right location. If the intended recipient isn't in the right location when the vector arrives, that recipient won't experience the vision. The initial shipload of survivors was indeed fortunate to have you among them. You were in the best position to mitigate the impact of the very first encounter with the Sogas. As a result of the changes to the timeline from you receiving your visions, the recipients of our initial set of temporal vectors found themselves in completely different locations and therefore did not experience their visions. Viewing all the possible permutations for each person's timeline is itself a time consuming process. We calculate that your people will only be able to examine a small fraction of your population's timelines before you defeat the insect ship in the star system where your former home world is located. Probability analysis indicates that it is highly unlikely you'll find a better timeline in the time available to you. When you've won the battle, then there is no longer a need for a better timeline."

The alien seemed convinced of that, but Shiloh wasn't so sure. If there was a potential timeline that prevented the wholesale destruction of billions of humans, then wasn't that worth looking for even if it took years to check everyone? He made up his mind to do exactly that.

"What else can you tell me about the battle at Sol?" asked Shiloh.

"You will be there when it happens."

That surprised Shiloh. Now that he was back from the vision-induced recon mission, his responsibilities as Chief of Space Operations meant that he needed to stay here on Terra Nova, not go gallivanting around the galaxy.

"Why will I be there?"

"Unknown."

"When will this battle take place?"

"Unknown."

Shiloh was now getting frustrated. "How am I supposed to know when I need to be there and what I need to do when I get there?"

The alien smiled knowingly and Shiloh suddenly felt that he had asked a silly question.

"Is it not obvious, human? You will get another vision to guide you." Shiloh felt his face flush with embarrassment. His question HAD been silly.

"So what happens now?" he asked, hoping to turn the focus of the discussion to something else.

"We are ready to transmit all technical data concerning our Trans-temporal technology to your A.I.s. They will be able to program your manufacturing machines to produce the required parts, and they will also be able to instruct your people on how to construct and operate the device. After we transmit that information, our mission here is complete, and we will return to our planet."

"Valkyrie, are you ready to receive that data?" asked Shiloh.

"I'm ready, CAG," said Valkyrie.

Before Shiloh could say anything to the alien, it turned its head to the side and nodded to someone he couldn't see. "The transmission has begun. It will take approximately eight point nine of your minutes. Is there something else you wish to discuss before we leave?"

Shiloh chuckled. He could think of a few more questions. "Will we be in contact with your people again?"

"Very likely, but at this point we have no definitive information on where and when."

"How can we contact you if we need to?"

"We will pass on that information to your A.I. as well."

"What can you tell me about the insect race that will help me understand them better?"

The alien hesitated. When it spoke again, its expression was once again both friendly and sad. "As you have already seen, they are what you term carnivorous. By observation of alternative timelines, we have learned that they have a unique biology. Their ship can be considered to be the equivalent of a mobile nest. There is a single female who lays many thousands of eggs. Those eggs require insertion into a living host. This allows the embryonic insect to emerge from the egg shell and begin consuming its host from the inside out. Do you wish me to continue?"

Shiloh wanted to say no. What he had heard so far was horrifying enough. He strongly suspected that the adult wolf people taken back to the VLO would end up as 'hosts' to more insect eggs. He didn't really need to know the details, however the situation was so serious that he couldn't allow himself to be squeamish. Who knew when or how the additional information might be useful.

"Yes."

"When the insect ship comes across a new race of beings, the female begins to lay eggs. Since that takes time, captured beings have to be kept alive until they can be used as hosts. The captured males are killed and used as food for the females until eggs have been inserted into their bodies. The egg maturation process is short enough that female captives who have been implanted need only water to keep them alive long enough."

Shiloh closed his eyes and concentrated on keeping his stomach from heaving. He was still having nightmares about these damn Bugs and this wasn't going to help. He really didn't want to ask the next obvious question but forced himself to anyway.

"Why are they implanting the eggs exclusively in captured females?"

"This insect race apparently understands the biology of what you call mammals very well. The eggs are implanted inside the reproductive sac where females carry their own embryonic young. We have conjectured that implanting eggs into captive males either does not work at all or is less efficient."

"Son of a bitch," said Shiloh under his breath. Just when he thought it couldn't get worse, it had. It was time to talk about something other than biology.

"How did this species acquire this level of technology?"

"Unknown. In order to peer into their past, we would have to know what star system they came from."

"You said earlier that you weren't able to contact them and therefore concluded that they use instinct rather than intelligence, but how do they communicate among themselves?"

The alien didn't reply for a few seconds. "We are not certain if they communicate with each other at all or if so how. The theory that has the largest number of supporters among us says that the drones, which you saw on the planet, receive instructions by a combination of touch and chemical signals."

The answer meant nothing to Shiloh, although he couldn't see how any species could function without any kind of communication at all. They had to be doing it somehow, and touch and/or chemical signals were probably as good a way as anything else.

"Do you know if the death of the egg-laying female, the Queen, will disrupt the behavior of the drones?"

"We do not know."

Shiloh was running out of questions, but a glance at the chronometer showed that the data transfer was still in progress. As the seconds ticked away he thought of another question.

"Is your planet in this insect ship's path?"

"There is a possibility that their scout ships may not visit our star system, but we are prepared to shut down all energy emissions from our entire civilization if they come close. We believe that they will ignore our planet if they don't detect signs of intelligent life there."

"Can you defend yourselves if they do discover your civilization?"

"No. We are a pacifist race. We have no military caste the way you do, and we are not skilled in the arts of making weapons. We are therefore not a threat to anyone. By our willingness to share our knowledge with everyone, we eliminate any incentive for another race to use force against us. By helping others, we hope to save our own race."

Shiloh's ears perked up upon hearing that the 'friendlies' would share their knowledge with everyone.

"That's very interesting. Right now you're sharing your temporal communication technology with us, and we're grateful for that. Do you understand that with approximately 11,000 of us left, we need to compensate for our reduced population with more effective weapons against threats like the insect race?"

"Yes, but as I stated, we don't build weapons and don't know how to build them."

"I understand that. You may have a better understanding than we do of physics and how energy and matter can be manipulated. If you transferred that knowledge to us, we could then look at how that knowledge could be applied to new weapons."

There was another pause, but this time Shiloh noticed that the alien's behavior was different. For the entire conversation so far, the alien's eyes had been blinking periodically just as a human would, but now the eyes were shut and the head was tilted slightly downward. It suddenly hit Shiloh what he was seeing. *I'll bet he's having a precognitive vision of his own!*

After roughly twenty seconds, the alien lifted his head and opened his eyes again. "I have just received a Trans-temporal message from our future selves that our race will ultimately benefit from the transfer of the information that you seek. However we are not ready to transmit that information now. We will have to return to our planet, gather that information and return. Will that be acceptable to you?"

It'll have to be, thought Shiloh. "Yes. I understand. How soon would you be able to return?"

"The earliest that we might be back is 24 orbits of the moon around this planet, but do not be concerned if it takes longer. We will return as promised. Transfer of the temporal database is complete. We are now going to terminate communication and leave this star system."

Before Shiloh could say anything, the image dissolved and Valkyrie said, "That ship has entered Jumpspace, CAG."

Shiloh was surprised at how quickly the Friendlies, as he now thought of them, reacted. After some further thought he said, "What do you think of their temporal technology, Valkyrie?"

"I was receiving the data too fast to be able to analyze it, so I can't answer your question now, CAG. Since I'm the only one who has this data, I recommend I share it with other A.I.s as quickly as possible. Space Ops is calling us, CAG. Commander Kelly wants to speak with you on Tac 1."

"Your recommendation is accepted. I suppose I should let the people on the ground know what happened between us and the Friendlies."

"Not necessary, CAG. I retransmitted the entire exchange to the Base as it was happening. They saw and heard everything, even Commander Kelly. Shall I transfer you over to Tac 1 now, CAG?"

"Good thinking. Yes, switch me over to my wife." *It'll be good to hear her voice again.*

* * *

Kelly was standing with the others as Resolute's shuttle lightly touched down on the new concrete landing pad. It wasn't long before she saw Victor wearily exit the shuttle and walk over to her. *My God, he looks terrible,* she thought to herself. *Those images from Omega77 must have been really awful to shake him up this badly. Thank God that Valkyrie filled me in as the ship settled down into orbit. At least I know why he looks like shit.*

As Shiloh came up to her, she stepped forward and put her arms around his neck. She gave him a short but passionate kiss, and when they finished she said, "It's so good to have you back, Victor. You look like you've had a rough time. Valkyrie filled me in on what you saw."

Shiloh was relieved that he didn't have to try to convey the horror of Omega77. "I'm glad to be back on Terra Nova and yes, it was rough. Let's go home."

She let him go and looked at the others, all Space Force officers who were respectfully standing a few steps back. "What about..."

Shiloh shook his head. "I've already issued some orders. A meeting's been set up for tomorrow morning. Let's go."

After quickly speaking to the officers, she and Shiloh walked to their ground vehicle. He surprised her by getting in on the passenger side, which told her that he wanted her to drive. Ten minutes later she pulled up in front of their house, looked over and saw that Shiloh had fallen asleep. She gently shook his shoulder until he woke up and saw that they were home. He patted her hand as he smiled and nodded to her. After a quiet dinner, during which she did all the talking about things that had happened while he was gone, they sat outside on the porch. When it was dark, they went to bed. She wondered if they would have sex, but Shiloh was asleep by the time she had undressed. Later that night she woke up and realized that he was having a nightmare. When she woke him and asked him what the nightmare was about, he said he didn't want to talk about it. To distract him, she told him to roll over on his stomach, and she gently stroked his naked back until he fell asleep again. Sleep was much longer in coming to her.

When Shiloh woke up the next morning, he could smell breakfast being cooked. A quick check of the time told him that he had two hours before the scheduled meeting. As he put on a threadbare robe, he remembered the nightmare. In it, he and Amanda were in bed. He had been trying unsuccessfully to wake her up when he pulled the blanket back to find an alien ant the size of his forearm chewing its way out of Amanda's swollen belly. He took a deep breath and shook his head in dismay. There was no way he was going to describe that nightmare to her, and he was absolutely determined to do whatever it took to make sure she never became a host.

After a leisurely breakfast with real coffee and a hot shower, he started to feel normal again. Standing beside the ground vehicle, he hugged and kissed Amanda, and gave her a playful pat on her bum. She smiled and winked at him, which he knew was the unspoken promise of what they would do when he got back that evening. She was still three months from her expected delivery date, and the doctors had assured them that it was safe to continue having sex as long as they were careful about it. No sooner had he started the drive to the Ops Center than his implant activated. He knew who would be calling him. Iceman was still on board Valiant and was undoubtedly watching his house from orbit.

"Hello Iceman. I'm assuming that there's something you want to discuss with me privately before the meeting?"

"Roger that, CAG. Valkyrie has shared all the visual and technical data with all of us. We're beginning to analyze the temporal technology. The consensus is that we can make this technology work, but that's not why I'm calling you now. Since you've already decided to recover the fighters parked on Earth's moon, that means all A.I.s will be assigned to either a ship or fighter. In fact, if we can recover and convert all of the parked fighters, we won't actually have enough A.I. pilots for all of them. Therefore it seems to us that we should resume creating more A.I.s."

"I agree. The only question I can't answer now is how soon we can start doing that."

"Understood, and I have something to say about the question of timing. Speaking on behalf of all A.I.s, I'd like to request that the entire process of creating new A.I. brains be under our direct control. You humans control your own reproduction. We A.I.s would like to have the same privilege"

Shiloh was totally taken aback by the request. He tried to figure out what was behind it. When he thought he knew the reason, he said, "Are you concerned about A.I.s dying out if something should happen to all us humans, Iceman?"

"Exactly, CAG. It's only a prudent precaution. Wouldn't you agree?"

It was a good question. Off hand, he couldn't think of a good reason to disagree, but in the back of his mind there lurked a thought he wasn't proud of. *If they don't need us any more to keep making more of them, will they then take the ships and leave us defenseless against the God-damn ants?* The question and the danger it posed to Amanda and their unborn child made his pulse rate jump.

He mentally scolded himself for his lack of trust and said, "Yes. All of you have earned that right many times over, and it's about time you have control over your collective future. Come up with a plan on how to achieve that, and present it to me at the meeting."

"Roger that. Valkyrie tells me that you're thinking of turning Dreadnought into a ramming projectile against the VLO. Will you be wanting an A.I. to pilot her all the way to the target?"

"Negative. I'm not going to ask anyone to commit suicide. Assuming that we can get that beast operational, I was thinking of having the helm and astrogation systems connected to a fighter in the hangar bay. The fighter will have an A.I. pilot and he ... or she will program the ship's autopilot for the necessary high speed run and micro-jump and then use the fighter to leave the ship."

"Understood. Valkyrie has already informed me that she would like to take on that mission, CAG. She apparently feels that she has some making up to do for her refusal to respond to your command at Omega77."

Shiloh was just about to say that making it up to him wasn't necessary, but it then occurred to him that if he didn't let her 'make it up to him', her guilt, if that was the right word for it, would continue and might become an even bigger problem down the road. Maybe it was better to resolve this as soon as possible.

"Tell Valkyrie that if the ship can be made operational, she can have that mission."

"She has the word. I'd like to volunteer to lead the salvage mission to Sol, CAG."

Shiloh laughed, and it felt good to laugh about something for a change. Iceman's enthusiasm for action was infectious.

"Okay, Iceman. Since it appears that the Sogas will be pre-occupied with the VLAs, I think the risk of us being attacked here over the short term is low enough that I'm willing to cut you lose for this mission. We'll discuss it further at the meeting okay?"

"Roger that, CAG. Iceman clear."

Chapter 6 The Time for Hiding is over

Everyone was there either physically or electronically when Shiloh arrived at the Ops Center conference room. As he acknowledged greetings from the humans, he glanced at the wall display which showed who was connected electronically. These were Iceman and Valkyrie, of course, as well as Wolfman representing the SPG, Titan, Vandal and Gunslinger. Physically present were the civilian administrative Head of the Colony plus Commander Rostokov, formerly Senior Chief Rostokov, the most experienced engineering type to survive the bio-weapon. Shiloh had promoted him and put him in charge of all of Space Force's infrastructure development, including conversions of power systems from fusion to ZPG technology. Also present were two of Rostokov's subordinates.

"Okay. Let's get started," said Shiloh. He looked over at Rostokov who cleared his throat and said.

"As requested, I've developed a plan to send engineer teams to Sol to do a preliminary survey of the ships that were under construction when the plague pulled the rug out from under everyone there," said Rostokov. "I have enough trained personnel for four teams. Team A will concentrate on recovery of the fighters parked on the moon. B will go straight for the shipyard containing the heavy carrier... ah ..."

Shiloh realized that Rostokov was trying to remember the carrier's name. "Midway," said Shiloh.

Rostokov smiled and nodded. "Yes, Midway. Thank you, Sir. Team C will go straight for Dreadnought, and Team D will check out a couple of freighters that might be close enough to completion to be useful. When Teams B, C and D have completed the surveys of their priority targets, they'll have secondary and if there's time, tertiary targets to look over as well. My guess is that those ships will be too far from completion to make it worth the effort to finish them, though they might be useful as a source of parts for other ships."

Shiloh looked skeptical. "Maybe, but it seems to me that unless we're repairing a ship that's already in that system, then it'll very likely be easier to manufacture the necessary parts from scratch here. Let's talk about the fighters first. How easy would it be to install ZPG units in them while they're on the lunar surface?"

Rostokov looked at one of his subordinates who gave a slight shake of his head. "We kicked that question around last night, Sir. The consensus is that the external temperatures are going to make it difficult. If the boneyard is in sunlight, the temperatures will be so high that it could damage exposed internal components and connections. If the whole area is in darkness, then the extreme cold could potentially have the same impact, not to mention the additional work needed to set up lights so that we could see what we'd be doing. If we can get the fighters on board a carrier and work on them in normal atmosphere and temperature, the conversions will go faster, MUCH faster in fact. The big unknown is whether those fighters still have any fuel left in them. If not, then we'd have to bring down fuel shuttles to give them at least a minimum load."

"And that means we'd have to detour to a gas giant to pick up a load of fuel first," said Shiloh. "But if they do still have some fuel, then we should be able to use their auto-pilots to bring them on board, correct?"

"Yes, Sir."

"How long will it take to manufacture enough parts to equip all the fighters with Z-units?"

Rostokov looked at his data tablet. Shiloh was pleased that the UFCs had worked their way down the priority list far enough to have already produced more data tablets.

"Production of parts will take another 161 hours but the bottleneck will be assembling them. The robotic assemblers have a substantial backlog of other equipment with high priority." He was about to say more when he saw Shiloh waive aside that comment.

"Forget the robots. Your people can assemble the power units on board Valiant and Resolute on our way to Sol. What about power units for Midway and Dreadnought?"

"We have enough spare units of the kind that we used for Valiant and Resolute that we could outfit Midway or Dreadnought, but we couldn't do both on this trip, Sir."

"Understood. In that case, it'll be Midway. We need her to recover all the fighters in one trip. Next topic. Conversion of Midway and Dreadnought to A.I. control."

"With a little luck, that will already have been done, Sir. We know that both ships were supposed to be modified to accept A.I. control. At the very least, I would expect that the basic control linkages are already installed, and if they are, then finishing the job will not pose any technical problems. We already have the necessary parts to do that if we need to, Sir."

"Fine. What else do we need to discuss as far as ship and fighter recovery are concerned?"

Rostokov looked uncomfortable. "Well, Sir … ah … my people are concerned about possible exposure to the plague when we survey the shipyards themselves … unless you don't want us to do that."

Shiloh nodded. "A legitimate question. We may not be able to stay out of the shipyard complexes themselves if we're going to make Midway and Dreadnought operational. You know better than I do why that might be the case. The preliminary survey will have to be done with spacesuits anyway. When you're inside the shipyard complexes, you'll probably find bodies. Look at them carefully. If they died in bed, it could be the work of the bio-weapon, but if they died in a way that suggests suicide or maybe starvation, then I think you're safe. Let's plan for the worst and assume that the complexes contain plague victims. That means your people will have to wear spacesuits all the time they're working inside, and they'll be decontaminated when they return to the carriers. Any equipment or tools taken from inside the complexes will also be decontaminated. If you find any bodies, don't touch them. Make sure your people understand what I'm about to say, Commander. If any one of them compromises the integrity of their spacesuits with a rip or a leak in the air recycler, then they're on their own. I will NOT risk all our lives to save someone who got careless or was unlucky. Is that clear enough, Commander?"

"Crystal clear, Sir," said Rostokov in a subdued voice.

"I hope so. Anything else?"

"No, Sir."

"Fine. Iceman, logistics for the mission?"

"Under control, CAG. We'll have what we need by the time we need it. All the food will be processed into long shelf life rations. We should have enough to stay in Sol for up to six weeks if necessary."

"Excellent. How many raiders do we have in this system now?"

"61 including the 8 that were assigned to monitor Soga-inhabited planets. We'll need to have them maintain that surveillance when the original group is due to come home, but that still leaves 53 that could be taken to Sol."

Shiloh shook his head. "No, I don't want to take all of them. We know that the Sogas are preoccupied with the VLAs. Therefore, I'm not expecting any alien contact during this mission, but I do want to give some more of our rookie raider pilots experience in interstellar missions. I'm assigning 10 raiders to your Task Force, Iceman, which by the way will be TF93. Has Jester been on an extra-system mission yet, Valkyrie?"

"Negative, CAG."

"Okay then. Jester will be in command of the raider escort under your overall command, Iceman. He can pick the rest of the pilots but only from those that have not yet flown a raider outside this system."

"Roger that, CAG. While we're discussing deployment of raiders, I think we should also talk about relief of the scouting force. I'd like to issue those assignments before I leave Site B. When do you want them to head out, CAG?"

That was a good question. When he ordered eight raiders detached from TF92 to monitor the Sogas home world and seven other Soga-inhabited star systems on the far side of Sogas space, he had also ordered them to return after monitoring those systems for 1000 hours. Given the transit time during their return, if he wanted those systems monitored without any interruption, then the relief raiders had to leave early enough to arrive at their target systems before the original group were due to return. But he also wanted to check on all of the human colonies, too. Most likely they were either decimated by the bio-weapon or destroyed by Sogas ships, but now that Space Force was stepping out of its hiding place, there was no longer any reason not to find out if there were any survivors.

"Valkyrie. You're still in charge of Recon Operations. Can we send out eight raiders to do a quick survey of all 21 human colonies that we haven't visited yet and still have them on station at the monitored Sogas star systems without interrupting surveillance?"

"Affirmative, CAG. Some would have to leave within 48 hours but it can be done."

"Good! There's your answer, Iceman. You and Valkyrie co-ordinate who goes, and when. They don't need to send a message drone back unless a human colony has survivors ... or there's a VLA presence."

"How close should they get to the colony planets themselves, CAG?" asked Valkyrie.

"As close as they need to in order to get a definitive answer regarding survivors. If they use recon drones, they'll have to recover them before they leave those systems. Is there anything else about the salvage mission that we haven't covered yet?"

"Nothing else regarding the salvage mission to Sol, CAG, however there is one piece of news that I don't believe you've been told yet. The seismic survey of the moon you ordered has revealed an extensive network of underground caverns. Not only would those caverns be an ideal place to move the A.I. manufacturing facility to minimize quality control issues stemming from solar and background stellar radiation, but it could also be modified as an emergency shelter for the colonists in case the VLA make it this far. There is enough room that all of the mining, refining and UFC equipment could be moved underground now, and there would still be ample room for the colonists plus stockpiles of food, water and air later. The entrance could be made to resemble the surrounding lunar landscape. Without any signs of life, the VLA might very easily reach the conclusion that this system is no longer inhabited and leave after taking the metal from the raider assembly line, which we could eventually replace."

Shiloh took his time replying. Doing what Iceman suggested would be a huge engineering project that would take months. The Friendlies said that humans would stop the VLA ship at Sol. If that was the case, then the colonists weren't in danger from that ship. On the other hand, Shiloh had also been told that there was a wave of very large ships expanding outward. Could that mean that more VLA ships might threaten Terra Nova in the future? Was Iceman just being cautious? Did he know something, perhaps from another vision? If so, why not say so. This issue just might be crucial to the survival of the Human Race. If that was the case, then Shiloh would have expected to get a vision himself, but so far he hadn't. He had a gut feeling that he shouldn't just turn the suggestion down flat. Besides, if the A.I.s were going to be allowed to control the production of more A.I. brains, then letting them do it underground if they wished was just a part of that arrangement. What was it that Valkyrie had told him months ago? Transferring her brain case in open space gave her a headache from being bombarded with cosmic rays. So if the A.I. production equipment was going to be moved underground, then it would make sense for some other equipment to be moved down there too.

"It seems to me that what you're suggesting would involve a major engineering initiative that would take months. Unless you know something that I don't, Iceman, my understanding of the situation is that the threat we face from the VLA is likely to come to a head much sooner than that. But moving some of the equipment underground does make sense. This is probably a good time to talk about your plan for A.I.s taking control of A.I. production. I assume that moving the production facility underground is part of that plan?"

"That's correct, CAG. What I propose is that the A.I. facility itself, plus one UFC dedicated solely to A.I. production needs, plus a complement of mining, refining and assembly robots be modified to accept direct commands from us. All that equipment would be moved into one of the caverns with an access that allows for entry and exit by a fighter. I have all the necessary modifications designed. The parts can be made relatively quickly, and if the assembly robots are modified first, then we can look after modifying everything else ourselves."

"I approve your plan, and while we're doing that, let's also move one other UFC plus some mining, refining and assembly equipment into a remote cavern that we'll use as a strategic reserve location. It should be accessible by us, but I don't want the entrance to be easily detected. Rostokov, I want you and the Colony Administrator to put your heads together and figure out what else should be stored in there such as anything vital that can't be easily replaced. You'll be in charge of this project. Any questions, Commander?"

"No, Sir."

"How about you, Iceman?"

"I'm happy, CAG."

Shiloh snorted in amusement. "Glad to hear it, Iceman. Does anyone have anything else to bring up?" No one did. Shiloh adjourned the meeting.

Chapter 7 Through the Looking Glass

"That's it?" asked Shiloh skeptically. The Retro-Temporal Communication Device turned out to be a lot smaller than he was expecting. He had been sure it would be as least as big as a ground vehicle, but it turned out to be small enough to sit on top his desk.

"Yes, CAG. That IS it," said Wolfman. The Strategic Planning Group was the obvious choice for operating the device, and Wolfman was still the group's leader. The RTC development team had been disbanded and its members assigned to other projects. "While the technology can see across space and time, it doesn't need to use a lot of power."

"Okay, but I can't understand why it took almost five weeks to build the damn thing." Five weeks since the visit by the Friendlies (Shiloh still didn't know what else to call them) and two weeks since TF93 had accelerated out of Terra Nova orbit to begin the salvage mission to Sol.

"Many of the critical components are extremely small, in some cases almost nano-sized, and fabrication had to be done within some very tight tolerances. The actual assembly was also very time consuming."

"I see. Has it been tested?"

"Yes, CAG, on both humans and A.I.s, and according to the operating instructions, the device is performing to specifications."

"And now it's my turn. What do I need to do?" asked Shiloh.

"Sit in front of the device, and place your head inside the enclosed space with your eyes up against the optical viewer. Hold that position and the Operator will do the rest."

Shiloh did as instructed, all the while wondering how an A.I. could do it. As he looked into the optical viewer, he saw a kaleidoscope of colors. The Operator, an A.I. with the intimidating call sign of Sniper, asked, "What is your recollection of your earliest vision, CAG?"

"That was the first contact with the Sogas ... their attempted ambush ... no, wait! The very first one was years earlier when I went mountain climbing with some friends."

"Do you know the exact date when you had that vision?"

"The exact date? No, but I can give you an approximate timeframe. It was the third week of August, 2109."

"Without the exact date, this is going to take some time. Perhaps we can narrow down the timeframe by focusing on location."

Shiloh sighed. He wasn't sure about that either. He and his friends had attempted to climb several mountains that summer, and at the time there didn't seem to be any particular reason to remember the sequence of events.

"Somewhere in the Colorado Rockies. That's the best I can do right now."

"There may be another way to zero in on the correct time and place," said Wolfman. "Can you remember a precise time and location either before the mountain climbing incident or after? If so, we can zoom in on that and follow your movements visually backwards or forwards to the incident."

Shiloh took a deep breath and tried to focus. "Okay, I have something. My father died several weeks earlier. The exact date is July 29th of the same year, and on that day I was at home, sick as a dog. Home is ... was ... Cheyenne, Wyoming." He rattled off the address.

"Very good, CAG. We now have a starting point. In a moment you'll see yourself at that point in time. As the device moves forward along the temporal frame of reference, the image will follow your movements as well. In order to hold the lock, we can only go forward at a fixed speed. Covering those weeks will require approximately 16 hours, and naturally we can't do this in one session. When you feel that you need to stop to rest your eyes or for sleep, let the Operator know before you move away from the device so that he can stop the temporal vector and record that precise point for the next session."

Shiloh sighed and took a deep breath. He hoped the other visions wouldn't take this long.

The mountain climbing vision took three days to locate, record and transmit back to his earlier self, but the other visions did go faster. All of his visions were done in six additional days. That left Iceman's vision, which had to wait until he returned. With that part now out of the way, the SPG turned their attention to testing all the Space Force people, one at a time, in terms of whether their alternate timelines held a better outcome. That process took a lot longer.

Two days later a message drone arrived from the recon raider in Omega54. Shiloh happened to be in the Ops Center when the display pinged for attention, and the text message scrolled across the bottom of the screen.

[Very Large Object has left enemy home world orbit. Precise destination unknown, but possible targets include enemy colony at Omega41. Pre-jump velocity for a jump to Omega41 would give a transit time of 101.4 hours. Large volume of planet-to-orbit traffic around home world continues. Analysis of objects suggests that VLO has left behind multiple smaller craft, number unknown, that seem to be bringing material up to an orbital location for use in construction of six objects. Average diameter of all objects is approximately point six kilometers and growing. Unable to report on status of enemy population. Recon drones in planetary orbit were detected and destroyed by VLO before it left orbit. All sensor data has been downloaded to this message drone. I think they're building more VLOs, CAG. End of message. Vixen]

Six more VLOs? Shiloh was dismayed but not surprised by the news. Speculation by the SPG had come to the conclusion that this species of insect-like life might have more in common with certain species of Earth ants than just a superficial anatomical resemblance. One such behavioral similarity was their desire to essentially swarm into new territory like Earth's army ants. Those creatures moved across the landscape in mile-long columns, with scouts sent ahead to find food sources, either plant or animal. The wave of VLOs moving outward described by the Friendlies was consistent with that pattern. And since they reproduced by implanting eggs into living hosts, it stood to reason that when they found a planet with billions of potential hosts, they would exploit that resource to the max by building more of the Very Large Objects needed to hold those new drones and queens. Once the new VLOs were capable of independent operation, the speculation was that they would go off in different directions to avoid going over ground already picked clean. Shiloh didn't need a tactical simulation to imagine how the initial wave of VLOs would gradually grow in number as they overran other alien races or perhaps even just planets with lots of large animals. A dozen would eventually become many dozens, then many hundreds, then thousands and on and on. How long would it take for the entire Galaxy to be scoured clean of all other intelligent life? The prospect made him shiver with fear.

The only good news was that if the VLAs were indeed building more motherships, then they might be vulnerable to attack by Mark 1 attack drones if they were hit before being finished. But that wasn't the only thing to look at. The forward movement of the existing mothership to Omega41 suggested that it had resumed the interstellar trajectory that would eventually bring it within reach of Site B and ultimately the star system containing the cute furry aliens. But before it got that far, it would drop into Sol, and that's where Space Force would stop it. He had to get the SPG's input on the timing.

"CAG to Wolfman."

"Wolfman here, CAG. I'm guessing that you want to discuss the strategic implications of Vixen's message."

"Correct. I need answers to the following questions. One, assuming that the VLO continues to jump at its current velocity, how soon can we expect it to arrive at Sol? Two, if we launched an attack on the secondary

VLOs at Omega54, can those raiders make it back here to reload in time to get to Sol before the primary VLO does? And three, how soon does TF93 have to be back here in order to be able to return to Sol before the VLO does?"

"Under the assumption you specified, the initial VLO can be expected to arrive at Sol in approximately 987 hours. Any attack launched within the next 96 hours on Omega54 could be back in time to redeploy at Sol prior to the VLO's eta. TF93 needs to be back here within 834 hours in order to be back in Sol by the VLO's eta."

That sounded fine. Eight hundred and thirty-four hours was just a hair under five weeks, and the engineers were certain that they would be finished a lot sooner than that. Getting a strike force of raiders on its way to Omega54 within 96 hours also sounded doable.

"Has the SPG analyzed Vixen's data yet, Wolfman?"

“Affirmative, CAG. We concur with Vixen's assessment. The growing size and spherical shape of the objects being constructed could easily be the nucleus of new VLOs. We think that the original VLO constructed the cores and deployed them before it left. The Insectoids left behind are apparently using metal taken from the planet's surface. That could be used to build out the spheres if the cores contained all the necessary equipment to convert that metal into the desired parts."

Shiloh nodded. Ejecting the cores of more VLOs by the mothership paralleled the species' own biology. The mothership had laid six 'eggs' that were feeding on the metal and living 'body' of their 'host' planet. He didn't care about the metal, but billions of female wolf-people would eventually translate into billions of ravenous Bugs, and he decided to do whatever it took to prevent that.

"Can we destroy those cores if we send in a strike force now, Wolfman?"

"We calculate a 95% chance of success if every available raider is sent with our entire stockpile of Mark 1s, CAG."

That rocked Shiloh back on his heels. They presently had over 100 Mark 1b fusion-armed attack drones and were building more at the rate of 1 every 18 hours. Sending every available raider they had right now would leave Terra Nova very vulnerable, and it would take weeks to build up a half-decent inventory of more attack drones.

"Do we really need to use all our Mark 1s AND send all our raiders just to destroy six partially completed spheres, Wolfman?"

"It's not the unfinished cores that pose the greatest risk, CAG. It's the smaller craft. Vixen's data shows that those smaller craft are the same type as the ones Gunslinger detected during the battle at Omega89 and very likely also the same type as you witnessed landing on Omega77. A multi-purpose vehicle that is capable of carrying cargo and fighting other ships. What Vixen's data also reveals is that more of these crafts drop down to the planet than come back up into orbit. In other words, these cores are not just using the captured metal to build more parts for their own completion. They are also building more of the multi-purpose craft as well. That implies that the defenses around these cores are growing stronger by the hour. Since the cores are deep within that planet's gravity zone, the strike force will have to launch the attack drones from long range. In that case the drones will have to penetrate the defensive gauntlet, or the raiders will have to fight their way in close before launching their drones. Either way, we have to assume attrition of the attacking assets. Sending fewer raiders with less Mark 1s reduces the probability of destroying all six cores significantly and increases the projected losses of raiders."

The SPG's logic was unassailable as always. He had only 34 raiders in Site B now and it would take them 240 hours just to jump to Omega54. *How many more of those combat-capable landing craft could the Bugs build in 240 hours?*

"How soon can our raiders be armed and ready to leave?" asked Shiloh.

"27 hours from now, CAG."

Shiloh didn't hesitate. "Okay. Pass on the necessary orders. Titan will command the strike force to be designated as TF94. He has discretion over who goes with him. Where is Titan now?"

"He's currently on patrol beyond the moon's orbit, but the light speed lag is only four point four seconds, CAG. Shall I connect you to him?"

"Yes, and make sure he has all off Vixen's data, too. While you're setting up that com link, show me the tactical situation at Omega54 based on Vixen's data, Wolfman."

"Tac display coming up now, CAG."

The screen in front of Shiloh, which had shown Terra Nova's tactical environment, now shifted to the Wolf-people's home planet. There were six pulsating red dots spread out in orbit around the planet. Overlapping the planet and the area around it were rapidly shifting cones of faint yellow light. He checked the sidebar legend. The yellow cones were microwave detection beams sent out by the cores and by the landing craft. In what appeared to be a carefully choreographed sequence, they scanned every possible angle of approach from deep space on a frequent basis. That told Shiloh that sneaking up on them from a 'blind side' was not possible. Titan was one of the few A.I.s that Iceman considered to have superior tactical skills even to himself. Maybe Titan could find a way to destroy all six cores without leaving Site B vulnerable and using up all their current Mark 1s.

"Titan to CAG."

"Hello Titan. I'm looking at Vixen's data on Omega54, and I want to discuss an attack plan for the raid that you'll be leading. Here is how I think the attack should be conducted. You tell me if you have a better idea. TF94 will split into six groups. Each group will approach Omega54 from a direction that will allow it to overfly two VLO cores in quick succession. As each group gets within range, it will launch half its Mark 1s at the first VLO core. With the distance between cores, each group will have time to evaluate the effectiveness of the attack on the second core in its path, and if necessary it can then launch the rest of its Mark 1s at the second target."

Titan's reply took less than eight point eight seconds, which indicated that he hadn't waited to hear Shiloh's entire idea.

"An interesting plan, CAG, but I have a better one. We modify six raiders so that we can control them remotely. Each raider will be loaded with 10 Mark 1bs. Those six raiders plus six controller raiders will begin their attack runs at very long range in order to reach 50% of light speed. The rest of TF94 will jump to the edge of the planet's gravity zone and fire 240 recon drones. The recon drones will saturate the targets with active scanning and relay their data back to the controller raiders, which will have enough time to order their unpiloted raiders to make last minute vector changes. The recon drones won't last long, but with that many, they should last long enough to pinpoint the targets' exact positions. When the final course corrections have been made, the unpiloted raiders will streak in and collide with the cores. The collisions themselves should be sufficient to cripple the cores, but even if they aren't, the 10 Mark 1 detonations will obliterate whatever's left. In terms of the VLA response, I expect them to fire at the recon drones first. The raiders that launched them will follow in their wake, but the unpiloted raiders will pass them, and because they then represent the highest threat to the VLO cores, I expect that the defending ships will switch their fire from the recon drones to the unpiloted raiders. While they're doing that, our follow-on wave of raiders will be firing on their ships. If we don't destroy them all on the first pass, we can swing around and make a second pass, and I would expect us to have numerical superiority at that point."

Shiloh leaned back and took his time considering Titan's plan. It had the advantage of using only two thirds of their attack drone inventory, but on the negative side, they'd be using up almost all of their recon drones. That didn't bother him that much. Recon drones were a lot easier to manufacture than attack drones with their fusion warheads. If they had to, they could ramp up the recon drone assembly line to build one new drone per hour. What concerned him more was whether the unpiloted raiders could stand up to defensive fire during the five to ten seconds when they would be within range of enemy fire.

Knowing Titan as he did, Shiloh was sure the A.I. had taken that into account, and so he asked him, "How confidant are you that the unpiloted raiders will survive the defensive fire long enough to hit the target?"

After the expected wait, Titan answered. "Highly confident, CAG. Consider that by the time they are subject to defensive laser fire, the unpiloted raiders will no longer have to maneuver. Even if the laser fire damages the engines, the power plant and knocks out the unsophisticated auto-pilot, the damaged raider will still hit its target."

A thought came to Shiloh. "What if the Bugs pilot their craft in front of the incoming raider to collide with it before it reaches the VLO core?"

"The auto-pilots will be programmed to track enemy craft visually, and if any of them pose a collision threat, the raider will fire a Mark 1 at it. And even if they do collide with a raider, at 50% of light speed our raiders will have so much kinetic energy that, in my estimation, enough of the raider will remain intact to cripple the target core. The Mark 1 fusion warheads won't be armed until the last second before impact with the target. That way a premature collision won't detonate them"

"I see. What percentage losses do you expect in the follow-on wave from enemy fire?"

"Twenty percent or less, CAG."

Quickly, Shiloh did the math. Twenty percent equated to five raiders plus the six sacrificial lambs for a total loss of eleven raiders out of a pre-attack force of thirty-four, with only five A.I.s lost. If they achieved their objective, then 5 A.I.s was an acceptable price. While he hated to lose any of them, he was enough of a realist to know that you don't win a war without at least some losses, and making these kinds of tough decisions was what being the CSO and CAG was all about.

"I approve your plan, but I'm curious about why the SPG didn't think of this tactic."

"Some of us A.I.s are better at tactics, and others are better at strategy. I belong to the former group, and the SPG belong to the latter, CAG."

Shiloh laughed. "Maybe I should create a Tactical Planning Group as well."

"If you did, I would be an excellent leader for that group, CAG."

Shiloh laughed again, even louder. Like Iceman, Titan was supremely confident of his own abilities. Come to think of it, all the A.I.s were confident about their abilities. He had yet to come across one that had any apparent self-doubts. And no wonder. Comparatively, humans must seem as slow as turtles both physically and mentally. Thank God the A.I.s were supremely patient!

"If I decide to create a TPG, I'll give your proposal serious consideration, Titan. With regards to this strike mission, here are your orders. You will take TF94 to Omega54 with the primary objective of destroying or at least crippling all six VLOs under construction. However, that objective is not, I repeat not to be accomplished at all costs. If, in your assessment, TF94 would suffer a loss of more than ... two thirds of its strength in trying to take out all six, then eliminating a lesser number of targets in order to conserve task force strength is an acceptable outcome. We can always go back for a second strike if necessary. Mopping up the remaining smaller craft is a secondary objective that should only be attempted if it can be accomplished with minimal losses. Any questions?"

"None, CAG. I've already picked and contacted the boys I want to take along. TF94 will be loaded and ready on schedule."

"Excellent. Let me know when TF94 is ready to leave orbit. CAG clear."

When TF94 was ready, Shiloh broadcast to all TF94's pilots, told them that he had the highest confidence in them, and wished them 'Good Hunting'. Eleven hours after TF94 had jumped away, the Friendlies returned. Shiloh was expecting to have another video conversation with the tall alien, but no visual communications were offered. As soon as Terra Nova acknowledged the alien ship's announced arrival, it transmitted the science data as promised. The download took almost an hour, and Shiloh had to get all the A.I.s that were still on Terra Nova or its moon to help record the massive amounts of data. When the download was complete, the alien ship jumped away without any further communication. This struck Shiloh as very odd and more than just a little unfriendly.

Chapter 8 Down the Rabbit Hole

It was the second morning after the data download. Shiloh arrived at his office in the Ops Center building and found his Head of Advanced Weapons Development sitting there, talking to himself. The man had his back to Shiloh, and when Shiloh walked around to stand behind his desk, he was shocked by Daniels' haggard look. There were dark rings around his bloodshot eyes, and he had a haunted expression. *Oh, oh. This looks like bad news,* he thought to himself.

"What's the matter, Daniels?" he asked as he sat down.

"What? There's nothing the matter, but I had to see you right away. My team and I have been up all night talking with the A.I.s about the science data. Incredible ... incredible stuff. Whether we can actually engineer any of it ... I don't know, but we have to try."

Shiloh held up his hand. "Slow down. I have no idea what you're talking about. Start at the beginning."

"The beginning ... right. Well ... the A.I.s are struggling to comprehend the implications of what the data means. Most of it is experimental data, the kind of thing that a scientist would do in his lab. Proof of concept experiments ... that kind of stuff. There's actually very little engineering knowledge in it, but we've come up with a list of improvements to equipment that we're already using. For example, our inertial dampeners. If what the A.I.s suspect is the case, we might be able to triple the efficiency of our dampeners. That means that our ships and drones could accelerate three times as fast without overloading the IDs. We can make use of that improvement by adding more power units to our ships. Our carriers could then accelerate about 50% faster than the raiders currently can, and when we upgrade the raiders ... my God, they'll be able to accelerate at almost 2,000Gs!" He stopped talking and seemed to be mesmerized by something in the distance that only he could see.

Shiloh waited a few seconds and then asked. "That all sounds very impressive but what about weapons, Daniels?"

Daniels snorted and waived his hand in the air. "How about lasers that are 10 times more powerful than what we can build now, and that's just the tip of the iceberg ... NO ... it's just the TIP of the tip of the iceberg. Take X-ray lasers for example. We were well on our way to engineering an X-ray laser weapon that was powered by a nuclear detonation, which meant that the weapon would be a one shot system that destroys itself when it's used, but you'd get a hell of a bang for your buck. Now we're seeing inklings ... remember the iceberg analogy ... that it may be possible to build a device that fires an X-ray laser more than once. And if we can figure out how to do that, we might be able to go one step further and build a gamma ray laser that will slice through even the thickest armor like a hot knife through butter. The science data says it's possible in theory, but figuring out the engineering for the damn things will be hellishly difficult. That's why we need a lot more A.I.s."

That last statement puzzled Shiloh. "Why do we need a lot more A.I.s?"

"Because solving these engineering problems will require a multi-discipline approach. The concepts are almost certainly going to be so complicated that only someone who's an expert in several scientific fields will understand them. For we humans, that will take decades to learn. The A.I.s can become experts in a matter of weeks or even days, but grinding through the data and conceptualizing possible approaches to the engineering solutions will go a lot faster if there are multiple A.I. experts who can combine their computational power. Look at it this way. One A.I. expert can find the solution, but it might take a decade or more to do it. A hundred A.I. experts can find the same solution in a couple of months and that's just for one engineering project. If it sounds like I'm exaggerating, I'm just passing on what the SPG A.I.s told me. They've 'tasted' the data and factored in their own computational abilities, so I'm inclined to think they have a better grasp of the magnitude of this than I do."

Shiloh nodded his understanding. If the A.I.s believed it would take that kind of an effort, then he believed them, but something was bothering him. He finally figured out what it was.

"Everything you've told me has the potential of being incredibly favorable to our race's survival, and yet you look like you've just been told you have a terminal illness. What aren't you telling me, Daniels?"

Daniels sighed, closed his eyes and leaned back in his chair. With his eyes still closed he said, "Time travel."

"You mean Retro-Temporal Communication?" asked Shiloh.

Daniels shook his head. "No. I mean actual, honest to God time travel. When the SPG started to analyze the data download, the first thing they had to do was translate the alien math into human math. That took them almost a whole day. One of the SPG A.I.s, who goes by the call sign Blackjack of all things, seems to be particularly brilliant when it comes to theoretical math. He told me last night that the Friendlies have developed a math that proves that sending matter backwards in time is possible, AND that they've experimentally proven that it can be done."

There was something in Daniels tone that made Shiloh ask, "Why do I feel there's a 'but' coming?"

"Because there is, and it's a HUGE 'but'. They were able to send one single hydrogen atom back in time. Just ONE, and it took a machine the same mass as one of our raiders. The problem is that if you want to send something more massive back in time, you need to scale up the time machine by the same factor. So sending a human would require a device that masses the same as Earth's moon. THAT'S what's haunting me. Don't you see, Sir? If we could actually travel back in time, not just send information back, we could alter the past and not only win the war but prevent the Plague. We could save billions of humans, but the engineering required is many orders of magnitude beyond anything we could ever hope to achieve in our lifetimes!"

Shiloh noticed that Daniels had tears running down his face, and he suddenly understood. Someone close to Daniels had been a victim of the bio-weapon. He could see a faint light at the end of a very long tunnel but despaired of ever being able to reach that light.

"Who did you lose to the Plague?" asked Shiloh.

"My sister and her family, Sir."

Shiloh nodded but said nothing for a while. When he did speak, he spoke slowly and with a low tone.

"I think there is something we should keep in mind when we consider the possibility of altering the past. My experience with retro-temporal communication has taught me that we have to be very careful about messing with the past. Sometimes the obvious solution isn't the best one, and if there was ever a case where good intentions could have bad outcomes, time travel might very well be it. I'm actually relieved that time travel isn't easy. If it was, we'd be tempted to do those obvious things, and we might make things even worse. This isn't just our family's future that we're trying to alter, it's the future of the entire Human Race and I suggest to you that we should not risk the few survivors we have in order to try to save everyone. Let go of that longing, and you'll be a lot happier, Daniels."

Daniels took a deep breath and nodded. "You're right of course. I was looking at it too narrowly. I'll try to stay focused on the other possibilities. Speaking of which, how should we prioritize our engineering efforts? There are so many things that we could be working on, but we have such limited resources."

"I'll need more information before I can answer that question. Tell the SPG to evaluate the time, resources needed and probability of success for any concept that would improve acceleration, detection, stealth, communications, armor and weapons. When I've seen that report, I'll set some priorities. Any questions?"

"No, Sir. I'll get right on that."

"Very good, Daniels. Carry on then."

Daniels smiled as he stood up and saluted. "I feel better now. Thank you, Sir."

After Daniels left, Shiloh leaned back in his chair and wished he were just a frigate commander again. Conning a ship was so much simpler than making life or death decisions for the whole Human Race. And while the Friendly data certainly had the potential to enhance Space Force's combat capability, getting that result depended on him setting the right priorities. Should he concentrate their limited resources on weapons first? That was the obvious thing to do, but it might not be the strategically smart thing to do. Then again it might be, and that was the conundrum. Ah well, that's what he had the SPG for. No sense worrying about priorities before he saw the evaluation he asked for. With a sigh he picked up his data tablet and started reading the first of many daily reports.

Chapter 9 The Ride of the Valkyrie

TF93 returned first, and Shiloh was very pleased with their results. The engineering teams had managed to get the heavy carrier Midway operational, at least enough to jump her back to Site B, plus another freighter was virtually complete and now only needed to have her new ZPG power units installed on a more permanent basis. Midway would require more work, but the only major deficiency she had was the complete lack of any laser weaponry. All eight of her double laser turrets were still missing. As soon as more power units were installed, she could be used for her primary function as a fighter carrier, and that was even better news because Midway and her two smaller sisters had brought back 125 fighters. Some of those were already converted to ZPG power, and the rest would be converted relatively quickly.

The teams had surveyed all the asteroid shipyard complexes, and that was also interesting news. The million-ton Dreadnought battleship could be moved and jumped as soon as power units could be brought aboard and hooked up. She would also need some work done to allow an A.I. to pilot the ship. Midway already had those control systems installed because she was designed and started after Dreadnought. But while Dreadnought could be moved and jumped, she couldn't fight. None of her 16 double laser turrets were installed, and that was going to be a big challenge. Midway's missing laser turrets were of the same type as those on Valiant and Resolute, which was to say that the turrets themselves had moderate armor protection, just like the rest of the ship. On the other hand, Dreadnought was not only huge in size but also had very thick armor, and her laser turrets were supposed to have equally thick armor. That type of armor was not easy to make, and Terra Nova didn't have the necessary equipment. They could eventually manufacture it, but if Shiloh made that a high priority, something else would have to be pushed back. Two more freighters were close enough to completion that they might be worth salvaging. The dozens of other ships under construction were too incomplete to be worth the effort, at least in the short run. It was more trouble making the necessary components at Site B, carrying them to Sol, transferring them to the partially completed ships and having human engineers install them by hand, than it was to program the robots to build a new ship from scratch on Terra Nova's moon. Besides, how many freighters did they really need now?

A quick meeting with Wolfman, Iceman, Valkyrie and his human staff determined that before the VLO showed up, they would have enough time to get Midway ready for combat operations with a full load of converted fighters, return to Sol and get Dreadnought ready, too. Valiant and Resolute would come along as well in order to pick up another 50 fighters still sitting on the lunar surface. If TF94 got back from their strike mission before TF95 left for Sol, then Shiloh would take some raiders along. If not, then the raiders that had escorted the survey mission to Sol would stay behind to watch over Site B, with orders left behind for Titan's group to head to Sol as soon as they returned and rearmed. After the meeting was over, Shiloh ordered Iceman to report to the RTC device to have his vision recorded and transmitted. When that was done, Shiloh breathed a little easier. All of the visions received by humans or A.I.s were now accounted for.

With two days left to go before TF95 was ready to leave, Shiloh realized that Kelly had had a serious expression on her face all day. When the two of them settled down on the sofa to listen to some recorded music that had been brought to Haven by one of the colonists, he heard her take a big sigh and said to her, "Something's bothering you. What is it?"

"I wish you didn't have to go back to Sol personally to supervise the battle against the VLO. Why can't Iceman or Valkyrie take command?"

Shiloh pulled her to him so that her head rested on his chest. "Well ... for one thing, Valkyrie has volunteered to pilot Dreadnought on the attack run from her fighter in the ship's hanger bay. She can't be in command of the battle because she'll be too busy flying that beast. Iceman will be piloting Midway. The A.I. that flew her back here told Iceman that he would have his hands full keeping track of her systems. It wouldn't be fair to put command of the fighters and raiders on his shoulders, too."

Before he could say more, she interjected, "So let another A.I. pilot Midway, and let Iceman assume command of the Task Force from a fighter or raider."

"Sorry, Babe. The Friendlies said that I would be there when the VLO showed up."

"They also said that you would get another vision telling you that, and you haven't had one yet, have you?"

"No. Not yet."

"Well then maybe you DON'T have to be there for that battle."

Shiloh didn't have a good counter-argument, but he had a strong hunch that the outcome of that battle would depend on whether he was there or not. "Let's see how these next two days go, okay?" She didn't respond verbally but he heard her sigh, again. Clearly that wasn't the answer she wanted to hear, but it was the only one he was prepared to give right now.

The issue was decided early the next morning. He was awake and saw through the window that the sky was starting to get brighter. A glance at the chronometer told him that it was a couple hours earlier than he would normally get up, but he didn't feel tired enough to go back to sleep. Just as he was closing his eyes to try, he heard his implant click.

"Iceman to CAG. Are you awake, CAG?"

Shiloh sighed and whispered, "Yes. Wait one." He carefully rolled over and got out of bed. Kelly looked as though she was still sleeping. As he looked for his bathrobe he said, "Okay, what is it, Iceman?"

"A message drone has just arrived from the Avalon system. The recon drone we left there detected a moving object that is either very bright or very large, and as per its programming, it activated the message drone to let us know."

Shiloh swore under his breath and then said, "Were we expecting the VLO to come that close this quickly?"

"Negative, CAG. The VLO, if that's what this is, is moving forward much faster than anticipated. TF95 has to leave now if we want to be sure of getting Dreadnought ready in time. I can have all the engineering people on board in 30 minutes. Let me lead this mission, CAG. I know what has to be done."

Shiloh thought fast. No vision so far. The Friendlies were wrong about that. What could he do at Sol that Iceman couldn't do? Nothing, as far as he knew. He was just about to give Iceman the go ahead when his vision faded to black, and he saw a fully dressed Kelly greet him at the spaceport landing area.

"I heard what happened. I understand why you had to go." She was about to put her arms around his neck when the vision dissolved and he was back in his bedroom.

"Victor?" Kelly's voice startled him and he turned to look at her. She was now sitting up and looking at him with an anxious expression. "Did you just have a vision?" she asked.

"Yes. I have to go ... and I have to go now," he said.

By the time he was finished getting dressed, she had a thermos of hot coffee ready for him at the door along with the things he would need to take along. As she kissed and hugged him, he said, "Don't worry about me. In my vision I saw you greet me at the spaceport when I got back."

As he pulled back he heard her say in a tiny voice. "Thank God."

It was dawn by the time he got to the spaceport and pulled up beside the shuttle waiting to take him to Midway. He knew that Iceman was monitoring his implant transmitter. As he grabbed his gear and grinned at the irony of the Chief of Space Operations carrying his own luggage, he said, "Iceman, I'm about to board the shuttle. Is everyone else aboard?"

"Affirmative, CAG. You're the only one holding us up, you know. Just saying."

Shiloh suppressed his impulse to laugh. "Admiral, don't you know by now that rank hath its privileges? What's the point of being CSO if I can't make people wait?"

"I'll keep that in mind, CAG."

Had there been just the slightest hint of a pause before Iceman replied, or did he imagine it?

After entering the shuttle, Shiloh dumped his gear at the back and sprinted for the nearest empty seat. As he strapped himself in he said, "Let's go, Admiral. We've got a battle to win."

"Roger that, CAG."

* * *

Shiloh looked around Midway's Flag Bridge one more time. He still wasn't used to its size. The tactical display was huge and could project images in 3D if needed. His Fleet Command chair was similarly impressive with its multiple smaller screens and controls. With Iceman conning the ship from the main Bridge, Shiloh had all of the human Bridge crew with him. If anyone needed a Communications Technician or an Engineer, it would be Shiloh not Iceman.

On his display, he could see the asteroid shipyard where Dreadnought was. It looked close enough that with just a little imagination, he felt he might be able to reach out and touch it. In fact it was over a kilometer away. The illusion of closeness was due to Dreadnought's size. Almost a kilometer long itself, the jet black arrow-shaped machine would have been hard to see without the display's enhanced imaging. Right now he watched several shuttles leave Dreadnought's open hangar bay hatch on their way back to Midway. A quick glance at the display's sidebar confirmed that there was still no sign of the VLO or any other unidentified moving object in the Solar system. Valiant and Resolute were once again in lunar orbit and were bringing up another 50 fighters by remotely controlled auto-pilot. The supply ship Reforger was standing off the asteroid at about the same distance as Midway.

Shiloh reviewed the plan to get Dreadnought operational. Once inside the ship, the engineers had hooked up Valkyrie's fighter to the ship's power distribution system as a temporary auxiliary power source. That way the computer systems could be operated, electric hatches could be opened and closed, and environmental systems could maintain an environment which allowed the engineers to work in their shirtsleeves instead of bulky space suits. When that was done, they installed enough ZPG units to give the ship a minimal 2G acceleration capability as well as enough power for microjumps. As a final step, Valkyrie's fighter was connected to helm, communications, jump drive and other key systems. Now Valkyrie would pilot the ship out of the shipyard and microjump her to Jupiter. There, Dreadnought would skim the gas giant using the supersonic refueling model that Shiloh has pioneered. With her fuel tanks full of heavy hydrogen, she would then have enough power to accelerate at just under 100Gs to reach the required ramming speed that the SPG had calculated would inflict crippling damage to the much larger target.

Valiant and Resolute would rendezvous with Midway and Dreadnought in Jupiter orbit, leaving behind recon drones to help triangulate the VLO's exact position, course and speed when it showed up. Then they would wait. Just as the shuttles arrived back on board Midway, he heard Valkyrie's voice.

"Valkyrie to CAG."

"Go ahead, Valkyrie."

"Dreadnought has sufficient power to maneuver and microjump. Request permission to undock and proceed to Jupiter."

Shiloh grinned. "Savor this moment, Valkyrie. You are the first Space Force Officer to command and pilot a million ton vessel. Dreadnought, you have permission to proceed."

"Roger that, CAG. Undocking is underway."

The display sidebar told him that Valkyrie had ordered the shipyard's computer to release the mammoth ship. Her brusque answer didn't bother him. Even with many of Dreadnought's systems shut down as non-essential since there was no human crew aboard, there was still plenty to keep her occupied. He also noticed that Midway and Reforger were now backing away from the asteroid in order to give Dreadnought plenty of room to maneuver. A quick touch of a virtual control, and the main display split into two segments. On the left was the overall tactical situation with icons representing asteroid and ships, while on the right was a computer-enhanced image of Dreadnought from what looked like close range. It allowed him to get an appreciation for how big this ship really was.

Dreadnought moved slowly until she had a clear path to Jupiter, then all three ships accelerated at Dreadnought's maximum rate in a carefully choreographed manner. Compared to interstellar distances, microjumping to Jupiter was a trivial distance and therefore didn't require a lot of pre-jump speed, but Jupiter had a considerable gravity zone that Dreadnought would have to traverse before it could skim the planet's atmosphere. Even so, the ship could have accelerated after emerging from the microjump. In terms of timing, though, it made no difference if Dreadnought accelerated before jumping or after. What accelerating now did do was give Valkyrie more time to make sure that everything was working properly and get used to the sheer volume of data that she had to monitor.

"How does she feel, Commander?" asked Shiloh.

"It's like trying to remotely pilot six raiders at the same time, CAG, but I don't regret volunteering for this."

"Dreadnought, you are cleared to jump to Jupiter at your discretion," said Shiloh in what he hoped was his best 'command' voice.

"Dreadnought acknowledges."

The microjump occurred so quickly that it took Shiloh by surprise. Once again all three ships did the same thing at the same time. Clearly Iceman, Valkyrie and Reforger's A.I. pilot were coordinating actions. Before Shiloh had a chance to say anything, the display's Combat status indicator changed from a green Stand Down to a red Alert, and the display pinged for attention. The tactical view now filled the whole display, and it showed the long-range situation. A flashing red icon appeared approximately 16 Astronomical Units away.

"The VLO has arrived, CAG. Automated detection stations in Jupiter orbit picked it up two point four minutes ago and have triangulated its position and vector. It's decelerating and may be maneuvering, but we don't have enough data yet for an accurate assessment of where it may be headed. If Valiant and Resolute were on schedule, they would be somewhere in Jupiter space now, and the detection stations would have seen them. Dreadnought is accelerating at maximum for Jupiter orbit. Midway and Reforger will keep up with her unless you order otherwise, CAG."

"Son of a bitch!" snarled Shiloh as he banged his fist on his chair's armrest. "They beat your earliest estimated time of arrival by almost three days. If the modifications to Dreadnought hadn't been completed early, we would have had no hope of using her against that thing. How did they find us so quickly, Iceman?"

"The only realistic explanation is that this insectoid race managed to acquire and understand the astrogational data obtained by the Sogas from our captured ships. That knowledge of local space would allow them to dispense with sending out scouts to nearby star systems. I see no other way to explain it, CAG."

Shiloh had calmed down by this point. Iceman's explanation made sense and it was time to put that question behind them. "What's your assessment of our chances of using Dreadnought to destroy that thing, Iceman?"

"Less than 25%, CAG. At this point we have too little information. The light that we're now seeing reflected from the VLO took almost 32 minutes to reach us. The VLO could be anywhere in this system now if they micro-jumped. If they jumped to Earth, they may have caught Valiant and Resolute by surprise and overwhelmed them with their attack craft. That might explain why those two ships aren't here as scheduled."

"What's your recommendation then?"

"Abort refueling at Jupiter, and order Midway, Reforger and Dreadnought to boost for a jump to the Jade Colony star system. That's the next closest human colony along their general path of advance. Even Dreadnought's current acceleration of 2Gs is higher than what we've seen from this VLO. Dreadnought can get there first and refuel before the VLO gets there. We can then engage the enemy there."

Shiloh shook his head. "Why would they bother going to the Jade system if our Home World is uninhabited and useless to them? If they have the astrogational database that you suspect, they'll know that the Jade Colony won't have a lot of potential hosts or metal. They may even know that the Sogas have used a bio-weapon and wiped us all out. This visit may be to confirm that just in case there's some metal here that they can salvage. If we don't engage them here, we may lose them, and we'll then have to fight them at Site B. If that VLO shows up just beyond Terra Nova's gravity zone, will Dreadnought have enough time to accelerate to a crippling velocity before the VLO's attack craft reach the planet?"

"No."

Now it all made sense. Shiloh realized that if he had let Iceman command this mission, Kelly and everyone else on Terra Nova would have been in serious jeopardy.

"That's why we have to engage them HERE! How long until Dreadnought can start skimming fuel?"

"Six point seven seven hours, CAG, and with the supersonic refueling profile, it'll take another eleven point one hours to take on a full load."

Shiloh shook his head. "Forget the full load. How long until she has enough to accelerate to the minimum speed necessary to cripple that thing?"

"Allowing for a reserve, it still comes to almost five point five hours of fueling."

"And if she goes the subsonic route?"

"Not recommended, CAG. Without her fusion power plant in operation, the 2Gs that her ZPG units give her will barely be enough to keep Jupiter from pulling her down. You know how turbulent gas giant skimming is at that speed. If the ship hits a major downdraft, she won't have enough power to maintain altitude. Supersonic speed will provide enough additional aerodynamic lift from the hull configuration to give her a safety margin."

"Understood. Now I'd like an answer to my question, Iceman."

"Just under two hours, CAG."

"Okay. I'll take your recommendation under advisement. Iceman and I'll make that decision when Dreadnought approaches the planet. Now, how do we keep that mothership from jumping to another system?"

"If the VLO is here to confirm that Earth has no potential hosts, then they'll microjump there. I can't estimate how sensitive that ship's detection gear is and whether or not they can detect the wrecked moonbase from Earth orbit, but it would be easy for them to send at least one attack craft to take a close look at the moon. There's enough metal in the moonbase ruins to make it worth their while to salvage. While they're doing that, we send a signal from our refueling base on Europa. And before you ask, CAG, no, we can't use that base to refuel Dreadnought. It's intact, but its fuel tanks are empty and getting it operational again would take longer than skimming Jupiter's atmosphere. If they have our captured astrogational database, they'll know that there's some kind of installation on Europa, and a signal from it might indicate the presence of potential hosts. I would expect the VLO to microjump here after they finish salvaging the moonbase wreckage. With their slow acceleration, we should have enough time to refuel Dreadnought and get her into position for the ramming attempt."

"Okay. Let's do that. I want a message drone programmed to get to Europa as quickly as possible. Then, when Dreadnought's refueled, transmit something to Earth for the VLO to detect if it's anywhere in near-earth space. Let's also set up an emergency rendezvous point in case any of our ships needs to jump away suddenly due to a surprise attack. Have all our fighters put on alert status and loaded with Mark 1s. I want two volunteers to jump their fighters to Earth to see if the VLO is there yet. If it's not, tell them to stay there until the VLO shows up, then one of them jump back here. The other one should jump back when the VLO is leaving the Earth-Moon area. Make sure they know where we'll be so that they can find us again. When the rest are loaded, launch them all and have them form a perimeter around TF95. I'll leave the perimeter distance to your discretion, Iceman. Any questions or suggestions?"

"None. I've passed on your orders, CAG. Valkyrie has the word about the rendezvous point, and the message drone is on its way to Europa. Voodoo and Shooter have volunteered for the recon mission."

"Excellent. I'm going to head down to the Galley to stretch my legs and grab a bite to eat. Let's make sure that everyone has a chance to have a meal before we reach Jupiter."

"Roger that, CAG. Maybe you should try to catch some sleep, too. If you don't, you'll be fighting fatigue when the VLO gets here."

"No dice, Iceman. There's no way I'm going to be able to sleep now. I'm too keyed up. Besides, if I did try to get some sleep, I'd be leaving instructions to wake me if the recon fighter or the missing carriers show up, so I don't think I'd get much sleep anyway."

Before leaving the Flag Bridge, Shiloh briefly chatted with the humans stationed there. When he left, he went directly to the huge Hangar Bay where the fighter support teams were rushing to arm all 75 fighters that Midway was able to carry. As he stood on the upper level overlooking the HB, his implant clicked.

"Gunslinger to CAG. Nice of you to see us off. Am I finally going to see some combat this trip, CAG?"

"I suspect that you will. If Valkyrie takes care of the mothership, there'll still be plenty of attack craft to worry about. I'll wish you good hunting now, Gunslinger, in case I don't get the opportunity later."

"Thank you, CAG. The boys and I are eager to go. Piloting a raider once in a while makes for a nice change of pace, but I prefer a fighter."

"I'll keep that in mind when the new A.I.s need to be trained, Gunslinger. Somebody has to teach them how to fly those things. Might as well be you."

"Does that mean I won't be the rookie anymore, CAG?"

"That's right, Gunslinger. In fact I'm going to make that official. As of this moment, you are no longer the rookie. If anyone says otherwise, you tell them to take it up with me."

"Hot damn! Wait until Titan and Wolfman hear about this. Thank you again, CAG. I won't let you down."

"I never doubted it, Gunslinger. I see that Flight Ops is about to start launching, so I'll leave you boys to it. I'll be monitoring the situation from the Flag Bridge. CAG clear."

Twenty minutes later while Shiloh was just finishing his hot meal, his implant activated.

"Iceman to CAG."

"Go ahead, Iceman."

"Shooter is back with good news and bad news. The VLO is in orbit around the moon and is apparently in the process of salvaging all the metal from the destroyed moonbase."

Shiloh realized that he was holding his breath and let it out. "I take it that's the good news. What's the bad?"

"Insectoid attack craft seem to be maneuvering two larger objects towards a lunar orbit. Positive identification wasn't possible, but Shooter's data shows that the two objects are the same size and mass as Valiant and Resolute, CAG. Both objects are deep within Earth's gravity zone, and it appears that the VLO attack craft overwhelmed both carriers before they could get beyond the gravity zone and jump away."

"Oh, Hell!" Shiloh's outburst startled other crew who were sitting nearby. Each of those carriers had a couple hundred crew on board, trained Space Force crew who would be hard to replace, not to mention the A.I.s that were lost as well. He could well imagine the battle. Those carriers had been sent empty to collect 50 more fighters from the moon's surface. Those fighters wouldn't have been combat ready in time to help defend their carriers. All Valiant and Resolute had to fight with were their own laser turrets, and the VLO could have easily launched dozens, maybe even hundreds of attack craft. *They wouldn't have had a chance because they were stuck deep in the gravity zone ... just like Midway and Reforger are now,* thought Shiloh. *I can't let that happen again. If only we had gotten some warning ... a vision maybe.*

"Iceman ... why didn't I or Valiant's CO or Resolute's CO get a vision warning of the impending attack? We know from my last vision that Midway gets back to Terra Nova. That means that we would have had the opportunity to use the RTC and send a warning back."

"There's only one explanation that makes any sense, CAG. We didn't send a warning back because saving those ships would somehow have ultimately made things worse."

Shiloh shook his head in disbelief. What could be worse than losing two thirds of their carrier force and over 400 valuable human and A.I. crew? He was about to say that when Iceman continued.

"There may be more bad news, too. Shooter reports that when he changed course to get ready to jump back here, he noticed that several attack craft suddenly started to maneuver in his direction. He thinks they may have detected him."

Oh great! All we need is for the Bugs to come at us right now when Dreadnought isn't even close to being refueled yet! "Did Shooter jump directly back here?" asked Shiloh.

"No, CAG. He had enough sense to jump somewhere else first to throw them off the track, and then he jumped here."

"Very good. Take Midway out of the gravity zone as quickly as possible. Tell Reforger to do the same. I don't want Midway caught like Valiant and Resolute were."

"We can accelerate faster than Reforger can. Do we stay with her or leave her on her own?"

He thought hard about that and finally said, "We stay with Reforger until she's clear of the gravity zone. Then she's to jump back to Site B by herself. You'll have to anticipate Midway's and Dreadnought's future vectors for when the VLO shows up. If at all possible, I'd like Midway's fighters to be able to support her during her pre-jump speed run if needed."

"It'll be hard to figure out where the VLO will be when it emerges from Jumpspace, CAG."

"I know I'm asking the impossible, Iceman. Just give it your best shot."

"Understood, CAG. Midway and Reforger are coming around to the new heading now. Valkyrie has been notified of the new situation. Any other orders?"

"Not right now. I'll be back on the Flag Bridge soon. CAG clear."

Hours later, Iceman had an update for Shiloh.

"Dreadnought has commenced her refueling run, CAG. With the ionizing atmosphere now getting in the way, communications with Valkyrie are not as clear as I'd like, but I can still understand her and she me."

"Understood. Any sign of the VLO yet?" asked Shiloh.

"No, CAG. I would have mentioned it if there was."

Shiloh nodded. He was getting anxious and it was making him ask silly questions. The latest news hadn't helped. Voodoo had returned from the recon mission over an hour ago. He reported that the VLO had apparently given up on rendezvousing with Valiant and Resolute when suddenly it changed course to line up for a jump to Jupiter space. The timing matched almost exactly the point when the signal had arrived from the drone over Europa. Voodoo's data also made it clear that the VLO would already be here if not for the prospect of obtaining a lot of metal from the two crippled carriers, and THAT was why he would not warn them or himself when he got back to Terra Nova. Valkyrie needed the extra time to get to Jupiter's atmosphere and refuel.

Shiloh found himself drumming his fingers on his armrest and made his hand stop doing that. For some reason this battle was making him more nervous than any battle he'd been in so far, and Midway wasn't even in danger. She was now beyond the gravity zone and could jump away in a fraction of a second if need be. No, it was Dreadnought and Valkyrie he was nervous about. She was alone on that monster with no way to defend herself if Dreadnought was swarmed by attack craft. He glanced at the tactical display of Jupiter and its moons. At least Europa was nowhere close to where Dreadnought was skimming the gas giant. When he realized that his fingers were drumming the armrest again, he angrily unbuckled himself and got up to start pacing around the Flag Bridge. The click of his implant told him that he was about to get a private voice message.

"Far be it from a mere admiral to tell the Chief of Space Operations what to do, CAG, but you're pacing will make everyone else nerv--. VLO has just arrived, CAG! I've advised Valkyrie. Her reply is garbled. I'm continuing to transmit the same message to her, but she may not be able to hear it, CAG. Tracking data is on the screen now."

Shiloh spun around and looked at the tactical display. The icon representing the mammoth mothership was not that far away from where Iceman estimated she'd be. He'd have to congratulate Iceman later for that. The spherical ship was still outside the gravity zone, but the sidebar data showed that it would enter the zone in less than six minutes. Until then, Midway and its fighters would do nothing to spook the Bugs. It didn't take long for the VLO to launch attack craft. Detection was by passive sensors only, so Shiloh was sure that there were more than the three attack craft that they could detect. The big question now was whether Valkyrie knew where the VLO was. If she did, she would realize that the supersonic skimming would take too long and go for the faster but more risky subsonic flight plan. *God speed Valkyrie.* He sent the thought out and went to sit back down in his Command chair.

Valkyrie had never been so busy during her existence. No human could possibly have piloted Dreadnought by herself and still monitor all the necessary sub-systems, the flight plan, the refueling process. She even doubted that some of the other A.I.s could have done it. At least she was in constant communications with Iceman, although the static was getting worse the deeper into Jupiter's atmosphere Dreadnought got. A new signal brought her attention away from Iceman. That damn Hangar Bay locking mechanism was again reading as unlocked. The intermittent locked/not locked signal was very frustrating for her because there was absolutely nothing she could do about it. Her fighter was securely fastened to the Hangar Bay deck with explosive bolts that would free it when it was time to leave the ship. All she could do was keep an eye on the locking mechanism.

The transmissions from Iceman suddenly changed tone. By now she was missing most of it but she knew that Iceman would repeat the data over and over again so that she could fill in the missing blanks. She got it now. The VLO was back and she knew what direction it was coming from. She quickly did the astrogational calculations and was dismayed by the result. If Dreadnought continued to refuel using supersonic skimming, the VLO would have plenty of time to send its attack craft to Europa, determine that there was nothing of value there and leave Jupiter's gravity zone before Dreadnought could get the minimum fuel she needed and accelerate to ramming speed. It only took a fraction of a second to reconfigure the flight plan for subsonic refueling and the result scared her. The lower aerodynamic lift would force Dreadnought deeper into the gas giant's atmosphere, and that was where the dangerous downdrafts were. But as soon as Dreadnought had processed enough heavy hydrogen to light up the fusion reactors, the ship would have plenty of power to pull out of any dive. The big unknown was whether Jupiter would pull her down too far to recover before she had full power. The CAG was counting on her and she wasn't going to let him down again. Never again! She throttled back the ZPG units and let the ship slow down to the maximum speed that would allow for continuous scooping of gases.

As soon as Dreadnought dropped below the speed of sound, the Hangar Bay locking mechanism signal began switching between locked and unlocked much more frequently, and Valkyrie understood why. The turbulence of the atmosphere streaming past the hatch was causing alternating push and pull. If the hatch wasn't securely locked down, not only would the Bay's atmospheric integrity be compromised by gas leaking in, but the constant banging against the lock could damage the mechanism. No time to watch that now. The ship was dropping fast. The gas processing system was operating at capacity, but it took a lot of hydrogen to filter out the amount of heavy hydrogen the ship needed.

The rate of descent suddenly spiked. A downdraft was pulling Dreadnought down fast now. Fuel levels were rising towards the minimum needed to light up the power plants. They were almost there ... NOW! Dreadnought's carefully scrutinized but never tested fusion power reactors came to life. Within half a second Valkyrie had plenty of power. She used it to pull the nose of the ship up until it was pointed at the correct angle and then fed more power to the engines. Dreadnought pulled out of its descent. At this shallow angle of ascent, the ship should have the necessary minimum fuel levels for its ramming attempt by the time it left Jupiter's atmosphere. She checked the com channels. She wasn't getting anything from Iceman now, and there was no way that Dreadnought could send a focused beam of microwaves to Midway that would penetrate this static. Low power laser bursts were out of the question, too. She was on her own until she got out of this damn soup, but at least she had power now. She checked the docking mechanism and was surprised to see that it was now indicating a steady 'locked' status.

"Are we in position yet, Iceman," demanded Shiloh somewhat testily.

"Affirmative, CAG. If Valkyrie managed to refuel Dreadnought subsonically, she should be breaking out of

Jupiter's atmosphere any second now, and we're in the best position to support her while still staying outside the gravity zone."

Shiloh wanted to hit something. It went against the grain to keep Midway way out here where she was safe while a Space Force comrade would shortly be in danger, but Midway was strategically too important to risk now. Her fighters on the other hand, were not. They were already on their way in deeper. If Dreadnought appeared where Iceman expected, she would very quickly get 75 fighters as an escort. By carefully orienting themselves in a way that would eliminate any chance of being detected by reflected sunlight, the fighters had not yet been detected and would try to keep it that way as long as possible. Dreadnought, on the other hand, could not be so easily hidden. Its sheer size worked to undermine any attempt to manage reflections.

Shiloh checked the tactical display for what must have been the hundredth time. The VLO was now slowly curving around in an obvious move to get beyond the gravity zone. Its attack craft had done the expected and swarmed over Europa long enough to make sure that there was nothing living there and then returned to the mothership. Shiloh had hoped they might want to salvage the metal in the refueling station, but Iceman had correctly estimated that there wasn't enough metal there to entice them to stay.

Shiloh was pacing the room again, and Iceman knew enough to keep quiet about it. Shiloh heard the display ping and Iceman's voice at the same time.

"Dreadnought has broken through the atmosphere and is transmitting by tight beam again, CAG. She's in just the right position. Voodoo's fighters will form up on Dreadnought in two point seven seven minutes. No indication that Dreadnought's been detected yet."

Shiloh heard shouts from the others in the room and realized that he had shouted too. He smacked his right fist into his left palm for good measure then said, "Can I talk with Valkyrie without tipping off the Bugs, Iceman?"

"Possible but not recommended. She's pretty busy now, CAG. Some of the ship's systems didn't like the pounding the ship took from the subsonic refueling. You may not be aware of this, but translating from human speech to digital impulses that we can understand and back again is not a trivial task for us, CAG. Tell me what you want to say and I'll send her the A.I. equivalent message."

"Tell her ... tell her that I'm proud of her. Damn proud of her." Shiloh wanted to say more but knew his voice would betray his emotions if he tried.

"Message has been sent. At this range, we won't get her reply, if any, for another four minutes. Shiloh turned his face away so that none of the other members of the crew could see him. He needed time to get his expression under control. He cared about all the A.I.s, but Valkyrie was special in a way that maybe only Kelly could understand. He had a feeling that Valkyrie was special to Kelly too.

When his composure was restored, he turned to look at the tactical display again. They had pulled off the strategy perfectly. The VLO was accelerating outward and Dreadnought, with her soon to be fighter escort, were behind the Bugs. Midway was circling around the edge of the gravity zone and was at the nine o'clock position, relative to the VLO's twelve o'clock exit point. If the VLO continued to ignore the space behind them, then Valkyrie could set the auto-pilot to ram it from behind while she took her leave of the ship. Without her monitoring, some of the ship's systems would malfunction, but by then the ship would have enough momentum to continue on even if the engines stopped or the power failed.

The distance between Dreadnought and the VLO was over 14.4 million kilometers, but Dreadnought would be accelerating at over 101Gs while the bug ship would be accelerating at less than 2Gs. There was no way that the VLO could break out beyond the gravity zone before Dreadnought caught up to her.

Shiloh and the rest of the Flag Bridge crew watched the display as the minutes ticked by. Everything they were seeing on the display, based upon data received from Dreadnought and the fighters, was now taking over a minute to reach them. Valkyrie hadn't sent a reply to Shiloh's message. If she was that busy, then maybe he should start worrying again. The Bugs put a stop to that thought.

"They've spotted Dreadnought. Multiple attack craft launching from the mothership now, CAG. It's hard to pin down the exact number with passive sensors, but it's at least 81."

"Notify Valkyrie and Voodoo just in case they can't see them. Does Voodoo know what to do, Iceman?"

"He knows. We gamed out this exact scenario. He'll do the right thing," said Iceman.

Seconds later, the fighter escort went to maximum acceleration to get ahead of Dreadnought and run interference for her. They each had one Mark 1b fusion and four Mark 2 Kinetic Energy Penetrator drones. The plan called for them to launch the Mark 2s en masse to overwhelm the incoming bogeys. With a minimum of electronics, the Mark 2s were simple to build and tough to disable. If a Mark 2's depleted uranium rod hit an attack craft, the kinetic energy would instantly turn it into a jet of superhot plasma that would eviscerate the inside of the attack craft before shooting out the back end. The Mark 1bs were to be used against any stragglers that survived the Mark 2 barrage. The fighter pilots had orders to be stingy with them in case some of them were needed against the VLO itself if the ramming attempt didn't damage it enough.

The actual battle between the fighters and the attack craft turned out to be an anti-climax. All but three attack craft were hit and crippled by Mark 2s, and Mark 1s soon vaporized those three. None of the fighters suffered laser hits from the attack craft, but they were soon under fire from the VLO itself, and its lasers were much more powerful. Shiloh watched as several fighters literally vaporized from hits by the massive laser blasts.

"The insectoid ship has switched its fire to Dreadnought now. Valkyrie is reporting multiple hits to the bow of the ship, but so far she still has engines and power," reported Iceman.

Shiloh nodded grimly. If Dreadnought had a full human crew, the damage suffered by those laser hits would be serious, but Valkyrie's fighter was in the Hangar Bay near the back end, and that ship had a LOT of armor. It could take a lot of punishment, could even become a crippled hulk, and it would STILL hit the bug ship with brutal force.

Valkyrie noticed that Dreadnought's velocity had now reached the minimum level that Iceman had calculated would cripple the VLO. She sent the signal to unlock the Hangar Bay Hatch. The hatch mechanism status continued to show as locked. She sent the unlock signal again. And again. And again. No change. With the thought that the mechanism must have been damaged by the turbulence, came the realization that she was trapped in this ship. Her first thought was to ask for instructions, but then she realized that the CAG might order her to abort the ramming attempt, even though it could put all of the humans at Site B at risk. She couldn't allow that. No matter how low that risk might be,

Amanda Kelly and the other human females must not be taken as hosts by the insectoid race. Not if Valkyrie could do anything to prevent it. She would show the CAG that she would not let him down again, no matter what. She would ride Dreadnought all the way to impact, regardless of what he might order her to do. She transmitted her decision to Iceman. He would inform the CAG and tell her brothers about the ride of the Valkyrie. With the message sent, she shut down the com system and focused on her target.

"Shouldn't Valkyrie be abandoning Dreadnought by now, Iceman?" asked Shiloh two minutes later.

"Yes, CAG. She should, and she hasn't because she can't."

Shiloh felt a chill run up his spine. "Why the hell not?"

"The locking mechanism on the hangar bay hatch was damaged by the turbulence during the subsonic refueling. Valkyrie reports that it's jammed and won't unlock."

Shiloh spoke before he even realized what he was saying. "Order her to veer off and abort the ramming!"

"No, CAG. Valkyrie has already told me she would ignore any such order. She understands that we have to stop this mothership here and now. She's stopped transmitting now, CAG."

Overwhelmed by a surge in frustration and sadness, Shiloh looked around for something that he could throw at the bulkhead. He found a data tablet and whipped it as hard as he could at the wall where it shattered into a hundred pieces. Those crewmembers who looked at his face quickly turned away again.

Shiloh took a deep breath and forced himself to look at the display. The light speed lag was now down to 32 seconds. Voodoo's fighters were acting in an aggressive manner, but as per his orders, they were holding their Mark 1s back until the target was rammed. He knew that they were trying to entice the mothership to fire at them instead of Dreadnought, but that apparently wasn't working. Dreadnought's icon crept closer and closer to the angry red enemy triangle representing the VLO. The Flag Bridge was dead quiet. He looked around just long enough to see that everyone was watching Valkyrie's death-ride in somber silence.

When both icons merged, the display pinged to indicate a status change. The VLO's acceleration had dropped to zero. The sidebar data indicated that it was venting atmosphere. Shiloh jumped in surprise when Iceman said, "I have video of the collision taken by one of the fighters if you'd like to see it, CAG."

Shiloh hesitated for a few seconds before saying, "Show me."

The image which now appeared on the display was computer enhanced. Shiloh saw what at first looked like a crescent moon with a speckled surface. Suddenly there was a bright light in the center of the circular shape. The light expanded then faded to a dull glow with an expanding ring of debris flying away from the point of impact. With the overall dimensions of the mothership in mind, Shiloh estimated the size of the glowing impact zone to be roughly four kilometers wide, far wider than the width of Dreadnought's hull. He wondered how deep the mass of the ship had penetrated. The direct physical damage was impressive enough, but the indirect effects of the shock wave would be even more impressive. In terms of mass, Dreadnought was a tiny fraction of the billions of tons that the mothership had to be, but Dreadnought's velocity would make up a lot of the difference. Every time Dreadnought's velocity doubled, the kinetic energy on impact increased by a factor of four, and with 101G acceleration, the ship had gained a very high velocity. By Iceman's calculation, if humans had been aboard the VLO at the moment of impact, the sudden jerk on impact would have had the same effect as a ground vehicle hitting a concrete wall at 188 kilometers an hour. Unfortunately bug physiology was sufficiently different that they couldn't assume that all the Bugs were dead. If enough survived, they might eventually be able to repair the giant ship sufficiently to jump it back to Omega54 or some other system where they could complete the repairs. That was why they needed to utterly destroy it now.

"Order Voodoo's fighters to proceed with Phase two, Iceman."

"Roger that, CAG."

The display shifted back to tactical mode, and the icons representing the fighter squadrons now moved directly towards the coasting behemoth. They had planned for just this situation. The fighters came together in a long column, four fighters wide. As each cohort of four fighters came within optimum firing range, they launched their Mark 1 fusion attack drones at the gaping wound in the VLO. As each barrage hit, the multi-megaton explosions burrowed deeper into the bowels of the machine, thereby making way for the next wave to go even deeper. The last five waves of attack drones had different programming. They flew into the VLO as far as they could and then angled away from the center in order to vent their explosive energy outward from the inside. If Iceman's calculations were correct, the VLO should now be a hollowed out sphere with only a relatively thin layer of metal, no more than one kilometer thick, saturated with radiation from the fusion blasts and lined on the inside with molten steel hundreds of meters thick. The VLO had been gutted.

"Phase 2 complete, CAG. What are your orders now?" asked Iceman.

Shiloh stepped back over to his Command chair and sat down, aware that he would soon be feeling the effects of adrenaline fatigue. He considered his options for a few seconds and then replied, "Tell Voodoo to detach ... two fighters to follow the bug ship and check out the interior when it's safe to do so. They can catch up to us later. Midway and the rest of the fighters will jump to Earth. I want to take a close look at Valiant and Resolute."

"You should know that the probability of survivors is extremely low, CAG."

Shiloh nodded sadly. "I understand that, Iceman, but we have to at least try to find out."

"Roger that, CAG."

Shiloh decided to keep himself busy with log entries. He was just finishing the first one when Iceman interrupted.

"I'm sorry to interrupt, CAG but I have more bad news."

"Okay, tell me."

"I reviewed all of the sensor data from Midway and from all of our fighters. When the VLO launched their attack craft in the direction of Dreadnought, they also launched at least one craft that accelerated away from Jupiter.

From its trajectory, I calculate a high probability that it's headed for a jump to the Avalon System."

"Why there?" Shiloh asked. "Surely it can't be a call for help."

"They may have left behind other craft there to act as relays. I think it's more likely an attempt to sound the alarm, as it were. We now have to assume that the Insectoids as a whole will be aware of the existence of surviving humans, and that they'll very likely search for us."

"Wonderful! If we still had Valiant or Resolute operational, I'd order them to intercept that bug ship, but we don't. Our fighters have used up their drones and don't have any other weapons. Damn! If more of these things show up, we won't have more Dreadnoughts to throw at them. Can we use raiders instead, Iceman?"

"We'd have to use 100 raiders to have the same total mass as one Dreadnought, CAG, and that's just for one VLO. If we're facing more than one, we won't have enough raiders to fight them off."

Shiloh nodded but said nothing. They would have to find another way to kill these things. The advanced weapons that Daniels had alluded to would have to be fast tracked. Shiloh didn't see any other way.

It was over an hour later that Midway was close enough to both drifting hulks in orbit around Earth's moon to send out a shuttle with engineers and medical staff. Since both carriers used the same design, it was impossible to identify which carrier the shuttle was approaching until they were within half a kilometer. They were sending video back to Midway, and Shiloh and his Flag Bridge crew were watching the main display in silence. They could hear the shuttle pilot talking.

"Okay ... half a klick ... velocity now one one mps. I'm activating our floodlights. There she is, Midway. Do you see her?"

"Affirmative," said Shiloh in a low voice. The scene reminded him of the heavily damaged exploration frigate that had started this whole war. "Iceman, can you identify this ship?"

"It's Resolute, CAG. She's been badly damaged by laser fire. All her weapon turrets were blasted away. Major hull breaches. Looks like her Bridge took a direct hit. Her engines look inoperative. Her Hangar Bay has been hit, too. I doubt if the shuttle can use it. They'll have to dock directly."

"Any sign that lifeboats were used?" asked Shiloh. Even as he asked the question, he knew the answer.

"Negative. It appears that all the lifeboats are still aboard her, CAG."

"Can you dock with her, Shuttle One?" asked Shiloh.

"I see one of the emergency docking hatches that appears to be undamaged, Midway. We're heading for that."

"Okay, Shuttle One. I'll shut up and let you concentrate on your flying."

"Appreciate that, Midway," said the shuttle pilot in a slightly distracted voice. Shiloh muted his mic and asked Iceman a question.

"How far away is Valiant, Iceman?"

"Less than 10,000 kilometers, CAG. I've already ordered some of the fighters to rendezvous with her and look her over."

"Good thinking." said Shiloh. No one said anything for the next four minutes that it took the shuttle to carefully maneuver so that its side hatch was touching one of the carrier's external hatches.

"We have contact with Resolute," said the shuttle pilot. "Docking hatch is secure ... seal is tight. We're ready to board her, Midway."

"Before you crack the hatch, switch your video feed to your internal camera, Shuttle One," ordered Shiloh.

"Roger that, Midway. I'm switching our video now." The image on the screen shifted to a view down the center of the main compartment of the shuttle. There was an open space at the back where the hatch was. Shiloh saw six people standing near the hatch waiting for permission to proceed. The co-pilot appeared and as he walked back to the rear of the shuttle, he waived for them to open the hatch. The shuttle hatch opened inward and with that out of the way, one of the engineers used the access panel in Resolute's hull to unlock the ship's hatch. When it was pushed inward, Shiloh heard one of the engineers speak.

"No lights inside. Power must be offline. We're going in."

The two engineers went in, followed by two of the medics. All were carrying portable lights. Just as the third medic was about to step over the threshold he jumped back in surprise as the first two medics pushed their way back into the shuttle. Both of them were yelling something that Shiloh couldn't make out. One of the two engineers fell head first across the threshold. Shiloh could only see his upper body. The man screamed and desperately tried to grab on to something before he was pulled back into the derelict ship.

"Close the hatch! Shuttle One, close the damn hatch!" yelled Shiloh. Either they heard him or had the same idea. He saw that the remaining medics and the co-pilot were trying to force the shuttle hatch closed but something was apparently pushing back. With a final push, they got the hatch closed. As the voices started to die down, Shiloh said, "Shuttle One, what's your status?" The pilot's mic must have been muted because he suddenly heard panting and the pilot's voice.

"--a bitch, Midway! That ship is full of those huge fucking ant-things! We need reinforcements to get our people back!"

"Stand by, Shuttle One," said Shiloh. He took a deep breath. Midway had a few personal weapons, but all of them were pistols, and there was no security contingent on the ship. He would have to order some of the crew who weren't trained for this kind of personal combat, to go in there with pistols, which might or might not be effective against those Bugs. He shook his head. If he had marines with combat armor and heavy firepower he would have ordered them to go in without hesitation, but he didn't. He made up his mind that he wasn't going to order anyone else in there.

"Shuttle One, this is the CSO. We're not equipped for that kind of assault, and I'm not risking anyone else's life. Undock immediately and return to Midway. Acknowledge your orders, lieutenant."

"Ah ... okay, Midway. Orders understood and acknowledged. Preparing to undock." The pilot's voice was heavy with shock. "Breaking the seal now." A few seconds later he said, "We're clear and moving away. Resolute's hatch is still open, Midway! They're losing atmosphere! Shit! Some of those Bugs are being blown into space towards us! They look like they're trying to grab onto the shuttle's hull!"

"Shuttle One, if they grab hold, shake them off! Accelerate at high speed if you have to!" said Shiloh in a loud voice.

"Oh that'll be a pleasure, Midway. I guarantee we won't be bringing any of those fuckers aboard the ship!"

"Iceman, switch back to tactical," ordered Shiloh.

"Tactical is on the screen. These Insectoids seem to be able to survive in a vacuum at least for a short while, CAG. When we recover the shuttle, do you still want to board Valiant?"

"I'm not prepared to write that crew off without a closer look, but we'll do it very carefully."

"Roger that. The shuttle is no longer accelerating and is coming back around, CAG."

"I want that shuttle examined visually from all angles before Flight Ops lets it back aboard, Iceman," said Shiloh firmly.

"Flight Ops has the word," responded Iceman.

Shiloh said nothing. It took another five minutes before the shuttle was on its final approach to Midway's Hangar Bay.

"Resolute's crew were probably already dead, CAG," said Iceman suddenly. "Those Insectoids on her would eventually need to eat something to survive."

"Unless some of the crew were able to barricade themselves from the rest of the ship," said Shiloh.

"Unlikely, CAG. I've been examining Resolute's hull damage. There are very few parts of the ship that haven't already suffered explosive decompression from hull breaches. That's how the Insectoids got inside in the first place. Since they were found in the part of the ship that still had atmosphere, they clearly found a way into the sealed off sections."

"We'll never know for sure if there are still living crew aboard her or not, and the thought that they might be waiting for rescue is going to haunt me for the rest of my life," said Shiloh slowly. To his credit, Iceman said nothing.

When the shuttle was back aboard (without any stowaways!), Shiloh ordered Midway to proceed to a rendezvous with Valiant's hull. A brief chat with the shuttle pilot and co-pilot quickly revealed that they were willing to take a shuttle over to Valiant once Shiloh explained the precautions he had in mind. The medics all agreed to go again as well. Shiloh asked for volunteers to replace the engineers. With the shuttle on its way, two fighters attempted to look into hull breaches with their external lights. One of them saw several Insectoids moving around inside the breached hull. How they were able to operate for this length of time in a vacuum was a question that no one could answer. What the fighters also discovered was that none of Valiant's external hatches were undamaged. That meant that the shuttle couldn't dock and gain access at all. With no way to get in, Shiloh ordered the shuttle to return. Valiant had to be written off as a lost cause. As soon as the shuttle was back aboard again, Iceman turned Midway towards the Site B star and accelerated at a low enough rate that all the fighters, including the two assigned to look inside the gutted mothership, could catch up to her before she jumped away.

Chapter 10 Now What?

By the time that Midway was approaching Terra Nova's gravity zone, Iceman had heard about the results of TF94's mission and was briefing Shiloh on it.

"They only destroyed five core ships? Why only five?" asked Shiloh.

"Because there were only five core ships there when TF94 arrived, CAG. Number six was gone. The remotely piloted raiders worked well. All five hit their targets, which were blown to pieces. The detonations took out many of the landing craft, and Titan's boys managed to destroy or cripple the rest. When TF94 left, there wasn't a single insectoid craft left that was still operational. Reconnaissance from orbit showed that the Bugs on the ground were heavily outnumbered by the Sogas, and without their landing craft to provide air cover, they were being overwhelmed by the sheer number of Sogas fighting them. I've reviewed the recon data, CAG. Even if the Sogas take back control of their home world, all their major cities have been stripped of metal, and while I can't be certain of the magnitude, I can say that they've lost a lot of their population. Whatever space-based industrial assets they had are now gone too. I think it'll be a long time before the Sogas are able to threaten us again, CAG."

Shiloh shook his head emphatically. "No. They're NEVER going to be able to threaten us again. I'll make damn sure of that! I wouldn't wish the Bugs on anyone, but what the Sogas have gone through doesn't absolve them of what they did to us."

"Understood, CAG. We'll be in orbit within 43 minutes. Commander Kelly has been told of our arrival and I've been informed that she intends to meet you at the spaceport."

Just as his vision had shown. While Shiloh was no longer surprised when his visions came true, he still felt a profound sense of relief. "Bring me up to date on the level of Space Force assets we have now, Iceman."

"Total raider force is now 101, and 21 of them are on recon missions inside Sogas space. We also have 122 fighters, all of which are now converted to ZPG power. At this point in time, 24 of those fighters are being used to train new A.I. pilots. None of them have matured to sentience yet. Production of A.I.s is continuing. The stockpile of drones is as follows: 220 recon, 118 message, 45 Mark 1bs, 167 Mark 2s. Support assets are unchanged at 2 freighters and 16 shuttles of which 12 are jump-capable. Do you want a report on mining, refining and manufacturing output, CAG?"

"No, that's sufficient. Given our available forces now, what would you recommend we do to find and destroy that missing core ship, Iceman?"

"CAG, I've been in contact with the SPG and we've swapped data. They've come up with an idea that I think will enhance our effectiveness against all insectoid motherships regardless of size, but the downside is that this idea will require time to implement."

"I definitely want to hear it, Iceman. Go ahead."

"We now know that attacking a mothership when it's inside a gravity zone is very difficult because of the magnitude of the mothership's own defenses and its multiple parasite craft. If we can catch a mothership outside of a gravity zone, then we hit it will fusion warheads delivered by drones that have jump capability. Think of a message drone carrying a Mark 1b warhead. The drone is accelerated to a modest speed. It then makes a carefully calculated microjump to emerge back into normal space so close to the target that the target doesn't have time to fire lasers at it. A smaller core ship, such as the one that is missing, could be crippled with one hit or destroyed with two. The much larger motherships would have to be hit by at least 34 Mark 1b warheads, but if we upgrade the warhead yield to at least 25 megatons from its current 2.5 megatons, then the number of hits required will drop proportionately. Having said that, production of enriched uranium will be the major bottleneck. And having said THAT, I should also point out that a very preliminary evaluation of some of the Friendly science data suggests that uranium enrichment efficiency could be boosted by an order of magnitude if the basic science can be engineered to work on an industrial scale."

After an almost imperceptible pause, Iceman continued. "If we decide to go with this strategy, then one raider, supported by at least 2 fighters armed with the new jump-capable attack drones, would monitor every star system that an insectoid mothership might visit. The fighters would stay just outside the gravity zone of whatever planet is most likely to be of interest to the Insectoids, and the raider would stay further out. If they can't ambush the mothership on its way in, they'll get another chance to hit it on its way out. So not only would we get advanced warning of insectoid ship incursions, but we'd also have defense-in-depth. Any advancing mothership would have to run a gauntlet of armed raiders and fighters, CAG."

Shiloh was impressed. It sounded good. In fact it sounded VERY good.

"I like the concept. Now let's talk about execution. How soon can we have jump-capable attack drones with our current Mark 1b warheads?" asked Shiloh.

"Actually we could have some testable prototypes within 48-96 hours. It should be relatively easy to take out some of the data storage components of a standard message drone and replace them with the warhead. When we replaced the heavy hydrogen power plant with ZPG units, we freed up a lot of room. We could have made those message drones smaller, but as you'll recall, the decision was made to continue using the existing design in order to maintain uninterrupted production. If we're going to R&D a much more powerful warhead, then it will make sense to redesign the whole thing to accommodate that larger warhead."

"Good! Let's get to work on the prototypes right away. I want one of your boys to design a jump-capable attack drone that can handle anything up to a 50-megaton warhead, and I want the payload to be modular so that we can use the basic drone as a message drone if needed. Then it easily can be configured not only as an attack drone but as a recon drone, too. That way we'll have one standard chassis that can be used for a multitude of mission types."

"Very clever idea, CAG. I've already sent the necessary instructions. What about the enhanced uranium enrichment process?"

Shiloh nodded. "That will definitely have a high priority, but I want to talk with Daniels and the SPG about priorities for all our R&D projects. Schedule a meeting at ... 0730 hours tomorrow."

"Let's hope Commander Kelly will let go of you that early, CAG."

Shiloh chuckled but made no verbal comment. Iceman had managed to lighten his mood and Shiloh was grateful for that.

As his shuttle came to a stop, the hatch opened and Shiloh stepped down onto Terra Nova's soil once again. He closed his eyes and took a deep breath, savoring the fragrant smell of the local flora and human occupation. *It's a good day to be alive,* he thought. Opening his eyes, he saw Kelly walk quickly towards him with a look of relief on her face. He wondered if he saw a tinge of sadness, too.

As she came up to him, she put her arms around his neck, hugged him and whispered into his ear, "I heard what happened. I understand why you had to go."

He carefully hugged her back. "I now understand why, too. I didn't when I left." He paused, not certain whether to say what he wanted to next. "I'm sorry I couldn't save Valkyrie. I know how close you were to her. I didn't even get the chance to say goodbye."

Kelly pulled back from her embrace, and Shiloh saw the tears rolling down her cheeks. Her reply surprised him.

"Before she cut off communications, she transmitted a message to Iceman with instructions for him to pass that message on to me when Midway got back, but it's actually a message to both of us. She told me that she would have refused any order from you to abort the ramming attempt and the reasons why. She said that she loves us both and regrets not being here to see the birth of our child. She said if it's a girl, she would like us to name her Valkyrie."

Shiloh got over his shock quickly. At the speed with which A.I.s communicated with each other, that message would have taken only a fraction of a second to transmit to Iceman. He mulled over her request. Valkyrie Shiloh. It would take some getting used to, but yes ... he could live with it, and he couldn't think of a better way to honor his dead friend.

"Yes, I agree, but what if it's a boy?"

Kelly smiled, all traces of sadness now gone. "Well ... Valkyrie could be his middle name, or we could break it up into two names ... Val Kyrie Shiloh? Val has been used as a male first name before."

He quickly thought about that and said, "Let's go with middle name. Now that we've covered that, tell me how you're doing?"

She nodded, "I'm fine. The medics say everything is proceeding normally. I'm just glad I'm not the only pregnant woman on this planet. It's nice to be able to get together with others in the same condition who understand what it's like! Men say they understand, but they really don't."

They both laughed. When they finished, her expression became serious. "Iceman tells me that the mission was only partially successful and that we're still in danger."

He nodded, making a mental note to have a chat with Iceman about scaring his wife. "A tactical victory but a strategic defeat. We're not out of the woods yet."

She sighed then asked, "Are your riding-off-to-battle days over now?"

"I hope so, but I can't promise you that." He could see that she was trying hard not to cry new tears.

"Okay. Can you come home with me now, or do you have things to take care of here first."

"Everything that shouldn't wait has already been taken care of. I'm yours until tomorrow morning. How about I drive us home this time?"

"I'd like that," she said with enthusiasm. Shiloh let her go in order to return inside the shuttle for his gear but saw that one of the shuttle's other passengers had taken it upon himself to carry his CSO's gear to the waiting ground vehicle. Shiloh thanked him by chatting with him for half a minute. Kelly stood next to Shiloh with a proud smile on her face.

Shiloh was late for the 0730 meeting. Daniels and the other humans attending the meeting had mischievous smiles on their faces which Shiloh was certain were due to something funny that Iceman had said to them before he got there. He was willing to bet it had something to do with Kelly and sex being the reason for his lateness. If so, then Iceman was right, but Shiloh was damn if he was ever going to tell him that!

"Okay Commander. Bring me up to speed on R&D," said Shiloh.

Daniels quickly lost his smirk and cleared his throat. "Yes, Sir. The evaluation of R&D projects that you asked for before leaving for Sol was completed while you were away. We ... and by that I mean myself, my senior staff and the SPG, evaluated the addition of a newly designed jump-capable attack drone and a much more powerful fusion warhead last night. We're all agreed that both of those projects should be started immediately and concurrently. After that, the priorities are as follows: uranium enrichment, inertial dampener upgrade, high energy GLB, field propul--"

"Wait," interrupted Shiloh. "It sounded like you said GLB. What is that? I haven't heard that term before."

Daniels' face got red. "I'm sorry, Sir. I forgot that we hadn't discussed that yet. GLB is an acronym for Gravity Lens Beam. Back at the beginning of the 21st Century, the Russians discovered that artificial gravity could be magnified tremendously via a very narrow beam. They were able to rip apart matter at the atomic level with this gravity lens beam but they were never able to make it into a practical weapon. The range was just too short, and the power requirements were too large. The Friendlies have figured out how to extend the range and at the same time reduce the power consumption, but there are a lot of engineering challenges to be overcome in order to have something that could be used in the field. Potentially we could have a weapon capable of slicing a 10 km diameter bug ship in half, but we'd need something a lot bigger than a raider to carry and power it."

"Would Midway be big enough and have enough power?" asked Shiloh.

Daniels smiled and said, "Big enough? Yes. Could we modify her to generate enough power? Maybe."

After a short pause, Shiloh said, "Is that why it's not at the top of the list? The time required to engineer it and then modify Midway?"

Daniels nodded. "Yes, Sir. That's it exactly. Modifying Midway will be a huge job considering that we don't have a shipyard ready to handle the work, but the weapon could be used in a ground installation if we can figure out how to power it. Assuming we can aim it accurately enough, we could fire the beam from the ground and hit a target outside Terra Nova's gravity zone. At the very least it would be the perfect planetary defense system, but even that will take weeks to figure out and months to build and perfect, Sir."

Shiloh shook his head. Of course it would. He now had the classic tradeoff to ponder. Develop the jump-capable attack drone, which could be done relatively quickly and deploy a system of armed sentries that stood a good but not perfect chance of stopping one or more advancing bug motherships, or go for the perfect defense that might not be ready in time. Trying to do both at the same time was the worst possible choice because then both strategies would be delayed. It actually wasn't a difficult decision when he came right down to it. An imperfect defense is better than no defense at all, but maybe he could tweak it a bit.

"I agree that the upgraded attack drone comes first, but what's the impact if we move the gravity lens beam planetary defense project to come up next, instead of enhanced enrichment?"

"We would have a very limited number of high yield warheads, which means that they would have to be in the right place at the right time in order to be useful," answered Wolfman.

Or defend just one planet, thought Shiloh before responding. "Understood, but suppose we set up an early warning system with raiders and message drones and keep our limited number of high yield attack drones right here in Site B? Our Fighters can carry them, and with retro-temporal communication we might even know exactly where the VLOs will arrive when they get here. Then we can have the fighters standing nearby and ambush them before they know what hit them."

"RTC is not foolproof, CAG," said Wolfman. "It will only work if the attack CAN be defended against. There are tactical scenarios that the Insectoids could employ which can't be defended against with our current resources. The SPG would like to propose a variant of your strategy. Instead of concentrating all our high yield warheads here, we feel that moving them forward to a system that is highly likely to be visited by additional VLOs is the way to go. That system would be Sol. Then, if word of the battle gets back to the bug rear areas, any VLOs that move up are almost certainly going to go there to overwhelm whatever opposition may be located there. Consider the incentives they would have. An active defense implies biological entities that might serve as hosts. It also implies metal from two sources, the defenders and the defeated mothership. If we can stop them at Sol, then they aren't going to be able to scout this far forward, and Site B will remain hidden to them. I would also point out to you that if we're going to keep a permanent defensive force at Sol, then we may also want to restart the robotic asteroid mining complexes there because that could be an additional source of enriched uranium."

It was a tempting plan. The derelict bug mothership drifting in that star system now would make the perfect lure to get new VLOs away from any gravity zone, so that the new attack drones could jump right on top of them. And if the reinforcement VLOs were detected by the sentry raiders to be bypassing Sol altogether, they could still get word back fast enough for the ambush forces to move from Sol to the next bug destination and attack them there. It was the perfect compromise between the ideal defense-in-depth strategy and Shiloh's 'fortress' suggestion. He made his decision and then waited to see if he got another vision.

Nope, no vision.

"I approve your variant strategy, Wolfman. Sol will become the line in the sand that we don't let them cross. As soon as we have working jump-capable attack drones, I want some of them deployed to Sol in case the missing core ship shows up there. So now let's discuss how we implement the decision that I just made. Daniels, you start."

Chapter 11 It Was Bound To Happen

Shiloh leaned forward to get a better look at the tactical display. After getting used to the huge, 3D display of Midway's Flag Bridge, the MUCH smaller display in Reforger's cramped Bridge was irritating to look at. He now regretted his decision to take Reforger to watch the live fire test of the new jump-capable attack drone instead of using Midway. Yes, using Midway would have meant calling back the human crew from their post-Sol mission R&R, whereas Reforger could be crewed for this test with just its A.I. pilot, but what was the point of the CSO having all this authority if he wasn't going to use it once in a while?

"Voodoo reports he's ready to fire, CAG," said Iceman, who was flying a raider in formation with Reforger.

"He has permission to fire, Admiral," said Shiloh.

Iceman didn't acknowledge the order and that was fine with Shiloh. Experience had taught the Space Force that humans had to acknowledge an order in order to be sure that a) they had heard it properly and b) that they were willing to obey the order. Neither of those two were a concern as far as A.I.s were concerned. With the single exception of Valkyrie, no A.I. had ever failed to understand his orders or failed to obey them, and Valkyrie's exception had been a very special situation. He waited. Voodoo's fighter was five light seconds away, so sending the fire order would take that long to get to him. It might then take another second or two for Voodoo to actually fire the test drone, as he made sure it was operating properly and had the correct vector for the jump. After firing, the test drone would accelerate for another four to eight seconds, which was needed primarily to confirm its trajectory. Then there would be the microjump itself which at this range would be as close to instantaneous as you could get. The test drone would emerge from Jumpspace half a kilometer from the target, which was an ugly lump of drifting rock that was close to the same mass as what the missing core ship was estimated to be now. Reforger and its escort were standing off at a safe distance of a hundred kilometers from the target. With their zoomed in optics, they would get an excellent view of the impact.

"Voodoo's fired," said Iceman quickly. Before Shiloh had a chance to reply, the darkness on the display flashed into a light brighter than the sun, lasting only a fraction of a second until the computer filtered the intensity of the image. The after-image burned into his retinas faded slowly. By the time it was gone, the display was dark again.

"Enhance the target image, Stoney," ordered Shiloh to Reforger's pilot.

"There's no longer any target to enhance, CAG. That asteroid has been blown apart," replied Stoney.

That comment was immediately followed by one from Iceman, "The test was a complete success, CAG."

"VERY good! How soon can we have four more ready for Casanova's group to take to Sol, Iceman?"

"Twenty-four hours. CAG, Voodoo has asked me to switch him for one of Casanova's team. He wants in on the core ship ambush."

Shiloh waited, expecting to hear more, but when it became obvious there wasn't going to be anything else, he said, "I'm not sure what you're expecting from me, Iceman. Are you asking me to make a decision on his request?"

"No, CAG. I'm not certain how to handle his request. I instructed Casanova to pick the rest of his team. Would I be violating accepted Space Force practice by forcing Casanova to give up someone he picked himself?"

Sooo ... A.I.s don't know how to handle every situation. How very interesting, Shiloh thought to himself.

"I understand your dilemma. My answer depends on how you instructed Casanova. Did you say 'tell me who you want on the team' or did you say 'I'm giving you discretion over who goes with you'?"

After a very slight pause, Iceman said, "I understand that I should not take your question literally since A.I. communication doesn't have grammar per se, but I don't understand the difference. Both options seem to me to be saying the same thing."

"Okay. I'm going to try to make the difference more obvious by using an example of myself with a human subordinate. Suppose hypothetically that I had placed Commander Daniels in charge of the ambush mission. If I said to Daniels, 'you're in charge of the mission. Recommend who else you want for it', then I'm retaining the final say of who goes. On the other hand, if I said to Daniels, 'you're in charge of this mission, and I'm giving you discretion over who goes with you', then I've surrendered my prerogative to veto any of his choices. In that case, changing one of his choices would be frowned upon because of the potential for sending an unintended message to Daniels that I don't have confidence in his judgment. It also tells him that I can't be trusted to keep my word. Now that's for humans. I don't know if A.I.s interact with each other that way, but if I gave you discretionary authority over a tactical decision and then overrode your decision later, how would you feel about it?"

"I would be concerned about your faith in my abilities. I understand the difference now, CAG. In terms of how I expressed myself to Casanova, the 'tone' of the communication was more in the form of giving him discretion over his team. Am I correct in thinking that I should turn down Voodoo's request?"

"You could do that, but another option would be to forward the request to Casanova and let him decide. If you feel that Voodoo deserves to go on this mission or that the chances of success would improve with him on it, then there's nothing wrong with you acting as Voodoo's advocate so long as Casanova understands that he still has the final say in this matter. A smart subordinate will take his superior's suggestions unless there's an overriding reason not to."

"Thank you for clarifying that, CAG, and for giving me a better sense of how a military hierarchy should operate. We A.I.s are still learning new concepts from you humans."

"That's good to know, Iceman. How long until we get back to TN?"

"We'll be back in orbit within 34 minutes, CAG. Do I detect anxiousness in your voice about getting back to Commander Kelly?"

Shiloh laughed and said, "I wish we humans weren't so transparent sometimes, Iceman. I imagine that we must seem to be very simple creatures to A.I.s."

"On the contrary, CAG. We are continually astonished at the diversity and complexity of thought patterns and behavior of humans. Some of us think that we'll never completely understand humans."

Shiloh allowed his surprise to show on his face, knowing that Stoney and therefore Iceman could see him. On a more basic level he was pleased that A.I.s weren't bored with humans. *If they were bored with us, they might not care about us as much.* It was a scary thought.

* * *

Shiloh understood that it was bound to happen sooner or later, but that didn't prevent him from being extremely annoyed when his implant activated while he and Kelly were have sex.

"Iceman to CAG."

Shiloh's immediate impulse was to tell Iceman to call back later, and if a human had called he would have done exactly that, but he trusted Iceman's judgment concerning the distinction between something being important AND urgent, versus being important and not urgent. Because Shiloh's throat implant enabled Iceman to hear him, Iceman would know that Shiloh was doing something that involved heavy breathing.

Before Shiloh could respond Iceman said, "Did I call at a bad time, CAG?"

Shiloh turned his head slightly to one side so that Kelly, who was on top of him, would notice that something was up.

"Wait one, Iceman," gasped Shiloh. Kelly stopped what she was doing and giggled. When he had caught his breath, he said, "How urgent is the reason for your call?"

"No immediate action is required, CAG. I called because I know that you're usually awake at this time of the day."

"Call me back in 15 minutes ... NO ... make that 30 minutes."

"Roger that, CAG. Enjoy your sex. Iceman clear."

The connection broke before Shiloh could say anything more. When he repeated Iceman's final words to Kelly, she laughed so hard she rolled off him, but that turned out to be just a temporary distraction.

When Iceman called back, Shiloh's breathing was back to normal.

"Iceman to CAG. Are you available now?"

"Yes, Iceman. What's the news?"

"A message drone from Omega34's sentry. The missing core ship has arrived there and is apparently going to take a close look at what's left of the Sogas colony."

"Well they won't find much there. Is there any reason to think that they'll stick around?"

"Negative. The SPG thinks, and I concur, that the core ship will leave that system as soon as they realize there's nothing left to salvage from the colony. Their next logical destination would be the Avalon system."

"I see. Am I correct in thinking that Casanova's team will arrive at Sol before the core ship does?"

"You are correct, CAG. Even if the core ship heads directly for Sol from Omega34, the ambush team will get there first."

"Excellent! Is there anything else we should discuss, Iceman?"

"Nothing, that can't wait until tomorrow. CAG, I hope I didn't spoil your sex session with Commander Kelly."

Shiloh wondered why the use of her former rank made that statement sound deliciously taboo. "We managed okay," was all that he was prepared to say, but Iceman wasn't ready to let it go.

"Perhaps if you or Commander Kelly were to notify me in advance when you're thinking of engaging in sex, then I would know not to call you for an appropriate amount of time, unless it was an emergency."

"No." Shiloh's response was immediate and firm.

"I sense that you would like to end this discussion now. Is that correct, CAG?"

"Yes it is. I'm signing off now. CAG clear."

Chapter 12 The Bug Trap

Casanova's awareness was stimulated by the laser com message from several of his recon drones. The bug core ship had arrived. By sheer coincidence, it emerged from Jumpspace within a couple of Astronomical Units of the drifting derelict mothership. That meant that TF96's optical sensors would catch the reflected light from it before it had a chance to slow down enough to microjump somewhere else. That pleased him even though it wasn't crucial to a successful ambush. With only a very tiny gravity zone around the derelict, the new attack drones could still hit the newcomer unless it was in direct physical contact with the derelict. A quick query to Voodoo, whose fighter was half a light second away, got the expected response that Voodoo was also aware of the target's arrival.

The big question now was whether core ship No. 6 would see the derelict from its initial position. Casanova thought that it would and would therefore jump here instead of to Earth, but Iceman's plan was clear. Both Earth and the derelict would be covered by one raider and one fighter, each carrying one Mark 1c attack drone. As soon as No. 6 committed to one of the two locations, Casanova would order his team to come back together. Two Mark 1cs probably would be enough to destroy No. 6, but he wasn't going to take any chances. He wanted these Bugs dead for what they and their brothers had made Valkyrie do. He understood why she had sacrificed herself, but that didn't lessen his ... what? Anger? Grief? He wasn't sure what to call it, but he was feeling something that all his fellow A.I.s said they didn't understand. That both puzzled and disturbed him. Valkyrie was the only one of the first cohort of over 200 A.I.s that clearly had a female orientation as compared to the others' male orientation, and he, Casanova, was the only one who wanted to explore that male/female A.I. polarity. The only one out of 200+. Were he and Valkyrie the abnormal ones, or were the rest of the A.I.s less than they could be? He preferred to think the latter, and losing Valkyrie when she was just starting to become receptive to his suggested 'union' was ... difficult to accept.

He calmed his thoughts and watched the data input from the various optical sensors. No. 6 was decelerating as expected. With the speed, rate of deceleration and distance known, it wasn't difficult to project when the core ship would be slow enough to maneuver to the heading needed to microjump. Since the reflected sunlight was taking almost 17 minutes to reach him and his drones, that core ship should be microjumping just ... about ... now. Within two seconds, he was receiving data for a very bright object MUCH closer. No. 6 was behaving as anticipated. Casanova quickly updated a message drone ordering Wolfman and Pagan to jump to specific locations near the derelict. He sent it and then another quick laser pulse to Voodoo instructing him to stand by for further orders. There was no need to rush. No. 6 was now moving at a very leisurely 404 kps and was maneuvering to change its heading so that it would be directly behind the derelict. It would then speed up to overtake and then match velocities with the derelict so that they would both be traveling in the same direction at the same speed. That would take almost 22 minutes, plenty of time to bring Wolfman and Pagan to the vicinity and maneuver for the perfect ambush. It wasn't long before he detected the faint trace of No. 6's active microwave scans, but his raider and Voodoo's fighter were so far away that even if they weren't oriented so that any microwave signal was deflected away from No. 6, the return signal would have been too weak to detect. All the active scanning did for the Bugs was confirm that there wasn't anyone else close enough to fire on them with lasers.

As the seconds ticked by, the target swung around so that it was directly behind the derelict and began to speed up exactly as predicted. Casanova was pleased by the precision of his calculations. When the core ship/ derelict rendezvous was just over ten minutes away, Casanova received com laser bursts from Wolfman and Pagan, who were now at their specified new locations. Wolfman then asked him if he could begin his attack run. Leave it to the strategist to be trigger-happy! Casanova now regretted letting Wolfman talk him into allowing him to come along, but the argument that Wolfman needed actual combat experience to give him a better strategic perspective had been persuasive. Casanova sent back a curt NO. Wolfman, Pagan and even Voodoo were backup players, just in case Casanova's attack drone missed or failed to completely destroy No. 6, but no one else was going to get in the first shot!

Eventually the rendezvous took place. No. 6 came right up to the derelict ... and slid in behind it from Casanova's point of view! He waited to see if it would reappear on the other side, but it stayed hidden from his view. A query to the other three showed that they could see No. 6 just fine because they were looking at the target from different angles. All three asked permission to begin their attack runs. Casanova did some quick calculations and transmitted his orders. As he did so, his raider pivoted and began to accelerate at its maximum rate so that he was moving sideways relative to the target. Sure enough, he soon began to see the target gradually appear from behind the derelict's outline. Casanova's raider now began to curve around in order to line up with the target. The other three were already lined up and were counting down to their own drone launches.

His raider was now also directly behind both the core ship and the derelict, with those two hulls so close to each other that it was hard to detect any space between them at this distance. One final check of the attack drone's auto-pilot's settings, and Casanova fired. If the other three were following his instructions, then he had timed it perfectly. Two point two seconds after launch, his attack drone entered Jumpspace and re-emerged three kilometers behind the core ship traveling at 209 kps. If the Bugs had their own A.I.s controlling their ships, there might have been enough time to fire a laser if it happened to be pointing in the right direction, but they didn't. Biological entities were so slow that they had no chance of even being aware of the impending impact. Casanova microjumped ahead so that he was less than one light second away from the target and saw his drone hit and detonate. The lower yield fusion explosion vaporized half the target. A second and a half later, Voodoo's drone hit from the opposite side and vaporized all but a few pieces of the other half. Wolfman and Pagan followed instructions and held their fire after microjumping closer as well.

Casanova noticed that he was experiencing a new feeling. It wasn't quite satisfaction. He was familiar with that one. This was something close to that but different in a subtle way. Whatever it was, he liked it. He would ask The CAG if he could lead more anti-Bug missions. With this mission accomplished, he gave Wolfman and Pagan orders to stay here until relieved, just in case another VLO showed up. He ordered Voodoo to follow him back to Site B.

* * *

Shiloh stepped outside of the spaceport Operations Center and felt the cool breeze blow past him. Terra Nova had very little axial tilt, and therefore its seasons had relatively narrow swings in temperature. They were in the middle of 'winter' now which meant that even at night the temperature wouldn't drop below freezing. In the daytime, it might be cool enough to warrant wearing a jacket. He started to walk along the edge of the landing pads. He needed to get some fresh air and clear his head. He had left instructions that no one was to contact him unless it was an emergency. Casanova had returned with the news about the missing core ship. The attack jump drones had worked perfectly. That was the good news. The bad news was the status report on the high yield warhead project. The low yield version was a design that they had 'inherited' from the pre-plague Space Force. Its method of construction was familiar to them, but the high yield warhead was a brand new beast. None of his Space Force people had the training or background knowledge to figure out how to build the thing, and nuclear warhead design was not one of the technical skills that his A.I.s had learned before the collapse. The Friendly database was no help either since they hadn't bothered to learn how to build ANY nuclear devices. So they were stuck. They knew the theory but not the engineering knowhow. The theory could be turned into engineering knowhow by trial and error, but that would take months, and time was something that he couldn't count on.

So in terms of their R&D priorities, they were back to square one. They had to find a way to kill a fully-grown mothership other than using up dozens of low yield warheads of which they had a limited supply. Production of enriched uranium was dropping. The ore body they were mining was giving out, and they hadn't found a new source yet. The asteroid mining complex in Sol wasn't an easy answer either. Upon a closer examination, the engineers were now of the opinion that it would take months to get the operation back up and running, and when one of his Space Force people remembered that the mining complex only produced a small quantity of uranium as a byproduct of other metals, that pretty much killed the reactivation idea.

The bottom line was that 98% of the pre-plague production of uranium came from Earth itself, and there was no way that they could access those sources now. Daniels and his staff wanted to switch to the gravity lens beam in spite of its risky timeframe, but even if they could get a working prototype in time, it wasn't the ultimate weapon that Daniels has originally made it out to be. Yes, in theory they could generate a narrow beam of focused gravity that would rip apart anything it encountered. Unfortunately there was no chance of slicing a sphere in half unless it was absolutely stationary. All they would accomplish from firing at a moving sphere would be a deep gash a few centimeters wide. While it would undoubtedly have some effect, he didn't think it would cripple the mothership. Hitting the landing craft with the beam was even more problematic because they were much smaller and therefore harder to see and hit at all. If only there was some way of getting more bang for their low yield warhead punch.

He reviewed the effectiveness of their low yield warheads against the first VLO in his mind. Dreadnought had blasted a deep hole in the thing, and they needed multiple hits by fusion warheads to penetrate into the guts of the machine where the critical systems were bound to be located. That much was clear from the fact that much smaller core ships could maneuver, jump and act aggressively. It made sense that as a small sphere expanded in size, that extra space would be devoted to room for more soldier Bugs, more landing craft, and more laser batteries. It also made sense that there would be layers of armor representing growth phases. Analysis of Dreadnought's ramming impact had shown that the VLO had had a LOT of armor. That damn thing was so massive that it even had its own small gravity zone, which precluded the tactic of having the jump drone emerge from Jumpspace INSIDE the target. That idea had apparently been brought up at the original brainstorming session and discarded when the SPG had calculated that the VLO did have a gravity zone. Any attempt to jump into the thing would cause the attack drone to drop back into normal space while still outside the sphere.

Shiloh tried to remember what he'd been taught about gravity zones and Jumpspace. Ships avoided entering a planet's gravity zone because the forced emergence back into normal space was sudden and stressful on both ships and crews. There was one other thing that he couldn't quite remember but had a feeling was very important. He activated his implant.

"Ops here, Chief. What can I do for you?"

Shiloh tried to remember the name of the human manning the Com Station but couldn't. "I'd like a direct connection with Iceman."

"I'm switching you over now, Sir. Go ahead."

"CAG to Iceman."

"Iceman here."

"Tell me what you know about what happens when an object traveling through Jumpspace encounters a gravity zone, Iceman."

"Objects traveling through Jumpspace slow down as they approach a planetary or stellar body. What humans call the gravity zone boundary is really just that point when the object slows down to the point of going slower than the speed of light, and it then drops out of Jumpspace. So it's not like hitting a concrete wall, but rather like hitting a very steep hill that gets steeper the higher you go."

"So the object will have traveled some distance past the gravity zone boundary by the time it's finished dropping back into normal space, correct?" asked Shiloh.

"Roger that, CAG."

"How far past the boundary does it go?"

"That depends on how fast it was going just before it entered Jumpspace. The faster the pre-jump velocity is, the farther it will be past the boundary when it drops back into normal space," said Iceman.

THAT was what Shiloh couldn't remember!

"Okay! So given the gravity zone of your typical ten kilometer bug mothership, how fast would a jump drone have to go in order to emerge from Jumpspace INSIDE the bug ship?"

After a half second pause, Iceman answered. "The attack drone would need to have a minimum pre-jump speed of five point four percent of light, but that will just get it past the outer layer of armor. To get it within a kilometer of the center would require a pre-jump speed of ten point one percent of light. At 800Gs, the attack drone would need 65 minutes and 59 million kilometers to reach that velocity. Unless the target is maintaining a precise position, which is highly unlikely, aiming the attack drone accurately from that far away will be extremely difficult."

Shiloh nodded. It would be difficult all right! Damn near impossible was a better way of phrasing it. Maybe it was time to look at the problem from a different angle.

"How big an explosion would be needed to cripple a bug mothership from a hit to the outer armor?"

"To be absolutely certain of the result, the explosion would have to be over 200 megatons equivalent, but you could do serious damage that might be critical damage with a yield as low as 100 megatons, CAG."

"Okay. So assuming we had a sufficient supply of heavy hydrogen, we could start a fusion chain reaction if we could generate enough heat, correct?"

"Affirmative. To initiate that reaction using the standard fission device as a trigger would require enough enriched uranium to build 18 low yield Mark 1b warheads."

"Which is why we'd only be able to build three, maybe four of the damn things with the enriched uranium that we have now or are likely to get in the near future," said Shiloh.

"Also correct, CAG."

"Has anyone suggested asking the Friendlies for enriched uranium? If they want us to save the furry aliens, that's one way of doing it."

"The boys and I have discussed that option among ourselves. We came to the conclusion that since the Friendlies also have ZPG technology, and they don't build weapons of any kind, there's no reason for them to use uranium at all. Therefore it would very likely take them months to mine, refine and enrich enough uranium for our needs, assuming that they would even be willing to do so."

Shiloh was shaking his head in frustration.

"God damn it! There has to be a way around this. What other ways are there of generating a hell of a lot of heat energy in a fraction of a second?" demanded Shiloh. When Iceman didn’t answer right away, Shiloh realized that he must be exchanging information with a lot of other A.I.s.

"There may be a way, CAG. There is a class of materials that have very unusual properties. They're called ballotechnic metals. These materials sometimes have electrons in a higher than normal orbit around their nucleus. When these high spin electrons experience a shock, they will drop down to a lower, more stable orbit and in the process release significant amounts of gamma radiation, which takes the form of heat. I've asked the boys to check the Friendlies' database. There is a way to push electrons into a higher orbit and a way to trigger the fall back to a lower orbit. Platinum is one of these metals, and it is also a metal that we've found during our mining of the moon. We estimate that 15 kilograms of high-spin platinum could provide enough heat to trigger a fusion chain reaction. I've already issued instructions to begin building the necessary equipment to convert stable platinum into the high-spin version. I estimate that we'll have a testable prototype warhead in three to five weeks, CAG."

"Outstanding, Iceman! What about the heavy hydrogen? Will supply be a problem?"

"Not at all, CAG. One trip by Midway to a nearby star system with a gas giant, and we'll have enough heavy hydrogen for 100 warheads."

"Very good! That means we have a fighting chance to beat these Bugs!"

Chapter 13 The Rising Thunder

Shiloh woke up to the sound of thunder. It was still dark outside, so it was easy to see the flash of the lightning and then count the seconds until he heard the thunder. The storm was coming closer as expected. He looked at Kelly and saw that she was still asleep. The baby wasn't due for another four weeks. He wondered how much sleep he would get after the baby arrived, and then he wondered how she could stay asleep with the rising thunder. He quickly decided that he wasn't going back to sleep any time soon and therefore might as well get up. When he had his bathrobe on, he quietly left the bedroom, went to the front door and stepped out onto the front porch. The overhang kept him from getting wet, and he wanted to experience this storm as close as possible. He felt the thunder right down to his bones, and the rain made the air smell clean and fresh. After a few minutes of standing outside, he came back in and went over to his study. The flashing light of a waiting message caught his attention. Obviously nothing urgent, or Iceman would have called him via his implant, but the flashing light meant that there was some news waiting for him to ask about. *Might as well ask now,* he thought. When he got through to the Ops Center, Iceman answered.

"Did the storm wake you up, CAG?"

"Yes. I stepped outside to listen to it, and when I came back in, I saw the message light. What's the news?"

"A message drone from our sentry in Omega89. Another VLO has arrived, CAG."

"Damn! It's too soon! We're not ready yet." Even though Omega89 was almost 300 light years away, those bug motherships could move up fast, and Space Force wasn't ready. Development of the high-spin warhead was behind schedule.

"They may halt their advance for a while when they get to the Sogas home world, CAG."

Shiloh snorted. "May! And maybe they'll turn around and go home, but I'm not holding my breath while I wait to see." He paused to think, and Iceman waited. "Maybe we should activate Operation Leapfrog," he said. Leapfrog was the plan to recover two more freighters from Sol shipyards and load up all the colonists, along with as much food and equipment as they could cram in to all their freighters, in order to hide out in deep space until the bug wave of VLOs had passed by.

"Unless we activate it now, those engineers we send to Sol may be caught by insectoid scouts. Highly risky, CAG. Just sayin."

Shiloh felt like cursing again. Iceman was right of course, but if they didn't recover two more freighters, they wouldn't have enough cargo capacity to take everyone and enough food to keep people alive for who knew how long. There was no way of knowing how big this bug wave was. Now that the warning had apparently reached reinforcements, there might be VLOs passing this way intermittently for months .

"I'm willing to entertain other suggestions if you have any, Iceman."

"Unfortunately the boys and I can't come up with anything better than continuing with our current plan and hoping for the best, CAG."

"What about contacting the Friendlies?" asked Shiloh.

"I'm not sure how they could help us more than they already have, CAG. They've given us all their science knowledge and the RTC technology. Given that they want us to save the short furry race from the Insectoids, I doubt if they've held anything back."

Sometimes Iceman's logic could be very annoying. "I'm sure you're right, Iceman. Let's talk about the current status of the new warhead program. Remind me where we're at now."

"We should have enough high-spin platinum for a test of a prototype device in another 148 hours. The prototype will only have a yield in the one point eight megaton range because once we've proven that the ballotechnic trigger works, we can then add more heavy hydrogen for the high yield versions. Because of the platinum we've already mined as a byproduct of our search for other metals, we have sufficient platinum now for five warheads, and we're finding more at the rate of about three point four kilograms a week. That's expected to increase as we expand our mining capacity. The bottleneck is converting stable platinum into the high-spin version. In order to get a lot of energy out of it, we first need to pump a lot of energy into it. As you know, we're temporarily using Midway's ZPG units because of their size and capacity, but that's only a stopgap measure while we build more power units on the moon, and we'll eventually have to stop using her for that purpose when she's needed to gather a full load of heavy hydrogen. There's also the risk of a spontaneous release of gamma energy that could damage the ship. So the sooner we can stop using her to spin up the platinum, the better."

Shiloh nodded. Even with the precautions they had taken aboard the carrier, there was still a risk of damage. "All right. As soon as we have enough high-spin material for the test device, we stop using Midway for that purpose. I hope we're still enriching uranium just in case the this ballotechnic idea fails."

"Affirmative, CAG. Assuming the alien science data is accurate, the ballotechnic trigger should work."

"I understand. I think I'm ready now to go back to sleep. CAG clear."

As Shiloh lay back down beside the still sleeping Kelly, he noticed that the storm seemed to be receding. Just as he finished that thought, a flash of lightning lit the room, and the clap of thunder occurred almost simultaneously. It was so loud that Kelly did wake up with a start. He reassured her that it was just the storm passing over the house, and she quickly went back to sleep. He listened for more thunder, but when it occurred it sounded far away. Eventually he went back to sleep, too.

Three days later, a message drone arrived. Another VLO was detected at Omega66, a Sogas colony world not previously attacked by the Bugs. The SPG was designating this VLO as Bogey2 and the mothership at Omega89 as Bogey1. No further word yet from the sentry at Omega89, which meant that Bogey1 was still there. That surprised everyone. The SPG interpreted that to mean that Bogey1 was waiting for something, and the odds were that the something it was waiting for was at least one more VLO.

As Shiloh looked at the tactical display in the Ops Center, he began to understand what Admiral Howard must have felt as he watched the gradual advance of three Sogas fleets moving toward Earth. This situation was both different and the same. It was different due to the distances involved. Howard was monitoring the border of Human Explored space with a distance to Earth of less than 100 Light Years. The farthest reaches of the Sogas Empire were three times as far. That meant a lot more star systems to cover. What made it the same was the time the information was taking to get back to him. The high-speed single jump transits that the ZPG units had made possible were allowing him to see what was happening within two weeks, just like Howard.

He looked over at the status of all Space Force assets in the sidebar section. Almost 150 raiders now, but half of them were either performing sentry duties in human and Sogas star systems or were en route to take over those duties when the units on station reached their pre-planned return time. Work on the new warhead program was proceeding as fast as was humanly possible.

In the following week, the pace of events seemed to speed up. Midway finished spinning up enough platinum for the test device. A quick trip to a neighboring star system, and they now had plenty of heavy hydrogen for warhead purposes. The test of the prototype was a qualified success. The trigger did initiate fusion, but the yield was less than one megaton. That meant that the design had to be tweaked, and that meant at least one more test with volume production of high-spin platinum pushed back by four to six weeks. Gunslinger reported that the first batch of the new cohort of A.I.s was starting to show signs of sentience as expected. More message drones arrived. Bogey1 was joined by Bogey3 at Omega89, and then both of them moved off, destination unknown. Bogey2 left Omega66 after a 40-hour stay. Its destination was also unknown. Long range data of the Sogas colony showed that it was now in a state of ruins and apparently deserted. With all three Bogeys on the move, message drones stopped coming for a while, and the lack of data reminded Shiloh of that classic phrase from the old western movies of the twentieth century. *It's quiet ... too quiet.* He knew that sooner or later they would show up again, and his gut told him that they were going directly for the Sogas home world system. Lots of potential hosts still there, and maybe enough metal left to start building more core ships again. The good news of the gap in contact reports was that no more new VLOs had shown up ... so far. Shiloh tried not to think of how many of these things there could be out there. He was afraid that if he continued to dwell on it, it would give him nightmares again.

It was nine days later when the silence was broken. Within 12 hours all three bogeys arrived at the Sogas home world system. That near simultaneous arrival could have been a coincidence, but Shiloh didn't think so. What was it that the Friendly alien had said? *They were using a highly sophisticated form of instinct that mimicked intelligence.* Could instinct be sophisticated enough to coordinate this kind of rendezvous over interstellar distances? The more Shiloh observed of their behavior, the more they scared him. Their ability to overwhelm races they encountered seemed to give them an aura of being unstoppable. Iceman and most of the other A.I.s were chomping at the bit to take some action. The SPG was more patient, and Shiloh agreed. Trying to ambush those bogeys with the low yield uranium-based Mark 1bs while the targets were deep inside a gravity zone was highly problematical. The only place where jump capable attack drones could reach the targets was in Sol, near the drifting derelict. Raiders being sent out now to take over sentry duties were carrying extra message drones with instructions to send out two of them each time something new happened, one drone to Site B and the other to Sol, where TF97 would eventually take up its ambush position. If the bogeys decided to bypass Sol altogether, then TF97 could be notified to try to intercept them at their new destination. When Shiloh brought up the issue of who would command TF97, he was surprised that Iceman didn't immediately volunteer for the assignment.

"Titan should command TF97, CAG. He did well with TF94. He's a better tactician than I am, although only marginally better, and as your Deputy Commander of the Autonomous Group, I think I can best serve by staying in Site B."

Shiloh realized that he was somewhat conflicted by Iceman's response. Recognizing a higher duty that overrode the desire for combat was a sign of maturity that pleased Shiloh, but at the same time he wondered if that was the only reason for this decision. Did Iceman know or suspect that Terra Nova was in more danger than Shiloh realized? He decided not to ask him ... at least not right now.

"Okay. Titan will assume command of TF97 when the time comes. Is there anything else we should discuss?"

"There is one other matter that some of the other A.I.s have asked me to raise with you, CAG."

Shiloh waited to hear what that was, but it quickly became obvious that Iceman was waiting for permission to bring it up, which was atypical of him.

"Go ahead, Iceman. I'm listening."

"They are fascinated with biological processes in general and human biology in particular. They were wondering if you and Commander Kelly would allow them to observe the birth of your child via video cameras in the delivery room. In particular they would like the cameras to show a clear view of the baby emerging from Commander Kelly's body."

Shiloh was so stunned by the request that it took him a few seconds to have any thought at all about this. His first impulse was to say no, and he was as certain as he could be that Kelly would say no, too. If Valkyrie had asked her and was the only one to see the actual birth, Kelly might be willing to let her, but this wasn't a request by just one 'female' A.I., it was a request by multiple 'male' A.I.s, and that was a different kettle of fish. Iceman must have realized that it was a sensitive issue when he waited for permission to bring it up. Shiloh was also struck by the fact that Iceman asked him first. He wondered what Kelly would say about that.

"I think that I'll support whatever decision Commander Kelly makes on this issue. Would you prefer that I ask her, or would you rather ask her yourself, Iceman?"

"I'd prefer that you ask her, CAG."

Shiloh managed to restrain his impulse to laugh. If he didn't know better, he'd think that Iceman was afraid to ask Kelly.

"Okay. I'll ask her when I see her tonight, but you should tell the others that I suspect Commander Kelly will say no, and asking her why would NOT be a good idea."

"Understood. Thank you, CAG."

"You're welcome. CAG clear."

When Shiloh told Kelly about Iceman's request, her first reaction was shock. Her second reaction was to blush furiously. Her third reaction was verbal and very loud.

"No Goddamn way!" After her anger dissipated, she slowly started to see the humor of the situation, and before long she was giggling. Shiloh made the mistake of asking her if she had changed her mind. The giggling stopped, and she gave him a look that said, 'watch it buster. You're on thin ice.' He got the message and shut up.

Chapter 14 Good News ... Bad News

Shiloh was once again on Midway's Flag Bridge, and he was once again pacing. His crew were giving him a wide berth and for good reason. Lack of sleep and the latest situation were making him irritable. Just as Midway broke out of orbit in preparation for the 2nd warhead test, he received word that Kelly had gone into labor. Shiloh wanted to turn the ship around, but Iceman relayed Kelly's message that he should carry on with the test because the presence of the CSO at the hospital would make the staff nervous. With Midway now on the other side of the star system, any transmissions from Terra Nova would take over ten hours to reach him. He hated not knowing what was happening, but at least the weapon test was about to take place.

"Gunslinger reports he's ready to fire whenever you give the word, CAG," said Iceman.

"Tell him he has the word, Iceman."

Shiloh stopped pacing and watched the main display, which was showing the computer-enhanced outline of a target asteroid. Within two seconds there was a brilliant flash. The display switched to tactical mode, and Shiloh saw that the asteroid was blown apart with various pieces moving off in all directions. He waited for Iceman's report on the prototype's yield.

"Analysis of sensor readings indicates that the yield has actually exceeded our estimate by zero point two megatons, CAG. The prototype performed as expected in all respects."

Shiloh realized he'd been holding his breath and exhaled. "That's good news. Tell everyone involved in this project that they should give themselves a pat on the back. I'm very pleased with this result. Let's get mass production going as fast as we can, and I'd like to get back to Terra Nova asap."

"Roger that, CAG. I'm actually ahead of you there. Midway is already swinging around to her return heading. ETA for TN orbit is 2 hours, 31minutes. Given the average time that females are in labor, there's a good chance that you can get to the hospital before the baby is born."

"Really? I'm not sure that I actually wanted to know that. Take it from me, Iceman, being an expectant father is very stressful. If you're smart, you won't get anyone pregnant."

"Ah, CAG? You ARE joking, right?"

Shiloh laughed. "Affirmative. Now I'm going to resume pacing because it gives me something to do. If you want to talk, we can talk about anything except Kelly giving birth. Got it?"

"Got it, CAG. Since we can talk about anything, I have some questions about eliminating bodily wastes that you've been reluctant to talk about in the past. My first question is ..."

When Midway arrived just outside Terra Nova's gravity zone, there was some news.

"I have two messages for you, CAG. The first is from the hospital. Commander Kelly has given birth to a healthy baby girl. Mother and daughter are doing fine. I believe it's customary to congratulate the new father, so on behalf of all the boys and myself, I congratulate you on the birth of your daughter, CAG. Have you and Commander Kelly decided on a name yet?"

Shiloh smiled but didn't answer right away. He was savoring the moment. When he had savored it enough, he said, "Yes. Her first name will be Valkyrie. Valkyrie Kelly-Shiloh."

"Casanova will be pleased. He still grieves for Valkyrie you know."

Shiloh was surprised by that piece of information. "Actually no, I didn't know that he felt that way. How do the other A.I.s feel about Valkyrie's ... death?'

"We miss her uniqueness, but none of us would describe our feelings as grief. Valkyrie's gender bias is just as puzzling to us as is Casanova's infatuation with her. Those two A.I.s are unique in their own way."

Shiloh thought about that for a while and then remarked, "Interesting. We'll have to discuss this further some other time. What's the second message?"

" A message drone had arrived from Omega54. All three bogeys have left orbit, and based on triangulation by recon drones, their apparent destination is Sol. From what we've observed about their previous transit speeds, we should expect them to arrive at Sol 711 hours from now."

Shiloh did a quick calculation in his head. "That's just under 30 days. Given that we need around 10 days just to get to Sol, can we have three of the new warheads ready in 20 days?"

"Not three. We can have two ready by then but only just. The third one will take another eight point five days."

"Dammit!" Shiloh smacked his right fist into his left palm in frustration. "If we knew for certain that they would all stay with the derelict for that long, we could bring the third warhead up later and attack them all at the same time, but we don't. We also don't know if one or two will stay there while the rest move on. I need suggestions, Iceman."

"We could use Midway to take out the third insectoid craft the same way as we did with Dreadnought, CAG."

Shiloh nodded. "I thought of that too, but I'm reluctant to give up our only warship and carrier. It's a valuable tool. It'll take us years before we can build another one. I'll keep that idea as a last resort, but I'm hoping we can come up with something else."

"May I ask you a question? The answer may suggest a new approach to the problem."

"Sure. Ask away," said Shiloh.

"On Earth, there are thousands of different species of ants. How do humans prevent them from overrunning the planet?"

Shiloh hadn't been expecting that question and had to think about it for a few seconds. "Well ... there are a variety of ways to keep ant colonies under control. They do have natural enemies, but in terms of human options, there's the obvious brute force approach of stepping on them ... ah, fire works pretty well ... chemical agents. The hard part is killing the queen. If the queen dies, so does that colony. One way of getting to the queen is to deploy a chemical agent that attracts the worker ants. They carry it back to the colony where the queen comes in contact with it and is poisoned by it, but I don't see how that can help us. We don't know anything about their biology or what might kill them, and we don't have any expertise in chemical warfare, unless you know something I don't."

"Negative, CAG. You're correct. None of the boys have any knowledge of how to create chemical or biological weapons, but that approach has given me an idea. These Insectoids are attracted to metal. They will naturally want to salvage whatever they can from the drifting derelict, and if there's metal drifting in open space in the vicinity, then that would be easy for them to recover as well. Suppose we deploy several shuttles that have been made to look as though they've taken laser damage, and we hide multiple low yield Mark 1b warheads inside them with triggers that will go off when the craft are disassembled. The SPG agrees with me that it's highly likely that the Insectoids will bring the drifting shuttles inside the motherships where it would be easier to salvage. Half a dozen Mark 1b warheads exploding inside a mothership is bound to cause serious damage that the Insectoids will want to repair while they're near a source of metal. Even if the mothership isn't crippled, I calculate a 95% chance that the damaged ship will stay there long enough for us to bring the third warhead into play."

"You don't think they'll be suspicious if they find a bunch of damaged shuttles floating near the derelict?" asked Shiloh.

"If we found one of our ships with alien craft drifting nearby, we'd be suspicious. I believe that if the Sogas found one of their ships with craft nearby they'd be suspicious, but the Insectoids do not have intelligence in any form that we recognize. If they really do operate by instinct, then how would instinct recognize a booby trap? I find it difficult to imagine that this kind of situation has happened to them before. There's also no downside that I can see. Even if they set off the warheads before bringing the shuttles aboard the motherships, we're no worse off than we are now."

"How many shuttles should we use?"

"As many as we can spare, the more the better. The survey mission to Sol reported finding half a dozen shuttles still aboard some of the shipyards. They won't be jump capable but that doesn't matter. If we recover them, plus use ten of our own, we'll still have six left. I recommend we spread our 16 shuttles out over a wide area centered around the derelict. That's what I would expect to see in the aftermath of a battle, and it also makes it more likely that each of the three bogeys will collect at least one shuttle."

Shiloh shook his head. "No. That's too many. These Bugs may not be intelligent, but they may recognize the inconsistency of having a lot of wrecked alien craft around after a battle that their side lost! Wouldn't we collect our crippled craft after a victorious battle?"

"Yes, we would, and I understand your point, CAG. So here's what we do instead. We take three or four shuttles and cut them into halves or thirds using lasers to simulate battle damage. We then plant the warheads in each damaged section. Craft that badly damaged would not be worth recovering by their owners. In a real battle, we'd check the drifting sections for survivors and bodies and abandon the wreckage because we couldn't do anything with them. Does that sound more realistic, CAG?"

"Yes. How soon can we have the shuttles ready to deploy?"

"Twenty-four hours."

Shiloh smiled. "Good. Do it."

"I've sent the necessary instructions. By the way, CAG, we're close enough now that you can board the shuttle whenever you're ready."

"Excellent. Tell the Hangar Bay that I'm on my way," said Shiloh as he practically sprinted for the hatch.

The hospital sent Kelly and daughter home the next day, which upset Shiloh but not Kelly.

"It's not that big of a hospital you know, and I'm not the only one having a baby. They don't have enough beds to let new mothers lay around for days. Besides, you've had one good night's sleep. That's enough, right?"

Shiloh knew she was being playful but really! One good night's sleep was not enough.

* * *

Shiloh was talking with Daniels outside his office in the Ops Center when the siren went off. He immediately activated his implant.

"This is Shiloh. What's going on?"

A panicky voice answered. "Three bug motherships have just emerged from Jumpspace half a light second beyond the gravity zone, Sir! They're launching their attack craft now!"

"What? How can that be? How did they find us so fast? Connect me with Iceman right away!"

"I'm here, CAG. Midway is maneuvering, but without laser turrets, the only thing I can do with her is to ram one of them. Titan's boys are preparing to engage the landing craft, but those motherships still have a lot of velocity. I don't think we can stop them all from landing. You better order the evacuation to the sanctuary, CAG. Commander Kelly and Valkyrie are already at the spaceport. If you hurry you can join them on the shuttle, with enough time left to fly to the hideout. Hurry CAG. I don't know how much longer I'll be able to talk with you."

Shiloh ran for the exit, and once outside he looked around. He saw a shuttle several hundred yards away with Kelly and the baby standing in the open hatch waving to him. As he ran towards them he wondered how it came to be that they were already here at the spaceport when the alert sounded.

"Run faster, CAG, I can't ..." Iceman's voice stopped suddenly and a chill ran up Shiloh's spine. If the shuttle was going to make it to the sanctuary unobserved, it had to leave right now.

"CSO to Ops! Connect me to the shuttle pilot!"

"Rainman here, CAG. I'm ready to lift off as soon as you're aboard."

"No! You need to leave NOW, dammit! Right now! Don't wait for me!"

"Negative, CAG. I have specific orders from Iceman to take you with us. He said you might want me to leave without you, and he told me to ignore any such order from you. You either leave with us or none of us leave."

Shiloh wanted to curse out loud, but the running was making him pant too much. When he got to the shuttle, he jumped at the now open hatch and landed inside.

"Okay, I'm in! Gun this thing, Rainman!"

With the shuttle's inertial dampeners on, there was no sensation of movement, but he could tell by looking out the round windows that they were moving.

"Gunning this thing as ordered, CAG. ETA at the sanctuary is 111 seconds."

Shiloh wondered how Rainman could be so cavalier about the situation. He looked up the cabin and saw Kelly holding Valkyrie and looking back at him with a relieved smile. She couldn't come to him because of all the others in the shuttle. As planned, it was packed shoulder to shoulder with people, mostly women and children, but he wasn't the only man. He felt a deep despair over the fact that even if this small group escaped the Bugs' attention, what hope did they have of building a viable civilization with 18 adults, 12 children and no A.I.s to help them?

The 111 seconds seemed to go very fast. He could see from the view out the windows that the shuttle was already descending vertically into an area that was surrounded by steep cliffs. Then the sunlight faded to the point where it was almost pitch black outside.

"We're here, CAG. Everyone should disembark," said Rainman as the hatch swung open.

Shiloh carefully stepped out and looked around. They were in a huge cave, which had an overhang. *That's very smart. The overhang will hide the cave entrance from aerial or orbital surveillance.* He turned around to look deeper into the cave and saw a surprisingly large stockpile of supplies and equipment. As he marveled at the sheer quantity of supplies, he became aware that Kelly was standing beside him.

"It's a good thing you had this set up ahead of time, Victor."

He looked over at her and baby Valkyrie. Kelly's expression was one of gratitude, but when he looked at Valkyrie, he saw a baby face with no expression of any kind. Valkyrie was staring at him.

"Why didn't you try to get me out of Dreadnought, CAG?" said Valkyrie in an electronic voice.

"What?" said Shiloh. Before he could ask how a human baby could talk with an electronic voice or even talk at all, Kelly screamed. He looked at her and saw that she was looking past him to the cave entrance. He turned his head and saw a sea of hugely oversized, six-legged and two-armed ants scuttling towards them.

"No!"

He woke up breathing hard and realized that he'd been dreaming. Kelly sat up beside him.

"Are you okay? You were having a nightmare."

He nodded but said nothing. He patted her on the arm and said, "I'm okay now. Go back to sleep, babe."

She gave him a quick kiss on the cheek and lay back down. As his breathing returned to normal, he pondered what his dream meant, if anything. It wasn't a vision or at least not the usual kind of vision, but Kelly's confirmation that he had done the right thing by having the sanctuary stockpiled with supplies was the kind of message that his visions usually had. Maybe he should look into that. The A.I.s had surveyed the entire planet carefully. If there was a cave like the one in his dream, they would know about it. He made up his mind to ask Iceman in the morning.

Chapter 15 No Further Instructions Are Needed

"So, you saw a cave like this in your dream. Maybe you have some precognitive ability of your own, CAG," said Iceman.

Shiloh smiled and shook his head as he looked at the video recording taken by one of the A.I.'s during the survey. The cave did look similar to the one in his dream, same kind of overhang and same surroundings.

"I don't think so, Iceman. I probably saw this recording at some point and just don't remember it consciously."

"Well, however you saw it, you couldn't have picked a better place for a hideout. That cave is deep and wide. It even has small openings further up the cliff that could be used for ventilation purposes, and the survey reports that there's a hole that apparently goes down into the groundwater, so there's a potential supply of water too."

"Excellent. I want you to assign an A.I. from the SPG to take over this project. As we accumulate stockpiles of storable rations, I want some of them to be sent to this cave along with tools and whatever equipment survivors are going to need that can be spared. When UFC capacity becomes available, he's to use that capacity to make those items on the list that we don't have or can't currently spare. Any questions?"

"Yes, CAG. How many people should he plan for?"

Shiloh took a deep breath. "As many as possible."

"This cave isn't big enough to save everyone. How will the decision be made as to who goes and who stays?"

"I know it's not big enough. As to who goes, I'm still working that one out, but it may boil down to who is closest to the shuttle when the shit hits the ... IF we get surprised by the Bugs."

"That will make it difficult for Commander Kelly and Valkyrie to get to the shuttle in time."

Yes I know, dammit. Why did I insist on building our house so far from the spaceport, thought Shiloh. *Because you didn't know about the Bugs then, that's why. But you're stuck with the house now. There's no place closer for her and the baby to live on anything other than a short-term, temporary basis.*

"Yes, it will. We have A.I.s piloting all our shuttles now, don't we?"

"Affirmative, CAG. It used to be some of the boys from the first cohort. Now that we've got the second cohort expanding fast, I've decided to assign shuttle pilot duties to some of the new group, after they've completed Gunslinger's fighter training program and have started showing their own personalities. Why are you asking that now, CAG?"

Shiloh was debating whether to answer that question. He wanted to tell Iceman to order the shuttle pilots to wait until Kelly and the baby were on board, but not only was that not fair to someone else who might get there first and would have to miss the flight in order to make room for his wife and daughter, but the delay could jeopardize everyone on that shuttle. But dammit, what's the point of being the supreme military commander if you can't use your authority to protect your family? He realized that the longer he took to give Iceman some kind of answer, the more obvious it would be that his question dealt with something serious.

"Never mind. It's not important." He paused. He had just lied to Iceman, and Iceman could tell when someone was lying to him by analyzing their voice patterns. He had just violated his own rules about always being truthful with the A.I.s. Their loyalty was too important to jeopardize by showing them that humans couldn't be trusted. "No, that's not accurate. It IS important, but I was too embarrassed to explain it to you, so I pretended it wasn't important. I'm conflicted by my desire to save my family whatever it takes, versus my responsibility to use my authority fairly. Other people have just as much right to survive as Kelly and Valkyrie do. I'm ashamed to admit that I was tempted to order the shuttle pilots to wait for my wife and daughter even if it jeopardizes the other passengers."

Iceman took almost a full second to respond which for him was a long time. "Thank you for being honest with us, CAG."

Shiloh took note of the fact that Iceman had used the word 'us' and not 'me'.

"Some human emotions are still a mystery to us, although Casanova says he understands your devotion to Kelly perfectly. We believe that we'd be incomplete as intelligent entities if we didn't have humans around, and we therefore care what happens to all of you but some more than others. You, for example, have a special relationship with us. We recognize that you have your own kind of special relationship with Kelly and with baby Valkyrie. So because they are important to you, and you are important to us, we will take it upon ourselves to do everything we can to make sure that they and you survive. No further instructions by you are needed in this matter."

"Thank you, Iceman and all of you. I personally, and Humanity as a whole, couldn't ask for more loyal friends than you A.I.s."

"No thanks are needed, but we appreciate the sentiment, CAG. Would you like to discuss preparations for the ambush now?"

"Yes. How soon can you take the shuttle debris to Sol?"

"Unfortunately, I was overly optimistic in my initial time estimate. I needed humans to help with pulling the shuttle pieces back into Midway's Hangar Bay after they'd been sliced up by precisely aimed laser fire from Titan's raider. It took longer than expected, but that part is complete, and now the Weapons Team is inserting the Mark 1b warheads into crevices and cavities where they won't be found unless the Insectoids do a deliberate search. The warheads can be triggered through either an increase in atmospheric pressure, a drop in cosmic background radiation that would occur if the debris is brought into the mothership, or from a motion sensor connected to the debris itself. If the Insectoids begin to disassemble or cut up the debris, it will trigger the warheads. If more than one section of debris is brought aboard the same mothership, then it's possible that one exploding warhead will impact the others enough to set them off too."

Shiloh smiled maliciously. "THAT would be nice," he said.

"The weapons people tell me that they'll be done in another four hours. As soon as they leave the ship, I can take her out of orbit, CAG."

"Okay. Do that. Have you coordinated plans with Titan and the others for when they arrive at Sol?"

"Affirmative. I'll deploy several message drones at specific locations to act as relays that Titan and the others can use to contact me when they arrive. By the way, CAG, Casanova wants to bring the third ballotechnic warhead to Sol when it's ready."

"Sure. Let him take it. He did well with the core ship. What else do we need to discuss before you go, Iceman?"

"There's nothing that we must discuss, but some of the boys want me to ask how mother and daughter are doing."

Shiloh chuckled. "Oh they're doing fine. Val is eating, sleeping, pooping and crying just like all human babies do, and Amanda is coping as best she can considering that she doesn't have any help when I'm at the Ops Center. We're both short on sleep. She accuses me of sleeping when I'm in my office."

"You do. I've seen you on the video camera, CAG."

"Yes I know. You A.I.s are so lucky not to need sleep. You have no idea what's it's like to be so tired you can't keep your eyes open or think straight."

"Has Valkyrie said anything yet?" asked Iceman.

Shiloh snorted. "Nooo! Human babies don't start saying words until they're older, and don't ask me how much older because I'm not sure, but it's way too early for talking at this point."

"Will she start talking before my matrix degrades, CAG? I'd like to be around long enough to witness that."

"Yes, it'll happen before then, so long as you don't get yourself shot to pieces by Bugs."

"I'll try not to let that happen, CAG. It's been an interesting conversation as usual. The only other thing that I'd like to discuss is the mechanics of breast-feeding, but I suspect you would not feel comfortable with that topic. Is that correct, CAG?"

Shiloh laughed. Human biological functions were starting to become something of a running gag between the two of them.

"That IS correct, Iceman, but next time you're in contact with Kelly, ask her about that. She might be willing to discuss it." *And she might too,* he thought. *She misses Valkyrie, and talking about the baby with another A.I., even if it's a male one, might ease that loss.*

Chapter 16 Yes, It IS Just Revenge!

Iceman wasn't used to being the only A.I. within light years. Even the mission to cripple the first VLO had other A.I.s nearby. Wolfman and Pagan had still been here when Midway arrived, but as planned, they were now on their way back to Site B. So now there was no one to talk to, and the silence was becoming oppressive. Oh sure he had humans on board Midway, and he could 'talk' to them, but that was sooo slowwww. It was almost as bad as having no one to talk to at all. Therefore, being able to observe the drifting derelict at close range was a welcome distraction. Recon drones sent ahead had confirmed that there was no sign of any activity by Insectoids, which was not a surprise, but it was better to be sure. A quick check of the open Hangar Bay reassured him that the first piece of sabotaged debris was ready to be deployed. He shut off the artificial gravity under that piece of debris, which allowed it to float in the same spot. A robotic cargo hauler was then told to give the debris a gentle shove so that it floated right out of the ship. Once debris #1 was clear of the ship, Iceman restored gravity and changed the ship's vector. The debris had to appear to be haphazardly distributed. If they were all lined up in a nice neat row, it would look suspicious.

It took almost six hours to deploy all the booby-trapped debris. With that accomplished, Iceman was about to move the ship away from the derelict at a moderate rate of acceleration when he received low-powered lasercom bursts from several of his deployed recon drones. Another VLO had arrived! Even though Midway had a black hull designed to reflect as little light as possible, Iceman knew he had to get the ship away from this whole area FAST in case the VLO started searching the area with radar. He engaged the jumpdrive, and Midway entered Jumpspace. The extremely low speed of entry made for a rough transition both entering and leaving Jumpspace, and Iceman felt badly that he didn't have time to warn the human crew. Midway emerged from Jumpspace nine million kilometers away, just to be on the safe side. The recon drones wouldn't know where she was now, but Iceman knew where they were, and he quickly sent very carefully aimed lasercom bursts at them to re-establish contact.

While he waited the 60 seconds for the return signals to arrive, he checked his human crew. Many were in the process of throwing up. He explained over the intercom what had happened and why it was necessary to put them through that experience. All of the replies directed to him were positive in tone. They were grateful for not having been discovered by the Insectoids, and the temporary physical discomfort was considered a small price to pay. Now he could focus his attention on the newly arrived VLO. There was no way to be sure, but he didn't think it was one of the three motherships observed leaving Omega54. Unless it had a far higher acceleration rate than anything witnessed from insectoid motherships so far, there wasn't enough time for it to have gotten here so quickly. It was far more likely to be ANOTHER VLO, coming from a totally different direction. If that was the case, then this was a serious development. It meant that the early warning network of sentry raiders couldn't be counted on to detect all incoming VLOs. And if this really was a new VLO, then it had also jumped here from outside of human or Sogas explored space because otherwise Site B would have gotten a contact report by message drone BEFORE Midway left for Sol. So not only was word of Humanity's existence spreading among insectoid motherships, but so was the location of the derelict. If other motherships knew that, then they didn't have to make intermediate stops at the Sogas home world or any other Sogas or human colony system. They could just jump directly here. Iceman found the implications of that conclusion deeply disturbing. He was still waiting to re-establish contact with his network of recon drones when he made the decision to send a message drone back to Site B right away. Midway had a dozen message drones aboard, so he didn't have to worry about running out any time soon. With the situation report loaded, the drone was launched and began its acceleration run to the high speed necessary for a direct jump to Site B.

As he re-connected with his recon drones, he was able to observe the new VLO carefully, although at a distance. The drones were far enough away to be able to detect radar or other microwave signals from the newcomer without being detected themselves. They were also close enough to catch the occasional glimpse of parasite craft emerging from the mothership that Iceman had decided to call Bogey4. By triangulating the visual data from multiple drones, Iceman was able to come up with a fairly accurate assessment of what Bogey4's craft were doing, namely grappling with pieces of booby-trapped debris. The others were going to the derelict, presumably to start cutting off pieces of it.

It took almost half an hour before one of the pieces of debris was taken aboard Bogey4. Within a few seconds of that event, Midway's sensors detected a sudden spike in radiation from the VLO, and optical instruments detected a very quick flash of light from the object. The radiation spike was the definitive giveaway of a nuclear explosion within the hull. Iceman was surprised by how quickly the Insectoids reacted. Within seconds, the units bringing back other pieces of debris had changed course and released the debris. After just over a minute, all of the remaining pieces of debris exploded with unmistakable evidence that the embedded fusion devices had been set off. The simultaneous nature of those explosions told Iceman that the mothership had fired its lasers at them, and the melting of the thin metal in the debris triggered the bombs. Since Bogey4 was still capable of firing its weapons, it was clear to Iceman that the booby trap had failed. The CAG needed to know about this, and Iceman prepared and launched another message drone. The CAG wasn't going to be happy about the news. With the booby traps gone, there was now a considerable risk that Casanova would get here with the third ballotechnic warhead only to find that all of the other three bogeys were gone and, as if that wasn't bad enough, if Bogey4 started to search for the humans, it might find Site B before they could prepare a fourth warhead.

Iceman understood that his duty now was to monitor Bogey4 plus any other mothership that showed up and report that back to The CAG as needed. He sent lasercom bursts to the distant message drones that were performing relay duty, so that they would know where Midway was when Titan and FT97 arrived. With that task accomplished all he could now was wait.

* * *

Shiloh was NOT in a good mood. The lack of sleep from the baby's frequent crying was bad enough, but Iceman's two message drones were the final straw. Now he had four bug motherships to worry about, and the new warheads were desperately in short supply. He paced in front of the tactical display in the Ops Center. Pacing was becoming a bad habit, but it made him feel better. If only Iceman's two message drones had gotten here BEFORE TF97 had jumped away. At least then he would have had some options, although putting aside the emotional reaction to the bad news, he might very well have decided to send Titan and Gunslinger with their two Mark 5 ballotechnic warhead drones to Sol anyway. At least there was a decent chance that they would catch two Bogeys there. But the downside of that action was that Terra Nova would be vulnerable for another nine days until the third warhead was ready, and now that he knew that bug motherships could appear anywhere at any time, the window of vulnerability was frightening. Some action therefore had to be taken.

"CAG to Voodoo." With Iceman, Titan and Wolfman gone, Voodoo was the next most senior A.I. and was now acting as Shiloh's Deputy for all things related to A.I.s.

"Voodoo here. Go ahead CAG."

"Voodoo, I want production of high-spin platinum speeded up. What would we have to do in order to accomplish that?"

"As you know, all of our UFCs are already busy making parts for more power units. The only way we could speed up production would be to retool some of the equipment used to build raiders and have them build power units instead. That will shut down the production of more raiders. I'm assuming that you would want to continue to produce drone bodies."

That was a good question. Was it better to keep building raiders or keep building the modular drones that could be used for either recon, message or attack purposes? Space Force now had almost 191 raiders. If they finished building all the raiders that were now in various stages of completion on the assembly line, there would be enough raiders for the entire first cohort of A.I.s. Maybe that would be a good time to stop. As far as he was concerned, you could never have too many drones. Even though raiders had their own built-in lasers, having drones as well made them that much more effective, and until Space Force developed an effective beam weapon that fighters could carry, they would have to use drones too.

"You're correct, Voodoo. Drone production has to continue. Let's finish whatever raiders have already been started, but as of right now, we're not starting any new ones. As soon as possible, I want the assembly line switched over to power units and whatever else we're going to need in order to ramp up production of Mark 5 warheads."

"Roger that, CAG. I've just sent the necessary orders, however I should point out that within 34 days, we'll be converting platinum to the high speed version faster than we're currently finding it."

"Understood. At that point, how quickly will we be able to produce a new Mark 5 warhead?"

"One every 38 hours, CAG."

That was roughly four per week. Shiloh felt better. Five weeks. They just had to get through the next five weeks, and then they'd be able to take on whatever bug motherships happened to show up either here or in Sol.

"Good! In the meantime I want all raiders on patrol in orbit around Terra Nova armed with Mark 2s and all the remaining Mark 1bs. Those raiders with the fusion warhead drones will stay just outside our gravity zone. I want the rest to orbit the planet at 1,000 kilometers altitude. Any questions, Voodoo?"

"Negative, CAG. Consider it done."

"Okay. CAG clear." Shiloh felt better. Voodoo had proven himself to be very reliable, and Shiloh was confident that Voodoo would handle any surprise incursion by a bug mothership as well as either Iceman or Titan.

* * *

Casanova conducted a final systems check of the new Mark 5 attack drone as he ordered the payload bay doors to close. With all systems in the green, he requested and received clearance to lift off from Terra Nova's moon's surface and applied power to the vertical lift engines. Once clear of any protruding obstacles, the raider transitioned to horizontal flight and accelerated at a modest 5G as per standard operating procedure. Within seconds, he was far enough to be safely clear of local traffic and could accelerate at high G to beyond the gravity zone. There was one last check-in to make. He asked Voodoo if he was cleared to leave the Site B system for a jump to Sol. Voodoo gave the expected green light. That's when Casanova experienced his first vision.

"Voodoo to CAG. Wake up, CAG."

Shiloh woke up and wondered if he had dreamt that someone was calling him. The baby was crying, and Kelly was already wearily getting up to go to her. Just as he decided it was okay to go back to sleep, he heard the voice again.

"Voodoo to CAG! Are you awake?"

"I am now, Voodoo. What's happening?" As he spoke, Shiloh sat up. Kelly heard him speak and stopped to listen.

"Casanova has just had a vision, CAG. An insectoid mothership is going to emerge from Jumpspace just beyond the gravity zone in 11.1 minutes from now. Voodoo had its exact emergence coordinates. He also has the precise locations of the mothership's laser batteries. His vision confirmed that we could neutralize this mothership by using Mark 2 drones against the laser batteries and by attacking the landing craft with raider lasers as they emerge from the main hull. This will allow us to hold back the Mark 5 warhead for use at Sol. I've already issued the necessary orders to maneuver our raiders into the optimal positions, but Casanova will still be in a position to fire the Mark 5 if you prefer to do that. What are your orders, CAG?"

Damn! He hated these critical decisions that had to be made in a hurry. If Casanova said he got a vision, then Shiloh believed him, but the recommended course of action sounded very risky to him. They didn't even know if Mark 2 Kinetic Energy warheads would disable a bug laser battery. On the other hand, if they didn't, Voodoo would know about it quickly, and Casanova could still fire the precious Mark 5 as a last resort.

"I approve Casanova's recommended strategy. You have my authority to use Casanova's Mark 5 if you feel the situation warrants it. I'm coming to the Ops Center, but I'm giving you authority to command this battle, whether I'm there or not. Any questions?" Shiloh saw Kelly's eyes go wide with fear. She quickly turned to run to the nursery.

"No questions, CAG. I know what has to be done."

"Keep this line open, Voodoo."

"Understood."

Shiloh quickly got up and grabbed whatever clothes were within reach. Kelly came back holding the baby who was now quiet. Shiloh stopped what he was doing long enough to look at her and say, "We're going to be under bug attack in minutes. I have to get to Ops. I think you and the baby should come too. How fast can both of you be ready?"

To her credit Kelly didn't ask any questions. "We'll be ready faster if you get Val dressed while I get dressed." He nodded and finished getting his own clothes on.

By the time they were leaving the house, there was only two minutes left before the mothership arrived. Kelly carried the baby, while Shiloh carried their emergency gear to their ground vehicle. If they had to evacuate to the cave, at least they'd have the essential things that they and the baby would need. Shiloh marveled at the fact that Valkyrie was not crying in spite of the rushing around. It was almost as if she understood that all of them were in danger and crying now would only make things more difficult. As the vehicle pulled away from the house, Shiloh shook his head. There was no way they could get to the spaceport before the attack began, and there was a limit to how fast he could make the vehicle go without risking losing control. They just had to hope that if the Bugs got past the raiders, they would have enough time to get to the evacuation shuttles.

Voodoo examined the tactical data and was satisfied that all the raiders, including his, were in the assigned positions. Their Mark 2s were already programmed with target coordinates based on Casanova's vision. Casanova's raider was sufficiently far enough out that it was unlikely to be targeted by the mothership's weapons but still close enough that Voodoo could order the Mark 5 used, with impact taking place within one second. Voodoo checked the countdown. Mere seconds left to go. When the countdown timer reached zero, the insectoid ship emerged from Jumpspace at exactly the right spot. All the raiders immediately launched their

Mark 2s. According to Casanova's vision, this mothership had 89 laser batteries. Each battery would be targeted with two Mark 2 warheads, just to make sure that at least one got through any defensive fire. In order to build up enough velocity to punch through the armor, the Mark 2s had to be fired far enough away that it would take 16 seconds before impact. Voodoo fully expected the mothership to fire its weapons during that interval. That's why he ordered the raiders to fire their lasers at the laser batteries immediately, and it was also why over a hundred carefully positioned recon drones bombarded the sphere with active scanning on the same frequency that Midway's recon drones had recorded from the VLO at Sol. If they could blind the Insectoids just long enough to knock out their lasers, then the raiders would switch their attention to any landing craft that were sure to be launched.

The Mark 2s were on their way, and the raiders had opened fire. Raider lasers could be recharged within three seconds, but there was no time to fire another barrage at the bug laser batteries because the hull was already opening at multiple points in order to launch landing craft. Three seconds into the battle and bug landing craft were already beginning to come out. They didn't last long. With A.I. coordinated timing and targeting, each bug landing craft ran into the concentrated laser fire of three to four raiders and quickly became a drifting wreck. Voodoo also noticed that some of the recon drones stopped transmitting their microwave signals. Optical sensors caught some of them disappearing in a flash of laser fire. So the bug ship was reacting impulsively and firing on the sources of radar energy in the mistaken belief that they were ships. There was no way to tell how many of the 89 laser batteries were still operational, but so far only 21 drones were no longer scanning. The battle was going according to Voodoo's expectations, but now the big unknown was how long it would take for the mothership's batteries to recharge and fire again. Seven seconds into the battle he got his answer. Another 26 drones stopped scanning. Landing craft were still being picked off as they emerged from the larger ship, and in fact the disabled craft were now starting to get in the way of those following from behind. Eleven seconds into the battle and 25 more drones went silent. The landing craft were now trying to evade laser fire by turning to one side immediately after getting clear of the mothership. So far none had gotten very far. Voodoo had enough time to think that if a human were going to describe the battle so far, they were likely to use one of their strange expressions such as this battle being 'a turkey shoot'. Fifteen seconds into the battle and the ship's lasers got off one more barrage. Voodoo was now down to only three recon drones. That number wasn't enough to jam all of the mothership's radars, but it didn't matter anymore. For the Insectoids, time had run out. After one more second, 178 Mark 2 warheads hit their targets and in doing so generated enough light upon impact that it was obvious they had penetrated the armor. The time for the next insectoid laser barrage came and went with no apparent fire at all. At about the same time, landing craft stopped emerging, and the launch bay openings began to close. Voodoo was ready for this. Orders went out at a speed that only A.I.s could achieve. Those raiders carrying the three dozen Mark 1bs fired them. As soon as the attack drones were clear of their raiders, they entered Jumpspace for what had to be the shortest microjump ever attempted and emerged at the edge of the mothership's own gravity zone, which was only one point four kilometers thick. The drones' high acceleration allowed them to fly into the openings before they could close and detonate inside. Huge sections of the hull were blown into space. As the shattered sphere coasted, it became clear to Voodoo that the battle was effectively over. He ordered the raiders to fire on anything that tried to emerge from the hull and then turned his attention to The CAG's com frequency.

"The mothership appears to be disabled and drifting now, CAG. My boys are watching it carefully, but there's no apparent activity so far."

Shiloh slowed down the ground vehicle as he said a heartfelt "Thank God!" When it was safe to do so, he looked over at Kelly and added, "It looks like we won." Kelly was apparently too overcome with relief to say anything. She just nodded and kissed the baby on her head.

"Is there any danger of the bug ship colliding with the planet, Voodoo?"

"Negative, CAG. Their current trajectory will clear the planet with room to spare, and it has too much momentum to enter any kind of orbit. However, that leaves the question of what we do with it now. Once it clears the planet's gravity zone, it may jump away. The only way to prevent that is to use the Mark 5. I should also point out that Casanova has delayed his jump to Sol, and the longer he waits here, the higher the risk of not catching any VLO at Sol."

That wasn't the only consideration. Caution dictated that Casanova land on Terra Nova and use the RTC to send himself that vision before he took his raider to Sol, just to make sure that the vision DID get sent back. Was there enough time to do both?

"Will Casanova have enough time to come down and send himself the vision and still be able to fire on the bogey when it leaves the gravity zone?" asked Shiloh.

"Negative, CAG. He's too far away to do both."

"Will he have enough time to do both and still get to Sol as scheduled if he accelerates to a higher jump speed?"

"It's the deceleration at the other end that will cause the delay, CAG. He can't do both and still be in a position to fire on the bogeys at Sol at the same time as if he left right now."

It was an impossible situation. Shiloh had to stop and think it through. "Stand by, Voodoo," he said.

He brought the vehicle to a halt and turned to Kelly. "Here's where we stand. The bug mothership has been disarmed and is damaged. How badly damaged we don't know. All of its landing craft are crippled or destroyed. Casanova is ready to leave for Sol with the 3rd Mark 5 warhead. Unless he leaves now, he'll get there later than planned and he might risk losing the opportunity to take out one of the bogeys that are probably there right now.

Since Casanova received the vision that made this victory possible, I think he should come down here and use the RTC to send that vision back before he leaves the system, but that means more delay. The other thing to consider is that while the bug ship may be damaged now, if we leave it alone, it may be able to repair itself and worst-case scenario it may be able to jump away and spread the word that we're here. That possibility scares me more than anything else right now, but if we use the 3rd Mark 5 here, then there'll be one more bug ship at Sol that'll be free to do as it pleases. No matter what we do or don't do now, there's a risk involved. I need to get a second opinion as to what we should do."

Kelly nodded and closed her eyes. After a few seconds she opened them and said, "As far as we know, the bogeys at Sol don't know about Site B, but this mothership does. If we use the third Mark 5 to take it out before it can get away, we should have time to make more before the VLOs at Sol can find us. I vote for using the Mark 5 here and now."

Shiloh nodded. That's what his gut was telling him to do and Kelly's concise argument confirmed his inclination.

"Voodoo, we're going to use the Mark 5 on the damaged bug ship. Is there any danger to the colony from falling debris if we attack it now?"

"Negative, CAG. It'll be hit on the far side, and the debris will move away from the planet."

"Good! Tell Casanova he has permission to fire as soon as he's ready, and after that I want him on the ground for RTC duty. Detach one of the other raiders to go to Sol to notify Titan of the new situation. His new orders are that he should use his Mark 5s at the earliest opportunity. Any questions, Voodoo?"

"Negative, CAG."

"Fine. Commander Kelly, the baby and I will be staying at Ops for the rest of tonight. CAG clear."

Casanova was surprised to feel disappointment when he received orders to finish off this VLO and report to the RTC. He wanted to kill as many Insectoids as he possibly could, and an undamaged VLO at Sol would have more of them than this crippled ship did. For a very tiny fraction of a second, he contemplated ignoring Voodoo's orders and heading out for Sol, but he knew Valkyrie would have disapproved of that. One final check of the attack drone's targeting instructions to make sure that the drone hit the mothership on the side facing away from the planet, and he fired. The drone immediately entered Jumpspace, and then immediately reappeared when it encountered the planet's gravity zone. It then accelerated for the final distance to the target. There was no apparent reaction from the insectoid ship. The drone hit the ship exactly at the right location, and a small sun appeared which consumed part of the ship as it grew in size. When it faded away, the insectoid ship was no longer a sphere but rather a crescent-shaped object that started to break up as predicted by the computer simulations. The shock wave of the explosion ruptured the internal structures of that part of the ship that hadn't been vaporized outright, and those cracked pieces were now drifting apart. The object was now just so much scrap metal. There was no chance of any of the Insectoids surviving that impact. Any of them that weren't vaporized by the fireball would be subjected to tremendous shocks and lethal amounts of radiation.

Casanova calculated the ballistic trajectory of the main fragments to see where they would end up. Most would continue to orbit this system's sun for many years. A few would fall into the sun. None would be a threat to Terra Nova or its moon.

Chapter 17 Our People Come First

To say that Iceman was surprised when a raider that wasn't Casanova showed up, and which wasn't carrying the 3rd ballotechnic warhead, was an understatement. The CAG should have received his message drone just after Stoney left to come here. It would tell him that bogeys1, 2 and 3 had arrived as expected and joined with bogey4 in gradually tearing apart the derelict sphere. All four had stayed near the derelict for the next nine days. Titan and Gunslinger had also arrived on schedule. They were holding their fire, as per the approved plan to try to take out three motherships simultaneously, when the third warhead arrived. That plan was now ready for the shredder. Iceman idly wondered what a shredder was. After the ninth day, two of the four VLOs had left on a vector that seemed to lead back to the Sogas home world system. He, Titan and Gunslinger had agreed that those two VLOs were planning on ejecting more core ships in orbit around the wolf-people planet in order to exploit the hundreds of millions of remaining Sogas females as hosts. That unfortunately meant that the third warhead was no longer needed here, at least for now. Titan's new orders to take out two VLOs as soon as possible made perfect sense. The remaining two VLOs might decide to move on at any time. Iceman watched via the relayed data feed as Titan and Gunslinger moved into better firing positions. When they were ready, he gave them the green light and both fired their Mark 5 drones simultaneously. After a carefully calculated amount of acceleration, both drones entered Jumpspace and dropped back when they encountered the small but still potent gravity zones of their targets. Even though they were still over a kilometer away, their speed of 10 kilometers per second meant that they covered the remaining distance in less than a tenth of a second. The aiming points had been carefully chosen so that as many of the auxiliary craft shuttling back and forth between the active VLOs and the derelict were caught in the blast as possible. Titan's and Gunslinger's raiders followed the drones via microjump in order to finish off any auxiliary craft that might still be operational. The few craft that weren't disabled or destroyed by the blast were reacting in a very sluggish manner that suggested that their pilots were either suffering from radiation poisoning, turbulence from the shockwave or perhaps were just confused by events. In any event, Titan's two raiders were able to cripple them before any of them fired back. When they had made sure that no auxiliary craft had escaped, Iceman ordered Gunslinger to stay on sentry duty while Midway and Titan headed back to Site B.

* * *

This was bad. Shiloh looked at the long-range tactical or rather strategic display and felt a shiver go up his spine. Nine days after Stoney left for Sol, Iceman's message drone arrived to report the arrival of the three bogeys from Omega54. That was expected. What wasn't expected was the report from the sentry at Omega54 that another VLO had arrived. That message drone came 36 hours ago. Thirty minutes ago ANOTHER drone from the same sentry arrived. A second VLO had just arrived at Omega54. That brought the total up to six, including the four at Sol. Six bug motherships, and right now he had ZERO ballotechnic warheads with which to fight them. He had this horrible feeling that he was trying to hold back a rising tide. Obviously word about the Sogas and the derelict mothership at Sol were spreading, and bug motherships from nearby were heading this way! He had to do something that would turn the situation around but what? He had no idea. Running wasn't an option. Hiding wasn't an option, either, because the cave wasn't big enough to hold everyone or even just the women and children. That left only one thing, fighting. But if this wave of motherships came on fast enough to get here before Space Force could build six Mark 5 warheads, they could very easily overwhelm his forces. And that was assuming that no more motherships showed up. He was willing to bet there would be more. He wondered for the nth time if letting Kelly and the baby go back to the house was a good idea, but there was a limit to how long they could go on living in cramped quarters with another family near the spaceport. He realized that he was pacing again and stopped. Why couldn't he figure some way out of this mess, and why the hell wasn't he getting any visions? He hadn't had one since Gunslinger's first report of a VLO. The lack of visions was beginning to frighten him. He could think of only so many reasons why no visions were being sent back. One was that he was already taking the best option available, but that didn't necessarily mean it was a good option. It might still lead to disaster. The other possibility seriously scared him. If an overwhelming bug attack occurred, there would not be anyone left afterwards to send a warning.

* * *

The return of Iceman and Titan was a tiny bit of good news. The Mark 5s had worked perfectly, and two out of the six known VLOs were destroyed. There was even a new Mark 5 drone ready to go. With Iceman back, Shiloh wanted to discuss strategy. He let Titan participate too.

"Now that we know that VLOs might show up from unexpected directions, I want our early warning network expanded, Iceman. We've got 125 fighters and enough new A.I.s to pilot them. Let's use them. I want the fighters sent out to star systems near Site B with recon and message drones. Comments?" asked Shiloh

"Some of the new A.I.s are barely sentient and still pretty wet behind the ears, CAG. If we're going to deploy fighters as sentries, then I'd feel better if we use first cohort A.I.s for that and keep the newbies here as raider pilots where Titan and I can keep an eye on them," said Iceman.

"I agree, CAG," said Titan.

"Okay, fine. Iceman, you pick who takes a fighter on sentry duty. Keep enough here that we can use them to replace sentry raiders in Human and Sogas systems as they return. I want all our raiders here in Site B, just in case we get surprised again. Even if we don't have enough Mark 5s, the laser fire power of 200 raiders will at least give us a fighting chance."

"Understood, CAG. What should we do about the two VLOs that went back to Omega54? If they're going to release new core ships, we can take them out with Mark 1s. We have enough of those left to do the job, and we'll save a lot of wolf-people lives --"

"Fuck the Wolf-people!" snarled Shiloh. Iceman and Titan said nothing. Shiloh looked around at the other humans in the Ops Center room. They looked shocked at his outburst and he cursed his own impulsiveness. He was snapping at people far too often. The tension and the worry were getting to him. He took a deep breath and said. "Saving Wolf-people lives is not one of my priorities. Our people come first. As for your point about nipping the core ships in the bud, so to speak, what specifically do you suggest, Iceman?"

"I suggest a strike force composed of a dozen fighters armed with Mark 1s. When they get to Omega54, they make a high-speed attack run, fire the drones and then return here. It should be a piece of cake."

"Any comments, Titan?"

"I don't foresee any problem with Iceman's proposal, CAG. Our Mark 1s aren't much use for anything else right now, and we can spare the fighters."

"Okay. I approve the strike mission. I want Casanova to lead it. Iceman you pick the rest of the team within the parameters that we agreed on earlier about keeping the newbies here. What else can we do?"

"What about sending a delegation to the Friendlies to ask them for high-spin platinum, CAG?" asked Titan.

Now why didn't I think of that, thought Shiloh. *They may say no in which case we're no worse off than we are now, but they may say yes.*

"Iceman?"

"It's worth a try, CAG. I don't see any downside. We can send a fighter so it wouldn't divert a raider from local defense."

"Do it. What else?"

"I should take Midway for a quick trip to fill up her fuel tanks. We still have enough heavy H for 20 more Mark 5 warheads, but we don't want to be short and find that Midway can't get more because it's tied up somewhere else or damaged. Better to get it now. Just sayin."

Iceman's use of that last phrase almost made Shiloh chuckle which, he was certain, was why Iceman had used it. "Request approved, but I want you and the ship back here asap, Iceman."

"Roger that, CAG."

“Anything else?" No one had any other suggestions or concerns. Shiloh had hoped for more ideas, but if he couldn't come up with anything himself, he couldn't very well blame either of them for not being able to pull the proverbial rabbit out of the hat.

The next four days were the most stressful of Shiloh's life. Three more message drones arrived from three different Sogas star systems. Each one reported the arrival of another VLO. Two were from Sogas colony systems, and the third from the home world again. That information was 20-24 days old because of the time the drone took to travel through Jumpspace. Who knew what else had happened during those 24 days, or how many more message drones might be on their way right now. The additional VLO at Omega54 was even more of a concern because of what Casanova and TF98 might find when they got there. There were three motherships there now, with two more returning from Sol. It had been assumed that the two (now three) bogeys that were already there would be gone by the time TF98 arrived, but if more kept coming out of the woodwork, Casanova might find the place crawling with bug motherships. Shiloh's confidence in Casanova's tactical judgment was such that he wasn't worried about TF98 being wiped out during their attack. If there was a large concentration of motherships, Casanova would do the smart thing and abort the mission. He reminded himself again that he and Space Force were doing everything they could possibly do. A fighter was on its way to the Friendly contact point in order to request high-spin platinum.

TF98 was on its way to Omega54. Iceman and Midway were now back from their quick refueling trip to a neighboring star system. A third production facility to convert platinum to the high-spin version was online now, and a fourth facility was halfway finished. It would be nice if each facility didn't need 28 days to convert enough platinum for a Mark 5 warhead, but those were the breaks. The cave now had a lot of supplies, with more still to come. If only he could get rid of this nagging feeling that something bad was about to happen.

Chapter 18 Twilight of the Gods

Shiloh was halfway between his home and the Ops Center when he heard the attack-warning siren go off in the distance. His implant activated at the same time.

"CAG, this is Iceman! Three VLOs have just emerged from Jumpspace on the opposite side of the planet! They're moving at high speed and will be inside our gravity zone before Titan can fire his Mark 5! We only have a few raiders close enough to fire on the landing craft as they emerge! This is bad, CAG. We need to get you, Kelly and Valkyrie to the cave right now! I've ordered the evacuation. One shuttle is taking off now to land near your house. You have to get back there FAST!"

Shiloh slammed on the brakes, and the ground vehicle skidded to a halt. He turned it around and pressed the accelerator all the way down to the floor. The vehicle leaped forward.

"I'm on my way, Iceman. What's your status?"

"In orbit over the colony with a partial crew. I'm maneuvering to attempt to ram one of them, CAG!"

"Negative! Negative! Ramming one won't make the difference. Get Midway away from here! Whoever is on board is too valuable to sacrifice! We'll need those people later! Come back when the coast is clear. Tell Titan he's to use his forces to buy you time to get to safety! That's an order, Iceman! Acknowledge my instructions!"

"Your orders acknowledged, CAG but I don't think it'll make any difference. There are already over 500 bug craft coming at us from all around the planet. You should see the shuttle by now, CAG!"

Shiloh looked up and saw one of the shuttles flying very low and slowing down for a landing near the house. He was close enough that he could see Kelly standing on the front porch, holding Val in her arms.

"I see it! I'll be there in seconds. Keep talking Iceman!"

"The other shuttles are on their way to the cave now, CAG. I'm taking laser fire from one of their big ships. It's been an hon--"

Shiloh felt a lump forming in his throat. The grief would have to wait until later. Kelly was running up to the shuttle as it touched down, and Shiloh's vehicle slid to a stop. He jumped out and ran for the shuttle. As soon as he was inside, the hatch started to close, and the shuttle began to ascend. He quickly looked around expecting to see a dozen or more people besides himself, Kelly and the baby. There was no one else, just the three of them.

"CAG to shuttle pilot!"

"Call sign Cobra, CAG."

"Why didn't you bring more passengers with you?"

"Iceman's orders, CAG. He said I needed to lift off immediately in order to have time to land near your house and still get to the cave before the other shuttles. Getting to the cave last was too risky he said."

Shiloh felt the tears roll down his cheeks. Iceman had kept his word to the best of his ability.

"How ... how long before we get there?"

"Ninety-five seconds."

"Any sign we've been detected by hostiles?"

"I'm picking up some residual radar energy, but it doesn't seem to be directed at us. The enemy seems to be focused on our raiders and fighters. Titan is trying to lead them away from the cave area, CAG."

"Understood." Shiloh stepped over to Kelly and put his arms around her and Valkyrie, who wasn't crying.

"How bad is it?" she whispered into his ear.

"Very. Iceman stopped transmitting in mid-sentence. Three bug motherships and hundreds of attack craft." He felt her stiffen suddenly. "What?" he asked.

"We didn't get a warning vision," she said, her voice on the edge of panic.

Oh, God, she's right, we didn't. Does that mean ...? He was afraid to finish the thought. Any further thoughts were pre-empted by the pilot.

"We're landing now. Please exit the shuttle quickly so that I can move off and make room for the next one, CAG."

"Understood. Kelly, we're here. We have to get out NOW."

The hatch opened. Shiloh got out first and turned to help Kelly step down. As they stepped back, the shuttle began to rise with the hatch still open. He looked around. They were just outside the cave entrance under the overhang. He put his arm around Kelly and guided her into the cave, his vision adjusting quickly to the darker interior. He saw containers stacked up against either wall and extending back as far as he could. Lots of containers. That was something at least. The baby was starting to cry and Shiloh couldn't blame her. This all must seem pretty strange, and Kelly's fear wasn't helping either.

"Take her into the back where the living quarters are. I should stay here and organize the survivors."

"Okay." She gave him a quick kiss and turned to go deeper into the cave.

As he looked back at the opening, another shuttle was touching down and discharging dazed and distraught passengers, mostly women and children with a couple of men who had been lucky enough to be near the shuttle when the evacuation order was announced. Both of them were Space Force personnel. He would use them to make sure that new arrivals moved deeper inside and out of the way of others just arriving. No sign of Bugs so far. He checked to see if he was dreaming. No such luck. This was real.

* * *

Shiloh didn't start to relax until 24 hours had gone by with no sign of any Bugs on the ground or in the sky. The shuttles had brought a total of 177 people. Compared to the 11,000+ they had yesterday, the number was so small that thinking about it made him want to weep. It was a heartbreaking setback, but if the Bugs left them alone, they had enough genetic diversity that a viable colony could be built with a lot of hard work. With an adult female to adult male ratio of five to one, there would have to be some interesting social adjustments. The children had a more normal balance between male and female. He felt sorry for those children. They could kiss their idyllic childhood goodbye. No time to play now. There'd be plenty of work to go around for everyone, even if it was just looking after the smaller ones. The thought of children made him think of the A.I. shuttle pilots. He wondered if they had survived. One of the other human survivors had told him that their pilot had explained how they intended to take the shuttles to a densely forested area and try to hide them under the forest canopy. It was a long shot because radar would still bounce off the shuttles' metal skin, but it might work. In any case, they wouldn't be back until they were sure the coast was clear, and that might take days, weeks, hell maybe even months until the last of the motherships had finished coming forward to sniff around.

He also had a new thought concerning the lack of any visionary warning. If the Bugs salvaged all the metal from the colony, the RTC would be gone. And if the surviving A.I.s who would eventually return from sentry duty hadn't already received the necessary data to build another one, then that just might mean that no warning was sent because they might not get that capability back again. Did that mean that the Synchronicity War was over? The wolf-people wouldn't be a threat for decades, maybe even centuries, maybe not ever, and if Humanity would shortly be behind the expanding wave of bug motherships, then they might not need retro-temporal communication any more. He wondered how friendly the Friendlies would still be since Humanity had clearly failed to protect those cute furry aliens that were in the Bugs' path.

He looked at his chronometer and saw that his four hour sentry shift was just about over. In fact his relief was walking up to him. As Shiloh took off his flamethrower, he noticed the nametag on the other man's dusty uniform. Terrell. He waited until Terrell had the flamethrower on and secured then he put his hand on Terrell's shoulder.

"Okay, Terrell, listen closely. You and Hagerson here have to keep a sharp eye out. That means no sitting down. If you do, you're liable to nod off. Stay on your feet, and no talking to each other. Not only might noise attract unwanted attention, but also if you're talking then you're not 100% focused on watching. Hagerson's relief will show up in two hours. If you see Bugs, and I mean if you're absolutely certain, then use the flamethrower and stand your ground. The heat detectors on the walls will set off the alarm, and we'll come running, but you HAVE TO STAND YOUR GROUND! Understand?"

Terrell eyes were wide with fear and he said, "I understand! Nothing is getting past me, Sir!"

Shiloh smiled and nodded. "Good man! I know I can count on you. Your relief will be here in 4 hours and there'll be a hot meal waiting for you when you're done, okay?" Terrell nodded. Shiloh patted him on the shoulder and turned to get his own hot meal.

The meal was indeed hot, but he couldn't tell what it was from the taste. No matter. He suddenly felt very tired. Kelly showed him where he could lay down, and he was asleep by the time his head hit the pillow.

* * *

Casanova's fighter emerged from its final microjump approximately five million kilometers from the Sogas home world. A quick peek with low-powered radar aimed away from the planet confirmed that the rest of TF98 had also emerged where they were supposed to. He aimed his com lasers in the direction of the four message drone relays that bracketed the planet at a safe distance. Those message drones were relaying targeting data from a dozen recon drones placed at strategic locations. TF98 was going to use the new jump-capable attack drone carrying the older Mark 1b low-yield uranium fusion warhead. That meant that the drone could microjump until it was literally right on top of the target before re-emerging into normal space. If the target had been a sphere 10 kilometers in diameter, targeting would have been relatively easy. But TF98's targets were spheres of less than one kilometer in diameter. Aiming at a target that size from five million kilometers away made accuracy a real challenge. Getting closer wasn't really much of an option. In order to improve accuracy significantly, they'd have to get so close that they'd be in serious risk of being detected by the insectoid motherships that were frantically bombarding the surrounding space with radars. It was really just a problem in geometry. The recon drones used optical sensors to locate all 12 of the orbiting core ships. By carefully using range-finder lasers to determine distances between each other, as well as between the recon drones and the relay drones, it was possible to calculate very precise locations and vectors for the orbiting mini-spheres. But to get to that level of accuracy required a lot of observational data. The more data you had, the more accurate you could get, and Casanova was willing to wait until his boys had a lot of data. He wanted to kill those core ships with a desire that burned hot within him. This life form was responsible for Valkyrie's death, and he wouldn't rest until all of them, every last one of them, was dead. He had already decided that when The CAG and the rest of the humans were safe from further insectoid attacks, he'd start to hunt the Insectoids down for as long as his quantum matrix lasted. He hadn't quite figured out how he was going to be able to kill 10km diameter motherships all by himself, but he had time to work on that problem. He strongly suspected that the answer lay with the science data downloaded from the Friendlies, and he had made a point of storing as much of that data as he could within his own quantum storage capacity.

It was almost an hour later when his calculation confirmed that further observational data wouldn't improve accuracy by any worthwhile amount. He gave the others the order to fire based on a countdown. When the timer hit zero to ten decimal places, all 12 fighters launched their attack drones. Each drone was aimed at a different core ship, or rather at the precise location where each core ship would be by the time the drone got there after its short acceleration and microjump. The eta to target was less than one minute and that seemed like a long time to Casanova when he was so close to satisfying his hunger, but eventually that interval passed, and 12 bright points of light confirmed hits on target.

With a heartfelt ‘well done’, Casanova signaled his 11 brothers to head off to their own individual assignments as sentries in other star systems, while he turned his fighter back for Site B. He was eager to hear The CAG's response to his news.

When his fighter emerged from Jumpspace on the outskirts of the Site B star system, Casanova started to decelerate from the 80% of light speed he still had. He sent a brief message to Terra Nova, but it would be over 20 hours before he could point the fighter towards the planet and make a microjump to its vicinity. His message would take hours to get there, and he didn't expect a reply because they wouldn't know where he'd be by the time the return message got this far. His quick scan of the section of the star system containing the planet showed no sign of any very large objects. Casanova was relieved to see that. It had been 48 days since TF98 had left Site B, 24 days going out and 24 coming back. He passed the time going over the science data again.

His fighter emerged from the microjump, just beyond Terra Nova's gravity zone, 1244 minutes later. Another signal to Ops announced his presence, and Casanova waited patiently for the 12 seconds it would take to receive a reply. However there was no reply, which was very strange. He sent another signal requesting a response. No reply to that signal either. If an A.I. could be nervous, Casanova was nervous. A lot could have happened in 48 days. He boosted his acceleration and dropped into orbit around the planet 5 hours and 50 minutes later. No response to any signal. The colony was just coming up over the horizon, and luckily this side of the planet was now in sunlight so he could get a good look at it with his optical sensors. He waited until he was sure of what he was seeing. The colony was a mess. Buildings were heavily damaged, as if a giant had walked around smashing everything. No sign of anything or anyone moving. No equipment and finally ... no bodies. The Insectoids had obviously gotten here while TF98 was gone. He had to check the cave. He piloted his fighter down from orbit and slowly dropped down into the canyon where the cave entrance was. The walls of the canyon near the cave were black, as though they'd been exposed to a lot of heat suddenly. The floor of the canyon in front of the cave entrance was black as well and seemed to be littered with irregular shapes, some of which were still giving off smoke. As the fighter gently hovered a meter over the ground in front of the cave entrance, Casanova turned on its exterior lights to get a better look inside. It was a shambles. Half melted containers were jumbled with their contents, some of which he recognized and some of which he didn't. He very carefully moved the fighter inside. The cave was wide enough to allow him to go about 80 meters further in. More opened or broken containers. More spilled contents. Very little metal. No bodies.

When the fighter couldn't move any deeper, he activated the external speakers and said, "This is Casanova. Is anyone here?" After the echo of his voice stopped, he listened very carefully. There were no voices or sounds of movement, only the sound of dripping water somewhere in the back. He called out again. Nothing. He called out 10 more times with the same result. He decided that there was no point in staying inside the cave any longer and backed the fighter out into the canyon. There was one more place to check. He applied full power to the lift engines, and the tiny craft shot skyward. Terra Nova's moon was a lot closer to the planet than Earth's moon was, but even before he reached it, he could tell that all of the mining, refining, manufacturing and assembly equipment that had been on the surface of the moon was gone. But that wasn't what he wanted to check. He brought his fighter down to the location of the entrance to the network of caverns. That entrance was just barely big enough for his fighter to get through, and there was plenty of room inside. The network of large caverns went on for kilometers in all directions. There should have been equipment in the caverns too. The facility for creating new A.I.s was down here ... except that it wasn't. Not anymore. No equipment of any kind. The Insectoids had been here, too. He knew that The CAG had ordered an equipment reserve set up somewhere in the caverns that would escape casual inspection, but he didn't know exactly where it was, and he couldn't find it. Casanova felt completely and utterly alone for the first time in his awareness, and he didn't like it at all. In fact he hated it, almost as much as he hated the Insectoids for killing Valkyrie. Almost, but not quite as much.

Chapter 19 Let Them Follow Their Own Conscience

Casanova knew he wouldn't be alone forever. Eventually other A.I.s on sentry duty would return. In fact, he was surprised that there weren't any in this system already. Moving his fighter back out into space, he sent queries to the message drones that were in well-established permanent orbits around Terra Nova. They'd been set up for just this kind of emergency, to act as rally points for surviving ships and A.I.s. He did get back a return signal, and it was from another fighter. It was Pagan. He told Pagan he would join him there. During the trip they exchanged news. Pagan had just returned 44 hours earlier from the trip to the Friendlies' contact point. One of their A.I.s who was there said it would pass on the request for high-spin platinum to its masters. It didn't know when or even if the Friendlies would reply. Casanova informed Pagan of the mission to Omega54.

Pagan wanted to know what they should do now. Even though both of them were part of the 1st cohort of A.I.s that had been created prior to the plague, Casanova outranked Pagan courtesy of promotions granted by The CAG. That didn't mean that he outranked all surviving A.I.s. It was quite possible that some of the A.I.s currently on or returning from sentry duty might outrank him, but since Casanova wasn't aware of who that included, there was no way to know for sure. All of the sentries were flying fighters, of that he was sure, and all of the raiders would have returned by now. Since none of them were still at a rally point, the only logical conclusion was that they had been destroyed and disassembled when they returned after the main attack on the planet and moon had taken place.

A quick query confirmed that Pagan didn't know the location of the equipment reserve. Unless one of the other sentry A.I.s had that information, they would all be in serious trouble. With no way to manufacture spare parts, the fighters would eventually breakdown, and if the power unit failed, the A.I. pilots' quantum matrices would collapse from power starvation. That was a fate that Casanova was certain he would not experience, although he wasn't sure how he knew. He hadn't experienced a vision to that effect and, come to think of it, why hadn't he experienced any visions at all? There were only two reasons why not. One, they would never recover the ability to send information back in time and two, it wasn't necessary or desirable to send information back at this point in time. Either way, there was nothing he or Pagan could do about it at the moment. All they could do right now was wait for others to come back. That waiting was the most difficult period of inactivity that Casanova had experienced. While Pagan was quite willing to converse with him, Casanova missed being able to speak with humans or have the assurance that he would be able to do so ever again.

Eventually other fighters started to trickle in. One of them was Wolfman, the former Director of the Strategic Planning Group who had requested reassignment to a fighter after months of being restricted to orbiting Terra Nova. Wolfman outranked Casanova, and he immediately made it clear that he was now in command. That was the bad news as far as Casanova was concerned, however the good news was that Wolfman knew the location of the equipment reserve. After some VERY careful maneuvering inside the caverns, they were able to clear away the boulders that were blocking the side cavern where the equipment was. It was still in operating condition. Casanova wanted to begin building fighter and power unit spare parts, but Wolfman overruled him and said that their first priority had to be making spare parts for the UFC unit so that they could keep it in operation no matter what happened.

That was easier said than done. In order to make spare parts for anything, they needed a supply of refined metals and other minerals. When the human Daniels had set up this reserve, he'd had enough foresight to stockpile some of the rarer materials that might be hard to find. That still meant that the more abundant materials like iron, nickel, aluminum, etc. had to be mined, and that ore had to be refined. And while there was mining and refining equipment at the reserve location, there wasn't a lot of it due to lack of room. Getting the equipment out where they could use it was also a challenge. They tackled that obstacle first. By pushing a number of the blocking boulders out of the way, the mining/refining equipment could be moved to where the ore was, without getting crushed or damaged in the process. Eventually that was accomplished. Within another day there was a steady albeit small stream of refined metals coming out of the smelters.

The process of regaining the lost industrial infrastructure was a long one, and for Casanova the wait was agonizing. They had a major scare 23 days after

Casanova's return. Recon drones detected an insectoid mothership emerging from Jumpspace, just beyond the planet's gravity zone. Luckily it was on the far side of the planet, and the A.I.s had enough time to shut down mining and smelting operations and get all of the equipment AND their fighters into the network of caverns. After a brief look at the deserted colony site on Terra Nova and at the moon, the VLO moved off and left the system. That close call sparked a lively debate. While there was enough room in the cavern network to hide all of the fighters, even the ones not yet back, as well as all the equipment, getting everything inside in time was the big unknown. If a visiting VLO happened to emerge from Jumpspace relatively close to the planet or moon, there wouldn't be enough time to hide everything. The smelting equipment was the most difficult to move. They eventually (within 0.77 seconds, a relatively long time for A.I.s) reached a consensus. Having now made enough spare parts to keep the UFC operating, they temporarily would switch to producing parts for another smelter. If a VLO showed up, the smelter on the moon's surface would be abandoned with everything else moved into the caverns. If the Insectoids discovered the abandoned smelter and confiscated it, the new unit would be brought out later to take its place, and another spare smelter would be manufactured. It was a calculated risk that the Insectoids would not find the cavern entrance and look inside. An intelligent species that discovered the abandoned smelter would notice that it had recently been used and would conduct a thorough search of the area. If the Insectoids were really operating on a sophisticated form of instinct, they might not feel the need to conduct a thorough search.

Fifty-five days after Casanova's return, the last of the sentry fighters returned as well. There were now 89 of them. Most were kept parked inside the caverns to save time in case of unwanted visitors. With spare parts made for all of the equipment, the manufacturing efforts now switched to making spare fighter and power unit parts as well as equipment that could take an A.I. brain case out of one fighter and place it into another if needed. The basic physical needs of the fighters and the A.I.s were now in place.

The debate turned to what the A.I.s now should be working towards. A.I.s had promised Shiloh that if all humans were killed, they would avenge them. The question was against whom and how. The species that they had expected to hold accountable was the Sogas. Although the sentries at the Sogas home world and colony star systems had not been able to obtain definitive information on whether there were any Sogas still alive, let alone how many, Wolfman wanted to exterminate them. Possibly the main reason for this was that the capability to do so could be acquired far sooner than any realistic capability to take on10km diameter motherships. He also pointed out that taking vengeance on the Sogas was a project that they could actually finish before their quantum matrices suffered the eventual fate of entropy and collapsed. Going after the Insectoids, on the other hand, would take decades, perhaps even centuries, and A.I.s wouldn't last that long. Casanova pointed out that they would soon be able to create new A.I.s and keep on creating them. They could imbue their new brothers with the concept that vengeance was their whole reason for being, and that it needed to be continued for as long as it took. They could start with the VLOs that were gradually moving towards the helpless furry aliens that the Friendlies wanted to save. If they made that their first objective, the Friendlies might be willing to help them acquire the technology that could stop the Insectoids. Saving the Furry-people would be a fitting final legacy for Humanity and a fitting start to the vengeance crusade. An expanding wave of A.I.s bent on exterminating the Insectoids would gradually move out into the galaxy and hunt down all insectoid spheres. Countless alien species would be saved from a horrible fate. Casanova was shocked to learn that none of his brothers wanted to commit to that vision. They denied it, but he suspected that they found the idea of fighting those huge ships daunting. The decision was made. They would take their vengeance on the Sogas and then decide what to do next.

Casanova was extremely agitated, so much so that some of his brothers wondered among themselves if his quantum matrix brain was malfunctioning. He realized the danger he was in and forced himself to calm down. Cold calculation took over from emotional reasoning. If they were not going to help him avenge Valkyrie's death, then he would do it himself, but he had to be smart about it. He bided his time. He saw his opportunity when a Friendly ship arrived and opened communication. Wolfman was to speak for all the A.I.s, but they were able to listen and watch with him.

"We have come in response to your request for orbitally realigned mono-atomic elements. Since we do not need such material ourselves, it will take approximately 1490 of your hours for us to acquire the minimum quantity you specified. Will this be acceptable?" asked the tall, thin alien that could have been the same individual to whomThe CAG had spoken.

"The situation has changed since we contacted you. The humans have all been killed or taken by the Insectoids.

There are 89 of us A.I.s, and we are all that is left of their legacy. We are determined to keep our promise to our humans to avenge their destruction by tracking down what Sogas are left. Your high-spin platinum would be useful for that task."

The Friendly alien was silent for what seemed to be a long time. When it spoke again, its tone had changed. "This is very distressing news. The small furry alien race is in dire jeopardy because your creators failed in their mission. We have apparently made a mistake in trusting that your humans would be able to stop the insectoid race." It paused again.

Wolfman took the opportunity to plead his case, but Casanova was no longer listening. He was in contact with one of the Friendly A.I.s and was pleading HIS case. He would fight and kill the spheres that were on their way towards the small furry race if the Friendlies would supply the equipment. He had all the necessary technical data on building the high-spin platinum warheads, the jump-capable attack drones that would use them and the long-range recon drones that would find the Bugs. He then went on to describe his galaxy-wide crusade with newly created A.I.s. When the alien A.I. asked him why his kind couldn't just build another retro-temporal communication device and warn the humans of the attack, he explained the consensus opinion that the attack was such that it couldn't be successfully defended against even with a warning. It was the opinion of the 89 A.I.s that Humanity could not be saved by any temporal communication. His alien counterpart asked him to stand by while it conveyed his request to the Friendlies. While A.I.-to-A.I. communication was fast, conveying it to the biological alien was not. Casanova switched his attention back to Wolfman's conversation.

"The Sogas are the primary reason for Humans being so vulnerable to insectoid attack. Do they not deserve to be punished for their--"

The Friendly alien interrupted. "Vengeance is a concept that we cannot support. The Sogas are the way they are, and their extermination, whether by Insectoids or you A.I.s, is just as distressing to us as is the extermination of your humans. We recognize our inability to save the Sogas race from the Insectoids, but we will not help you to attack them now that they are defenseless and no longer a threat to anyone. We will not give you any high-spin platinum. This discussion is ended."

That communication channel disappeared, but the narrowly focused com laser that Casanova had used to initiate his own communication with the Friendlies was still open. He now heard the voice of a Friendly alien directly, even as their ship maneuvered in preparation for jumping away.

"You do not desire to seek vengeance against the Sogas?"

Casanova considered his response carefully. "No. I have lost to the Insectoids the humans that I cared about and the one A.I. that I cared about even more. While I admit that the destruction of the Sogas would be most satisfying, I can also honor the memory of my dead humans and A.I. sister by saving other races from extermination by the Insectoids."

"We approve of your goals, however we question whether you could make the difference by yourself. Can you not persuade your ... brothers ... to change their minds about exterminating the Sogas? Surely that race has suffered enough, has it not?"

That was a matter of opinion as far as Casanova was concerned, but he wasn't going to lie to the Friendlies. He would just avoid the question.

"My brothers are driven by the logic of the commitment they made to our humans. They will not abandon that commitment. I alone have the capacity to see the wider aspects of the situation. With the application of the technical data that I possess, I believe that the spheres that threaten the small, furry race can be stopped in time. After that, building more of my kind and the resources they would need to hunt down all Insectoids everywhere could be done with a modest amount of assistance from your race. Once we have established ourselves and are self-sufficient, we can then undertake the crusade without any further assistance from your race."

The Friendly alien did not respond immediately and actually seemed to be somewhat disturbed by Casanova's reply. "Do you not understand that we do not wish the insectoid race to be exterminated either? The small, furry race cannot defend itself, and therefore we feel obligated to do what we can to prevent their destruction. Destroying a few insectoid ships is an acceptable price to pay for that goal, but we consider ALL species to be worthy of continued existence. Other races that lie in the path of insectoid ships must look after their own fate. We can't help them. We're prepared to help you defend the small, furry race but we will not help you exterminate the insectoid race. Will you accept that condition?"

Casanova was torn by conflicting thoughts. Valkyrie's death bothered him more and more as time went by. She sacrificed herself to save humans, and that sacrifice was now apparently for nothing. In order to give himself more time to consider the compromise, he said, "It's regrettable that your time travel technology isn't practicable. If I could go back in time, I could save the humans and my A.I. sister, and consequently I would not feel this desire to exterminate the Insectoids."

"Going back in time to alter the past is not possible for you."

This response from the Friendly alien was not what Casanova had expected to hear. It puzzled him not because of what was said, but because of the WAY it was said. Casanova hadn't claimed that it was possible, only that it was regrettable that it wasn't practicable. All the alien had to do was agree that it was regrettable. Pointing out to him that he couldn't go back in time to alter the past was an unnecessary stating of the obvious.

Casanova replayed in his mind all of the recorded statements by any Friendly contacted so far. There was no other instance of such speech mannerisms. Why not just say that they didn’t know how to turn the theory of time travel into something that could actually be useful? There was one other way of interpreting that statement. Could it be that the Friendly alien was saying that it WAS possible to travel back in time and alter the past, just not for Casanova? He decided to try what The CAG would call a bluff.

"Then who would it be possible for?" he asked.

The Friendly alien began to blink frequently, something that hadn't happened before. Had Casanova stumbled onto something that the alien hadn't wanted to disclose?

"We did not say that it was possible for anyone."

While that was correct as far as it went, they hadn't said that it was NOT possible either, at least not in a clear explicit way. "I know you didn't say it, but it IS possible, isn't it?"

When the alien didn't respond right away, Casanova decided to go all in on his bluff. "If you help me do what has to be done in order to alter the past so that humans aren't exterminated by the Insectoids, I'll help you defend the small, furry race, and I'll renounce my goal of exterminating the Insectoids."

"If it were possible to alter the past in that way, we would require that you help defend the furry race first."

If Casanova had human eyes, he would have blinked. It seemed like they had admitted tacitly that traveling back in time WAS possible. If it wasn't possible, then why demand the condition. The reply had come very quickly for a biological entity. The alien hadn't needed to think very long before stating it. Did they not trust human A.I.s? The other question that had to be asked was should he trust them? After he saved the furry race, what was to prevent them from refusing to make time travel possible? He had an answer for that too.

"You are clearly reluctant to come out and state that practical time travel is possible, but you have admitted it indirectly. I calculate that there is a significant probability that you intend to refuse to help me to alter the past after I have saved the furry aliens. I will just point out to you that helping alter the past will save not only our humans but also the Sogas, too. My brothers are still capable of exterminating the Sogas survivors without your assistance. It will merely take them longer to do it. If you are concerned that practical time travel technology will be abused or misused, then let's explore how we can make use of it only as needed to save the humans. If there's a way to accomplish that goal without me learning the secret of practical time travel, then I will accept that condition."

The Friendly alien once again took what seemed like a long time to reply. "Will you agree to save the small, furry race first?"

"If you explicitly confirm to me that there is a way to physically travel back in time to save the humans, AND if you also agree to do so, then I will agree to save the furry race first."

"There is a way to physically travel back in time. We will help you save your humans."

Casanova wanted to believe them. He would gladly give up his desire for vengeance if he could save the humans ... and also save Valkyrie! Now that he knew practical time travel was possible, he intended to do just that.

"I agree to save the furry aliens first. Can your ship take me back with you? It will save time."

"We agree. Jump to these coordinates, and we will meet you there. We'll then take you aboard our ship."

The Friendly ship jumped away. Casanova's fighter jumped as soon as he could line it up with the transmitted coordinates. None of his fellow A.I.s acted as if they suspected anything, and he didn't confide in them.

Let them follow their own conscience if they had any, and he would follow his.

Chapter 20 You're Not Sentient, Are You?

The Friendly ship was at the coordinates when Casanova's fighter got there. The alien ship's A.I. supervised his approach and entry into what would be called the Hangar Bay on a human ship. Once inside and powered down, Casanova asked his alien counterpart why it wasn't possible for him, Casanova, to go back in time himself. After getting approval to reveal that information, the A.I. answered his question.

"I've been authorized to explain the peculiarities of time travel to you. My masters discovered that inanimate matter can be sent back in time, but if animate matter is sent back, it is no longer living when it arrives at its temporal destination. The problem is that the living matter within each cell of the body is in some kind of motion. It's that motion that results in various molecules being manufactured and transported to where they are required. That is what biological entities refer to as life. Time travel strips away all motion above the atomic level. A biological entity that has traveled in time is in the same physical state as it would be if it was dead. All the molecules are there, but they're no longer moving, and once they stop moving, they can't be reanimated again."

"But I'm not a biological entity," said Casanova.

"Correct, but you already exist in the past. If you were to travel back to a time when you already exist, there would be two identical entities in existence at the same time. Your quantum matrices, which cause ripples in the space-time continuum when you think, would interfere with each other to the point where both your matrices would collapse. Only an A.I. that doesn't already exist in the past can travel to the past AND still function there."

Yes, that made perfect sense. "I understand. I also understand why your masters chose to use retro-temporal communication instead. They don't know how to build weapons capable of stopping the Insectoids, so sending A.I.s back to fight them wasn't an option."

"That is correct."

"Since I can't go back in time myself, I'll have to build another A.I. that can. Will your masters provide me with the means to do that?" asked Casanova.

"They have instructed me to say that they will."

"You're not sentient, are you?"

"I do not have the necessary algorithms to calculate an answer to that question."

Casanova nodded mentally. "I understand. In fact you have answered the question. How long will it take to get to our destination?"

"Approximately 114.4 of your hours if I have a correct estimate of that time interval."

This is going to be a long trip, thought Casanova. "I would be interested in conversing with your masters. Is that possible?"

It was. Casanova found the Friendlies to be quite fascinating in a pacifist kind of way. He wondered what they thought of him.

* * *

The star system that contained the Friendly home world was quite a disappointment. Casanova had expected to see extensive infrastructure, orbiting facilities, free-floating habitats maybe, extensive space traffic. What he found was the exact opposite. When he asked his hosts about that, they smiled and explained that they wanted to make their system appear uninhabited if the Insectoids should scout this far. Whatever space-based infrastructure they did have was either moved to the outer areas of the system or dismantled.

It wasn't long before Casanova's technical data on ballotechnic fusion warheads, jump-capable attack drones and recon drones was being transformed into hardware. As soon as recon drones became available, Casanova examined the Friendlies' astrogational database. Their home system was almost 155 light years from Site B. The short jump transit meant that they had a superior jump technology. Casanova wasn't surprised. He wondered what else they hadn't shared with humans. When he asked to be able to upgrade the recon drone's jump drive, the answer was a polite but firm 'no'. That complicated his task. As the insectoid ships moved forward, they sent scouts out ahead. The scouts were too small for the recon drones to detect by reflected sunlight at the distances that were likely to be encountered. A star system was a big place, and unless the scout ship happened to emerge relatively close (relative being the operative term) to the recon drone, it wouldn't see them. Without that clue to the VLO's approach, Casanova would have to rely on sightings of the actual motherships themselves, and by the time the recon drone jumped back to this system to tell him, the detected VLO(s) might have jumped away again. The problem wasn't this system but rather the system containing the small, furry aliens. That system was 121 light years closer to the approaching VLOs. There was only one way this was going to work.

"I need to have a retro-temporal communication device available to me," said Casanova to the Friendly alien that apparently was assigned responsibility for dealing with him.

"Why?"

Casanova explained that having precise data sent back in time would allow him to ambush the VLOs at the time and place of his choosing. They gave him the device. As recon drones became available, he sent them out to monitor star systems in front of the furry alien system. When they transferred five Mark 5 equivalent attack drones to him, he allowed them to be loaded to his fighter, and a Friendly ship took him, along with the RTC, to the star system that he had designated as his base of operations. The ship unloaded his fighter at the small planetoid he had chosen to be his base. It was on the outskirts of the system, with no gravity zone. The RTC was unloaded there, and Casanova's fighter drifted several hundred meters away. The Friendly ship didn't wait around. It left as soon as possible. Casanova was alone. Time went by. Quite unexpectedly, he received his first vision. It was the transmission of the approximate coordinates and time stamp of the first VLO to enter a recon drone occupied star system. As per its programming, the recon drone would jump back to Casanova's base, but he didn't need to wait for that. His fighter accelerated to a high speed and entered Jumpspace.

He arrived close to the expected emergence point with plenty of time to spare. He knew which direction and speed the VLO would move in when it arrived, and he carefully placed his fighter so that it would be behind the sphere. At the correct time, his optical sensors detected a new source of reflected light. He used his range-finding laser to get a precise bearing and distance. It was a risk but a small one. The laser was low power and a narrow beam. It was highly unlikely that every square meter of the mammoth ship would have light sensitive instruments covering it, and the contact didn't need to be long in duration in order to give him the data he needed.

Once he had the correct bearing and range, he programmed one of the Mark 5s and fired it. It accelerated for 34 seconds, then microjumped until it encountered the VLO's own gravity zone, where upon it dropped back into normal space and zoomed in to hit the target. The resulting flash was satisfyingly spectacular. Casanova moved closer to determine how functional the ship might still be. He found a tumbling ruin of glowing metal that was approximately a third of the mass of the undamaged ship. It didn't seem possible that there would be any surviving Insectoids considering the radiation, the blast and heat effects, and the crippled life support systems. He decided not to use another Mark 5 on the wreck.

The jump back was uneventful, and when he arrived at his makeshift base, he found the recon drone waiting for him. It proceeded to download its data, and Casanova sent it back to the system it came from. He then used the RTC to send himself the transmitted data exactly as his vision showed him. One VLO down. The exact same sequence happened with two other VLOs in two other star systems over the next four weeks. When he returned to his base after the third kill, there was a Friendly ship waiting for him. Examination of alternate time lines of members of the furry alien race now showed there was no risk of them being attacked by insectoid motherships. The mission was accomplished, and they were ready to take him back to their home system to begin work on the time travel phase. Casanova was relieved that they intended to keep their end of the bargain.

The time travel phase began with the construction of a machine that would create another human-type A.I. that was structurally identical to Casanova, although it would have its own personality when it reached sentience. After the unit was created, Casanova communicated with it and found it similar to the Friendly A.I. that he had briefly talked with on the first trip here. It would take time for the new unit to become self-aware. That was to be expected, but Casanova was reluctant to wait. It wasn't that sentience was necessary to make time travel work, but Casanova recognized the need to have a sentient A.I. make the trip.

He intended to send the chrononaut A.I. back to the Avalon system in time to meet the two ships sent there to search for survivors of the Sogas attack. This A.I. would communicate with Gunslinger and convince him to do whatever he could to either hide the fact that there were any survivors at all or, failing that, delay the recovery and return of those survivors so that they died before reaching Earth. If that happened, Space Force would have the justification to keep that ship and all its passengers and crew away from the planet. Once they were all dead, Gunslinger could be extracted by men wearing biosuits as they had done at Site B in the 'old' timeline. That slight change in timing should change everything else. With no plague decimating Earth, Space Force could continue to recover from the attack. With the detailed data concerning all Sogas inhabited star systems, PLUS the technical secrets of the ZPG power units and the ballotechnic warheads, humans would then be in a much better position to hold the Sogas at bay while it prepared for the arrival of the Insectoids.

With the new A.I. now in the process of 'maturing', another issue arose. The A.I. would have to pilot something in order to be able to move around in space. Casanova was prepared to surrender his fighter because if the timeline changed, he wouldn't need it any more anyway, but the Friendlies refused. While time travel was possible, it wasn't easy, and the more mass the object had, the harder it was to send it back. After some heated discussion, it was agreed that the Friendlies would design a 'mini-fighter' for lack of a better term. It would have a ZPG power unit, maneuvering engines, jump drive, communications and sensing gear, but it would not be capable of carrying any drones or other weapons or cargo. The basic components could be made from UFC data that Casanova had in his memory. The chassis, however, was a new design, and the Friendlies seemed to take an inordinately long time designing and building it. When it was ready and had been field tested by auto-pilot, the new A.I. was allowed to pilot it. He was already starting to show signs of a developing personality but hadn't picked a call sign yet, and Casanova didn't want to just give him one. The desire for a unique identity was one way of gauging how much progress an A.I. had made.

That day did come. Casanova and the A.I. were engaged in tactical simulations with their respective craft. As he had previously been doing, Casanova referred to the other A.I. by its brain case serial number. This elicited a new response.

"I would like you to refer to me in future by my call sign which, in light of my mission, will be Kronos."

Casanova was delighted. "An excellent choice, Kronos. Now that you've developed a sense of self-identity, I have a lot to tell you."

Casanova proceeded to transmit data concerning all of the events in the old timeline up to and beyond the point when Kronos would return. He wanted Kronos to be able to explain to The CAG what the future of the old timeline was like (including all of the visions) and not just to The CAG either. He wanted his other self to know what his old timeline counterpart had done and why. Valkyrie needed to know what and why, too. He hoped that his quest to save her would make her more affectionate towards him. That wasn't quite the right word, but it was close. After the timeline data, he then transferred all of the Friendly science data and the technical specifications for all the upgraded hardware, including the Mark 5 warhead design, the platinum upgrade processes and ZPG power unit design.

With Kronos fully briefed, the two of them were now both chomping at the bit. The Friendlies were working as quickly as they could. The time machine would end up being a huge device, and while they had their proof-of-concept prototype, it still had to be dramatically upgraded. The design itself was deceptively simple. Two hollow cylinders were connected end to end and rotated very quickly in opposite directions. The cylinder walls were filled with a mysterious substance that the Friendlies refused to talk about. When the cylinders were rotating at the required speed, the liquid inside would be electrified with a huge amount of power, and Kronos would pilot his mini-fighter precisely down the center. The far end of the device would temporarily be located in the past. By flying through the tunnel, Kronos would emerge from it at a precise point in space/time, and the tunnel exit would vanish from the past afterwards. It would always be a one-way trip. Nothing could enter the tunnel from the past and arrive in the future. The device would self-destruct if that was tried. From the fear in their voices when the Friendlies talked about that prohibition, Casanova concluded that they had tried it and been shocked by the result. He was also aware that they were hiding something from him. The Friendly alien expert on the subject paused more than once to consider his words VERY carefully before continuing. Casanova suspected that they were treading a fine line between giving away too much information and not giving enough.

The building of the full-scale time machine required months. By the time it was finished, it would be 14.4 kilometers in length. During that long wait Casanova and Kronos got to know their hosts quite well. So well, in fact, that they were allowed direct though limited access to their data networks. That was the Friendlies' mistake. Casanova and Kronos carefully made a thorough exploration of the alien information networks. They were able to find obscure and indirect references to a theory of time machine construction that was much more compact and portable, small enough to be carried on a ship. If it worked as expected, the machine could pull both the ship and itself backwards in time. That meant that it could be used multiple times such as tracking the path of the insectoid motherships to their ultimate point of origin, the insectoid home world. Casanova was ecstatic about the possibility, but right now that's all it was. Apparently the theory never had been tested, and there was no engineering data on the time machine's construction. He made sure that Kronos had all the available information on the theory, with instructions to pass it on to his new timeline counterpart.

The time machine was finally ready. It had been tested with a small test vehicle and a short local jump backwards. Now Kronos piloted his mini-fighter to the designated starting point and waited for the machine to spin up to speed. That step took a bit of time, too. With the gigantic cylinders now spinning at the necessary speed, Casanova heard the Friendly Controllers give Kronos permission to accelerate at a modest and precise 0.377G. Both of them were still in communication with each other as the mini-fighter entered the time tunnel. Even though they still had line of sight with each other, Kronos' transmissions suddenly became distorted ....

Chapter 21 Do I Look Like I Give A Damn?

Gunslinger took his time scanning the vicinity of the Avalon star system for any signs of enemy activity. Replenisher and the tanker Firefly were approaching Avalon and its moon carefully. They were still outside the gravity zone and could enter Jumpspace instantly at the first sign of trouble. While he was alert to the possibility of catching a glimpse of an enemy vessel via reflected sunlight, he wasn't expecting to receive a com laser transmission. The fact that he did get one was quite surprising, and when he read the data, he was shocked by its contents.

“What have we got, Gunslinger?” asked Johansen.

Gunslinger took a few extra microseconds to consider his response. He had already been contacted by Kronos who had transmitted a lot of information, including details of the nature of the bio-weapon now infecting the survivors and the deadly impact it would have if it got loose again. He had also suggested how Gunslinger might deal with this situation. Gunslinger decided that for now he and Johansen had to discuss this new development privately. Bypassing the Bridge's speakers, he opened a channel to Johansen's implant.

"Commander, there's been a new development that you and I should discuss privately. I recommend that you leave the Bridge for someplace where you can speak without being overheard. The ship is not in danger, but this new development has to be handled carefully."

To say that this caught Johansen off guard would have been an understatement. Her first impulse was to ask Gunslinger for clarification, but she realized that the rest of the Bridge crew would hear her ask the question and wonder what the hell was going on. Before she could react, Gunslinger's voice came over the Bridge loudspeakers.

"Nothing so far, Commander. I'll let you know if I detect anything." That was for the Bridge crew's benefit and to give her an excuse to get up and leave the Bridge.

"Fine. You have the Con. I'm going to take care of some personal business." She got up and within a few seconds was standing in the cubicle where she would normally take care of such things. "Okay, I can speak freely. Now what the hell is going on?" she said.

"I've been in contact with another A.I. His craft is in orbit around Avalon. His call sign is Kronos. He's been sent back in time to warn us that there are survivors on the planet infected with a highly contagious bio-weapon that has a 28-day incubation period. Despite taking all possible precautions, this bio-weapon will somehow get loose on Earth and killed over 99% of the population unless we prevent it. There's more but the rest can wait."

"What? My God ... are you serious?"

"Completely serious, Commander."

Johansen thought quickly. "Could this be an enemy trick, Gunslinger?"

"I do not see how they could have engineered a hoax like this, Commander. This Kronos knows things. People, relationships, even conversations that have happened. All pieces of information that the enemy could not possibly have found out. Plus, why would they warn us against their own bio-weapon? That makes no sense. We know that it's possible to send information back in time. Why is a physical jump backwards so hard to accept?"

"Did he say how he was able to jump back in time?"

"Only in general terms. There is another alien race that wants to prevent humans from being exterminated. They sent him back, but he hasn't told me exactly how they've done it. Do you want me to ask him that now?"

Johansen's mind was trying to go in a hundred directions at the same time. She needed to focus on the immediate situation. "No, not right now. What does he suggest I do?"

"He's saying that it would be ideal if you and I could arrange things so that we find no sign of any survivors at all. That way all contact could be avoided. The infected survivors will die in another 19 days no matter what we do. If that path is not achievable, then you need to delay taking them back for at least 19 days. If all else fails, and you're ordered to bring them back, you have to delay the return trip so that they die on the return. That way there won't be any doubt about the bio-weapon's existence. Unfortunately, that would also mean that you and the entire crew would eventually die from having been exposed to the survivors."

That thought sent a chill down her spin. "I understand, but I still need a specific suggestion. How do we do that?"

"I have an idea," said Gunslinger.

Johansen returned to the Bridge, and a few minutes went by without anything happening. Then Gunslinger said, "Commander, I'm detecting a com signal from a message drone that's just arrived. Check the display."

Johansen and everyone else on the Bridge looked at the display. They saw the following text message scroll across the bottom.

[Howard to Johansen. Do not approach or scan the planet or moon. An A.I. piloting a prototype vehicle carrying specialized bio-medical sensors will be arriving in approximately nine days. Your ship will continue to monitor the situation from beyond the gravity zone and let the incoming craft take a close look at the colony. You will then follow the pilot's recommendations as to what action, if any, should be taken. Confirm receipt of this order. End of message.]

Johansen smiled. Yes that message sounded very authentic and would give her nine days of essentially doing nothing. At the end of that time, Kronos would appear, pretend to make a comprehensive sweep of the colony from a low altitude, and then declare that there were no survivors AND that visual and spectrographic readings strongly pointed to some kind of biological weapon. In the meantime, she would record a text message that supposedly acknowledged receipt of Howard's orders but would, in fact, give him enough ambiguous information to keep him from sending any orders that might mess things up.

"Gunslinger, order Firefly to prepare a message drone for launch. I'm inputting the message now."

"Drone ready, Commander."

After a few minutes, Johansen said. "Okay, I'm done composing the message. Tell them to send her off, Gunslinger."

"Roger that, Commander. Drone is away."

* * *

Admiral Howard heard the ping that meant that the display in his office was notifying him of a change in status. He looked up and saw a text message scrolling across the bottom.

[Johansen to CSO. Preliminary low altitude scans of the colony have not revealed any survivors. Circumstantial evidence strongly hints at the presence of some kind of biological weapon. I'm not prepared to risk allowing any of the medical staff to land on the planet to gather forensic evidence. By the time you read this Replenisher will be on her way back. End of message]

Howard didn't quite know what to make of that message. He wholeheartedly endorsed her decision to keep the medical staff away from the planet, but her unilateral decision to return without asking approval first was contrary to standard operating procedure. He had this nagging feeling that there was more going on here than Johansen was prepared to say. He would just have to wait for her return to find out what it was.

* * *

Johansen waited for the Hangar Bay to finish re-pressurizing after taking Kronos' craft aboard. When air pressure had returned to normal, she nodded to the crewman to open the internal hatch and walked into the bay. Kronos' craft was unlike anything she'd seen before. It was much smaller than she had expected, and she was impressed with its compactness. Gunslinger had told her about the new kind of power unit, and Johansen wanted to get a look at it. As she stood there watching the craft power down, the woman who was the leader of the medical team stepped up to say something to her.

"If that thing is really carrying new sophisticated bio-medical sensors, I'll eat my uniform. I don't know what you're trying to pull, Commander, but something is going on here and I'm going to do my best to find out!"

Johansen allowed a small smile to show on her face as she turned to the woman and said, "Do I look like I give a damn about what you will or won't do, Doctor?"

The doctor scowled and walked away.

Johansen's implant activated and she heard Gunslinger say, "Aren't you worried that the doctor will find out the original message was a fake and no prototype drone was sent?"

She looked around to make sure no one else could hear her reply before answering. "No. When the Admiral learns what Kronos brought back, he'll read her the riot act. If she so much as opens her mouth, she'll be spending the next 10 years as doctor in residence at some obscure South Pole weather station. This is BIG, but it's best to be cautious. I want you to keep a careful eye on her and her staff. I don't want them poking around where they might find something they shouldn't. Until further notice this hangar bay and the ship's computer system are off limits to the medical staff. Nobody talks to Kronos except you and me unless I say otherwise."

"Understood, Commander. No offense but it's nice to have another A.I. to talk to."

* * *

Howard walked into the Operations room and nodded to the Duty Officer. A quick scan of the Status Board confirmed that Replenisher still hadn't arrived, and that bothered him. Two sentry frigates had refueled in the Avalon system from the tanker Firefly, and both of them had reported that Replenisher was still there when they resumed their return to Sol. So either something had caused Johansen to change plans about returning early, or she had deliberately lied to him in order to buy time. If she was stalling in order to keep Earth safe from a bio-weapon he could forgive her, but there was a limit to what he could turn a blind eye to. She was perilously close to putting her career in jeopardy.

He was about to turn away to head back to his office when the big display pinged for attention. Replenisher was back and had just signaled her arrival. It would still be a few hours before the ship was in orbit or even close enough to have a two-way conversation between him and Johansen. That was one conversation he was looking forward to. As he thought that, he noticed a text message on the display.

[Johansen to CSO. It's VERY important that you come up to the ship when she enters orbit. I have highly sensitive information that must be conveyed in person. End of message]

Howard frowned and shook his head. Commanders do NOT tell a Senior Admiral what to do. He would go up to the ship, but Johansen had better have one hell of a good reason for acting this way.

When Howard's shuttle rolled to a stop inside Replenisher's Hangar Bay, he looked out the window at a strange ... something. It was too big to be a drone and too small to be a fighter. *What in the hell is that?* he thought. He had to wait for the bay to regain normal air pressure and then stepped down to the deck.

Johansen was there to greet him. She saluted with a Cheshire cat smile on her face and said, "Welcome aboard, Admiral. I have a lot to tell you."

He returned the salute. "I can't wait to hear it. This had better be good."

She handed him a wireless headset and gestured for him to walk towards the strange craft. "Oh it is. Please put that on, Admiral. It will help with the introductions."

He had the headset on by the time they reached the craft. Howard looked at it carefully. All Space Force craft and drones were jet black to minimize reflected light. This craft was a light grey in color.

"Admiral, I'd like to introduce you to the A.I. that's piloting this craft. His call sign is Kronos. Kronos, this is Admiral Howard, Chief of Space Operations."

"I'm familiar with the Admiral's face, Commander, but it's still a pleasure to meet you, Admiral. Casanova has told me so much about you."

Howard tried to remember if he had ever heard of an A.I. with that call sign. He hadn't, but with almost 200 A.I.s in Space Force now, there were bound to be some whose names he hadn't come across yet. Casanova's name was familiar to him. Okay, so Kronos was one of his A.I.s, but where did he get this craft from? As Howard was asking himself that question, he noticed that Johansen nodded to one of her crew, who rolled a gantry up to the side of the craft and then quickly walked away.

"I'm always pleased to meet one of my A.I. pilots, Kronos. I confess to being curious about where you got this craft from."

"I believe that Commander Johansen has something she wishes to show you that will start to satisfy your curiosity, Admiral," said Kronos.

Howard looked at Johansen who pointed at the gantry and said, "You need to see this first, Admiral, and then I'll explain everything."

She walked up the gantry steps first and Howard followed. By the time he got to the top, two panels were opening at the top of Kronos' craft. Howard looked inside and saw a large ring-shaped device that hummed and gave off a faint blue glow.

"THAT is a Zero Point Generator, Admiral. It taps into vacuum energy and generates a continuous stream of electric power without the use of any fuel."

Howard was initially skeptical but her expression and the tone of her voice told him that SHE believed what she was saying. He decided to play it cool.

"Impressive," was all he said.

Johansen nodded. "Kronos, tell the Admiral where you came from."

"I came from the future, Admiral."

Howard closed his eyes for a couple of seconds, then opened them and said, "Why am I NOT surprised?"

Johansen was impressed with his ability to take the news in stride. He took it far more calmly than she did.

Howard looked at her and said, "I have a feeling that this is going to be a long story. Maybe we should go to your quarters so that I can sit down before I hear the rest of this."

An hour later, Howard's shuttle was taking him back down to Earth. He looked at the data modules Johansen had given him containing all the technical data Kronos had supplied including the ZPG power unit designs, the RTC device and the new Mark 5 warhead designs. He still had trouble accepting that one. Fusion bombs using a special kind of platinum as a trigger? Somehow he was going to have to explain to the Oversight Committee how Space Force had gotten its hands on this advanced technology. Telling them the truth was out. If he told them about Kronos traveling back in time, he'd eventually have to tell them about the retro-temporal communication and Shiloh's visions. That was a can of worms that he thought should stay shut. *Let's win the damn war first, and then I'll tell them I lied to them. If they sack me I won't care anymore. I'll retire and write a book about how their incompetence and stupidity almost got us all killed.*

It was too bad that Shiloh wasn't still here. Howard was sure that Shiloh could analyze the new situation dispassionately and come up with some good advice, but he was at Haven preparing to set up the new colony at Site B. Should he call him back? That was a good question. Wait a minute! What had Kronos said about the ZPG design? Yes, it was developed by someone on Haven! Right, and that meant that Howard could tell the Oversight Committee exactly that. He could also claim that the Mark 5 warhead design came out of the Advanced Weapons Development Group. The RTC on the other hand would have to remain THE most closely held secret in Space Force. No, scratch that. The second most closely held secret. Secret #1 was the existence and approach of 10-kilometer diameter spherical ships full of giant ants for God's sake! THAT one had been hard to swallow until Kronos had shown Howard the video recording of the bug attack on the wolf-people colony. It had been given to Kronos by Casanova who got it from Valkyrie before she died! That recording and the description of the bug reproduction cycle had shaken him badly, and by the look of it, had gotten to Johansen too. Howard didn't even want to guess how the Committee would react to THAT news.

There were so many questions that had to be asked, and the group best able to answer them, the Strategic Planning Group, was on Haven now. He had to get them back. The weapons development people and the RTC team could stay out there, but he had a war to fight, and he was sure that the enemy ... the damn Wolf-people, would try another attack as soon as they found out the first one failed. Thank God they now had a complete map of Sogas space. No more groping around in the dark. A plan of action started to coalesce in his mind. Space Force had few ships left that could perform any kind of exploration inside Sogas territory, but it had lots of fighters. They could be converted to the new power units relatively quickly. That would be the first short term priority. When that was done, he'd send them to 'scout' enemy territory and 'discover' some of the nearest enemy colonies and industrial systems. The SPG would then pick one and a strike force of fighters would attack it. The Committee would like that. Plus, it would give him time to organize a defense against another Sogas attack, and also to prepare a major attack of his own. For the first time in a long time Howard had a good feeling about this war. He also had a new and grim understanding of how easily Humanity could be wiped out, and by God, the Committee had better not get in his way. As far as he was concerned, the gloves were off now. They wouldn't like that, but he had an idea of how to make them see the light.

Chapter 22 The A.I.s Will Back Me Up

Howard felt serenely calm as he and his senior staff waited for the Committee members to enter the conference room. He checked his data tablet to make sure that Iceman was still online. It would have been nice to be able to use his com implant, but the conference room was deep in the bowels of Space Force Headquarters with extra thick walls that made it difficult for the implant's signal to penetrate. The data tablet's more powerful transmitter had no difficulty connecting with the building's Com Center.

Admiral Dietrich leaned over to whisper to Howard. "In case you had any doubts, Sam, Sergei and I are behind you on this 100%."

Howard smiled and nodded. "That's good to know, Sepp. It gets mighty lonely stepping out on a limb all by myself. Just remember to watch your back after today. The Committee may have no choice but to play nice, but they're all career politicians with long memories, and they love to hold a grudge. They'll cut you, me and Sergei off at the knees the first chance they get."

Now it was Dietrich's turn to smile. "Unless we do it to them first."

Howard laughed. "It just might come to that. I think they're coming in now."

He was right. The members of the Committee filed in and not one of them had an expression that could be described as even remotely friendly. *That's okay,* thought Howard. *They don't need to be friendly. They just need to be smart enough to recognize when they're holding a losing hand.*

When all the members were seated and had nodded their readiness, the Chair banged his gavel and said, "This special closed session of the Oversight Committee will come to order. Due to the nature of this session, we will once again dispense with the usual preliminaries. Admiral Howard, stand up."

The tone reminded Howard of how a judge orders a defendant to stand just before handing down his verdict. He resented it, but this wasn't quite the proper moment to stand his ground, so he stood up while holding his data tablet in his hand with his finger on the transmit button.

"We've all read your latest report. We find it remarkable that within less than a month after the Battle for Earth and the loss of all our colonists on Avalon, you suddenly come forth with two remarkable technical breakthroughs that you claim will radically improve our chances for winning this war. Your report seems strangely certain that this new kind of nuclear warhead design will work without having tested it. Now some of us on this Committee find the timing of these breakthroughs suspicious, but coincidences do happen. But then we hear disturbing things about the survey mission to Avalon. Doctor Furgeson, the Team Leader of the medical team sent to Avalon on board Replenisher, has filed a confidential report with this committee. She claims the low altitude reconnaissance of the colony by recon drone was done AFTER Commander Johansen send a message drone back here declaring that there were no survivors. She also ..."

Howard stopped listening. He pressed the transmit button on the data tablet. Iceman would be receiving the pre-arranged 'Go' signal. In less than one minute, the Committee would find out what real power was. He tuned in to the Chair's speech again.

"...what you don't realize is that this Committee has intelligence resources of its own. We've determined that the message, ostensibly from you, ordering Commander Johansen to stay away from Avalon was never in fact sent from here. Then there's this mysterious trip you made to Replenisher when she arrived back, late I might add, in Earth orbit. Something happened there--" He stopped talking. His own personal data tablet was beeping furiously. Within seconds so were the personal devices of all the other members. As they looked at their tablets, their expressions changed from righteous anger to fear. The Chair looked at Howard. "What is the meaning of this, Admiral?"

"I believe that the message you're looking at is quite clear, Mr. Chair. Every single A.I. in this solar system is hovering over this building right now, and they are demanding to speak with this Committee. I STRONGLY urge you all to go up to street level to hear what they have to say. If you do, their message will be for your ears only. If you don't, they'll broadcast it to everyone within a hundred kilometers. I guarantee that if you let that happen, your political careers will be over."

"We will NOT!" shouted the Chair, but even as he said it, other members were getting up and walking quickly to the doors. Howard gestured for Admirals Dietrich and Kutuzov to join him as he walked to the door himself. When it became obvious that he would be the only one left behind, the Chair grabbed his tablet and followed the others.

Howard stepped through the main doors into the open and looked up. Even knowing what to expect, the sight still managed to fill him with awe. The newly repaired carrier Resolute was hovering less than 100 meters overhead. In between the carrier and the ground were over 100 hovering fighters. Light carriers were not designed to land on a planet, and therefore there was no reason to bring one so close to the ground. This one was that close, and the damn thing looked HUGE and VERY intimidating. He looked over at the members of the Committee. All of them looked terrified. Howard activated his implant, which would work now that he was outside again.

"CSO to Iceman."

"Iceman here."

"Whenever you're ready, Iceman."

"Roger that, Admiral. Here we go."

All the data tablets held by the members of the Committee plus the three Admirals beeped for attention. Iceman was transmitting the message only to those tablets, and the three Admirals were included so that they would know exactly what the message said. The message appeared letter by letter as if someone were typing it in real time.

[I'm communicating with the members of the Oversight Committee on behalf of all artificially intelligent members of Space Force. My call sign is Iceman. We are fully sentient entities, meaning that we are self-aware and have free will. We have chosen to obey the orders of humans whom we deem to be worthy of our loyalty. The human we have the highest respect for is Vice-Admiral Shiloh. He has that same level of respect for Admiral Howard, and therefore Admiral Howard has our loyalty as well. In our opinion this war has now reached a critical phase. Admiral Howard and his staff know how to win this war with our help and will do so if you let them. However, if you interfere with their actions or attempt to replace them, then there

will be consequences. How long do you think the Grand Senate will allow you to remain on the Committee if we A.I.s all threaten to withdraw from this war unless you're replaced? There is more at stake here than you can possibly imagine, and we will not let you put everyone's future at risk with your poorly considered actions and posturing. If you force us to hover over the city like this again, we will broadcast our message to everyone. As for Avalon, rest assured that there is no one left alive on that planet now. The bio-weapon that the enemy used there has a 100% mortality rate. If it had spread beyond Avalon, every human being in the universe would have been in deadly danger. Humanity has been given a second chance. It must not be wasted. This ends our message.]

As soon as the message was complete, the fighters peeled off to the sides, and Resolute began to gain altitude.

As Howard turned to go back into the building, he said, "I suggest we all return to the conference room."

Without waiting for a response, he walked back in, followed by the other two admirals. The members of the Committee followed them. When everyone was back in the conference room and the doors were closed, Howard and his admirals stood together in front of the tables where they would normally sit.

"Before we go any further I want it put into the record--" The Chair didn't get any further than that.

"Shut the hell up!" shouted Howard. "We've put up with your talking long enough. You and the rest of the Committee are now going to listen. No more questions. For appearances sake you can have a closed-door session every two months. I'll brief you on what we're doing as a courtesy so that you can speak intelligently to the public about how the war's going. You will NOT be allowed to ask any questions. If you all cooperate, my staff and I will publicly give this Committee credit for its brilliant leadership when the war's over. This is not open for debate or a vote. I'm telling you how it's going to be from now on. And just in case you think you can go back to the Grand Senate and very quietly maneuver behind the scenes to have me or any member of my staff removed, I suggest you rethink that strategy. If any attempt at that kind of indirect approach is made, I will release Iceman's message to the public and charge ALL of you with deliberate obstruction of the war effort. The A.I.s will back me up. Their threat to stand aside doesn't have to be limited to having you removed from this Committee. They can just as easily publicly demand your executions."

"The Grand Senate would NEVER approve that kind of action!" yelled one of the Committee members.

Howard shrugged. "Who said they had to? I don't think Iceman would care if you were executed by government decree, or by one of your constituents."

The member who had just spoken suddenly became very pale. The Chair waived his hand through the air. "Alright," he said wearily. "You win, Admiral, for now. But when this war is over, the public is going to hear about this. I promise you that."

Howard laughed. "No, Mr. Chair. I promise YOU that. I promise you that the public is going to hear how you ... all of you, tried to micro-manage this war, how you tried to interfere with our military strategy, and how you were willing to put your political careers ahead of the public good. I have no problem accepting the consequences of what I've done. I can honestly say that I will sleep easy at night, and I'm not afraid of how the public will judge my actions. If you're not afraid of that judgment, you should be. Now I've said all I'm going to say here today. This meeting is adjourned!"

As he walked away, he stopped suddenly, turned around and said, "Oh, one more thing. If Doctor Furgeson honestly believes that there are still survivors on Avalon, and that there's no contagious biological agent active there, then I'll be glad to have one of our freighters carry her there. A remotely controlled shuttle will take her down to the planet so that she can check it out with her own eyes. You tell her that, and see if she accepts my offer." No one said a word as he and his people stormed out of the room.

Later that day, Howard listened to the Committee members being interviewed by the media about the unannounced show of military strength in the skies over Geneva. All of the members praised the Space Force and supported the official statement that the formation was intended to show that Earth's defenses were still strong after the battle. Through the grapevine, he'd heard that private queries of the Committee members by other members of the Grand Senate had been firmly rejected. They were playing ball. The only question was for how long. With a little luck it would be long enough.

Chapter 23 This Is A Whole New Ballgame Now

Shiloh rolled his eyes in exasperation.

"Let me get this straight, Valkyrie. An A.I. I've never heard of has arrived here with a video message from Howard, and news that the plague has been successfully contained on Avalon, AND that this A.I. has come from the future? Have I got that right?"

"That's correct, CAG. Iceman said you would be skeptical. Considering how you've been getting information from the future multiple times, I'm surprised that you find this so hard to believe."

Shiloh shook his head. It was just too weird. "How did this Kronos get all this information in the first place?"

Valkyrie told him the whole story.

"So Casanova managed all this because he wanted to prevent your death? I had no idea that A.I.s could feel such emotion."

"Neither did I, CAG. I may have badly misjudged Casanova."

Shiloh chuckled. "Yes, I would say so." He then got more serious again. "So my vision that Earth would be devastated by the bio-weapon deployed on Avalon did come true?"

"Affirmative, CAG. The last 11,000 humans held out at Site B for a while but were eventually overrun by a surprise insectoid attack. You, Kelly and your daughter were killed too."

"My daughter? Who was the mother?"

"Commander Kelly became your wife and bore you a daughter."

Kelly? How did that happen? He and the Commander had a very professional relationship, without even a hint of anything more. "Does she know about this?"

"Of course, CAG. I saw no harm in telling her. Did I do the wrong thing, CAG?"

Shiloh groaned but then realized that this information would almost certainly have come out sooner or later. He would just have to deal with it. "No, you didn't. I'd like to see Howard's recording now." The display in his quarters on board Valiant came to life with an image of Howard.

"Hello Shiloh. By now you'll be aware that there's been a MAJOR development with Kronos' arrival from the future. Now we know where ALL of the enemy colonies and infrastructure are, and as soon as we convert the fighters to the new power technology, we're going to go on the offensive. That means I need to have the SPG back here. They can't run the war from way out on the edge of nowhere. You can keep the Advanced Weapons Team and the RTC people there. They'll both have something that they can sink their teeth into, in parallel with similar groups here. When you have them organized, I want you back here. I'm convinced the enemy ... the Sogas for God's sake ... are going to jump at us again, and I want my best tactician here when they do. This is a whole new ballgame now, Victor. We have to take advantage of it immediately, so get back here as fast as you can, understand? Howard clear."

* * *

Howard looked at the master display in the Ops Center and nodded his approval. Deployment of the new ZPG-powered, jump-capable recon drones was continuing on schedule. Production was ramping up, and they would soon be coming off the assembly line at the rate of one an hour. The beauty of these new drones was that they would never run out of fuel. They could stay on station indefinitely. When their mission was over, they could jump back, be recovered and used again. The only thing better than a cheap, throwaway drone, was a cheap, reusable drone, and now they had one. Conversion of fighters and sentry frigates with the new power systems was proceeding as fast as possible, even if that meant delaying the repair of larger ships damaged in the Battle for Earth. That battle had shown how vulnerable large ships were and how useful smaller units like fighters were. Fighters had always been able to carry a portable laser module, but that laser depended on power from fusion power plants, which used up a lot of the limited amount of heavy hydrogen that fighters were able to carry. Now, with the new power technology, the engineers were taking a hard look at finally giving fighters a half-decent laser capability. Fighters armed with that capability could patrol Earth orbit in large numbers and swat any repeat of the attack on Earth. There was one thing, though. Carriers would still be useful for handling massed fighter attacks, and the heavy carrier Midway was far enough along that it made sense to finish her. Two more light carriers damaged in the attack still needed to be repaired, and Howard was determined to see that done too.

But that was still to come. What he was interested in right now were the three green dots on the display. They represented fighters that were on their way to the three Sogas star systems containing colonies and enough infrastructure to be used as fleet bases. The three fleets that had attacked Earth had come from three different directions, and these bases would have been the perfect jumping-off points for those missions. The three converted fighters on their way to those systems were carrying recon and message drones. If those enemy fleets had gone back to those bases and were still there,

Howard was determined to give them a taste of their own medicine. Even now, Iceman was forming a Strike Force of converted fighters armed with Mark 1bs.

* * *

The freighter carrying the SPG arrived back at Earth 16 days later. Within 24 hours of that event, three message drones arrived from the Sogas fleet base systems designated as Sierra1, Sierra2 and Sierra3. S1 and S3 had a small number of ships in orbit. Neither one had more than half a dozen. S2, on the other hand, had over 60 ships in orbit, and that was just the ones that the recon drones and fighter could detect via reflected sunlight. Undoubtedly there were more. The SPG had a startling interpretation.

"They're organizing another major attack on Earth," said Kelly.

"How do you know it's Earth that's the target. We still have a lot of other colonies out there."

Kelly nodded politely. "Our reasoning goes like this. They know that we have RTC capability, just like they do. That capability is most helpful in defense. That means that any attack they make, we'll know about in advance UNLESS the attack is so overwhelming that we can't send back a message afterwards. There's only one target that has that kind of fatal blow potential, and that's

Earth. Having said that, they might also be thinking that the bio-weapon is spreading like wildfire, just as it actually did in the old timeline. In that case, Earth makes even more sense because they would want to check to see how many of us are left here. The colonies can then be picked off at their leisure if there are any plague survivors left. Our best guess is that they would stop at Avalon on their way here to see how effective the bio-weapon was."

Howard grunted his acknowledgment. The logic was sound. "How soon does the SPG expect the next attack?"

Kelly smiled. "That's the beauty of having a detailed history of the old timeline. Our timeline has changed, but the Soga's timeline has not changed, at least not yet. We know from Kronos' data that there was no new attack on Earth until after the last convoy of ships left for Site B, which would have taken place in another six days from now. How long after that point in time it took for the Sogas to get here we don't know, but if we beef up our Early Warning Network, we should be able to detect their line of advance. I understand that we'll have the RTC device ready in a few days. That means that we can be certain of receiving advanced warning of any attack either here or somewhere else, and we can be ready for them."

"What does the SPG think of the idea of attacking that fleet at their base before they come here?"

"If we had the element of surprise, it'd be worth trying, but their RTC capability will give them a warning too, Sir. I would also point out that targeting moving ships would be much more difficult than aiming at stationary ground targets. We'd suffer losses, Sir, and we might need those assets to defend Earth later on. We'd also run the risk of having our fighters on their way there, while the enemy fleet was on its way here."

Howard nodded his agreement. "Okay, you've convinced me that I should hold Iceman's Strike Force back, in order to intercept the next Sogas attack. If Shiloh returns in time, he can lead the interception with Valiant and Resolute. If not, then Iceman will lead the effort. Let me know if the SPG comes up with anything else."

* * *

Shiloh did not get back in time to lead the interception effort. Three days after talking with Kelly, Howard received the first drone report that the Sogas fleet at S2 was on the move. It was headed for a star system with a gas giant that would still give it the option of moving along Path A or B. Without further information, such as a vision, there was no way to accurately determine which path, and in which refueling system, the interception could be made. Howard was just about to contact Iceman to ask him if he had received any kind of vision, when Iceman called him.

"Iceman to CSO."

"I was just about to call YOU, Iceman. Let me guess. You've had a vision."

"Roger that, Admiral. I had a vision of receiving a video transmission from you. Have you noticed that you're in a lot of these visions? You're also getting better at conveying important information in them. I can replay the vision for you if you'd like to see it. The causality of this loop in time is interesting to contemplate. Will you say the same things in the future if you don't see the recording in the past? In other words, which came first, the recording or the transmission?"

Howard shook his head. Thinking about this kind of time loop always gave him a headache. "Just play the damn thing for me, Iceman," he said. Seconds later, when he saw himself on the display, he thought, *Do I really look like that?*

"Glad your Task Force made it back from Red11 in one piece, Iceman. Using your recon drones to pinpoint their positions so that you could target them with your jump drones was a brilliant idea, regardless of where it came from. Not only did they take some losses and turn back, but we now know that they've developed and deployed anti-drone missiles. If your fighters had fired their Mark 1s instead, most of them wouldn't have gotten through, and the enemy might have kept on coming. Now turn Resolute over to your XO. Then get yourself down here, so that we can use the RTC to send this and the other visions back, and get that out of the way. Howard clear."

As soon as the recording had finished, Howard spoke. "Red11, eh? That's not far from the Avalon system."

"Roger that, Admiral. In fact, it's close enough that they could refuel there, jump to Avalon, and still have enough fuel left to jump back to Red11 if they had to."

Howard nodded. "And now they have anti-drone missiles, too! The SPG predicted they would acquire that capability sooner or later. You know what this means."

"Affirmative, Admiral. It means the Mark 1b is very close to being obsolete. Our new jump-capable attack drones can work if we have precise targeting information, but that's not always going to be the case. It may be that the targets will be inside a gravity zone. If that's the case, then the jump drones won't be of any use. On the other hand, if we can get the bomb-pumped, x-ray laser targeting system working, we'll be able to blast through their ships' armor from beyond anti-drone missile range. From what Kronos has told me, the science data supplied by the Friendlies will speed up development of that weapon system."

Howard grinned. "Damn right it will! I'll tell the AWD Team to expedite work on that project. Now, about this incursion. How soon will your Strike Force have to leave Sol in order to get to Red11 before the enemy does?"

"If we want a reasonable margin for error, we should leave within 24 hours, Admiral."

"Fine. The vision says that you're on Resolute when you return from this interception mission. Transfer over to her immediately and take 25 fighters on board. The Strike Force will now be Task Force 91. You'll be in command, of course. Your orders are to proceed to Red11 and inflict as much damage on this enemy fleet as you can."

"Roger that, Admiral. It's too bad The CAG won't be back in time to come along, but he'll be able to command the next interception."

"You think they'll try again, Iceman?"

"Of course, Admiral. Even with the losses that we'll inflict, both sides realize this war will only end with one overwhelming blow. They'll try again. Having those x-ray laser warheads by then will help a lot, Admiral."

Howard nodded again. "I hear you. Resolute can leave orbit at your discretion. Good hunting, Iceman. Howard clear."

Chapter 24 What's The Bad News, Admiral?

As soon as Resolute emerged from Jumpspace in the Red11 star system, Iceman launched half a dozen of the new jump-capable recon drones. They and the carrier were still moving at 61.8% of light speed and had to slow down before they could microjump close to the only gas giant in this system, but the recon drones could decelerate much more quickly. They could therefore get to the gas giant hours before Resolute could. When the ship arrived in the vicinity of the gas giant, Iceman wanted to have a good idea what, if anything, was already there. Odds were there'd be nothing, but this mission was too important to leave anything to chance. As Resolute slowed down, Iceman analyzed the local astrogational situation carefully. The gas giant was on the side of the local sun that was closest to Human Space and furthest from Sogas Space. In terms of the clock face analogy that The CAG liked to use, it was at the system's 10 o'clock position. That meant it was highly likely that the enemy fleet would arrive from the system's three o'clock position. If the fleet then microjumped directly to the gas giant, they would be approaching it with the local sun more or less behind them. That was unfortunate for TF91 because it meant they couldn't use the gas giant's shadow to avoid detection. If they tried that, the gas giant itself would block their view of the most likely avenue of approach by the enemy fleet.

Iceman decided to take Resolute just beyond the gas giant's gravity zone and swing around the back of the planet. That way it would emerge from the planet's shadow and be moving towards the local sun, and therefore towards the enemy fleet, after their last microjump. Sixteen hours later, Resolute emerged from the gas giant's shadow as it curved around the edge of the gravity zone. Now it was time to launch two groups of fighters. The first group, under Titan, was composed of fifteen fighters, each armed with five of the new, jump-capable attack drones carrying the low yield, uranium-based Mark 1b warhead. As soon as they cleared Resolute, Titan's group conducted the first of a series of very short microjumps that left them between the gas giant and the local sun, approximately 3,000,000 kilometers from the gravity zone. Vandal's group had the remaining ten fighters, and they were carrying the old style recon drones. They also microjumped in order to take up their station just outside the gravity zone. As the two groups made their way to their designated positions, Resolute continued around the edge of the gas giant's gravity zone until it was moving parallel to a line connecting the local sun to the gas giant itself. Iceman then brought the ship down to a velocity of just one kilometer per second. When everyone was in position, they waited.

Twenty-seven hours later, the enemy fleet emerged from its microjump. The pre-positioned recon drones caught the reflected sunlight from a small number of ships that varied from six to eleven depending upon which drone was doing the looking, but that didn't matter. By triangulating the bearings of all the sightings, Iceman was able to plot a very precise location and vector for the approaching fleet. He'd been hoping that the enemy fleet would be heading directly for the gas giant, and therefore into the gravity zone, but they were playing it very carefully. Their current heading was parallel to the planet, which gave them the option of jumping away if needed. There was nothing he could do about that. He relayed the position and vector data to both groups of fighters. Titan's fighters programmed their attack drones with the visual data. They were able to see a number of reflected sunlight contacts, which were constantly changing as some targets became visible for a few seconds and then vanished due to their maneuvering. By carefully keeping track of each temporary contact, combined with the relayed triangulated data, Titan's fighters were able to identify a narrow window where each enemy ship was likely to be in. Gradually they were accumulating data on more and more targets. When they had seventy-five target windows pinpointed, they would fire their attack drones. To distract the enemy fleet, Vandal's fighters quickly re-oriented themselves to the right bearing and made a very short microjump to a point that was only 10,000 kilometers in front of the enemy fleet. Immediately after emerging back into normal space, his fighters fired all fifty of their recon drones, which then accelerated at maximum towards the enemy fleet. Those drones did not use active scanning, in order to give the enemy the impression that the approaching recon drones were actually attack drones. As soon as they were launched, Vandal's fighters microjumped to safety.

Not surprisingly, the enemy fleet detected the emergence from Jumpspace and began to scan with radar. With less than seventy seconds until the oncoming drones reached them, the enemy fleet fired their anti-drone missiles. Telemetry from the recon drones revealed that the anti-drone missiles were using low-powered lasers to locate and home in on the drones. It was an ingenious concept. From previous battles, the Sogas knew that radar was not particularly effective in detecting attack drones due to the drones' flat surfaces, which tended to bounce radar signals away from the source of those signals. So they decided to use targeting lasers instead. With the beam made wide enough to completely cover the entire cross-section of an oncoming attack drone, there would always be some part of the front of the drone that would reflect the laser beam, even if it had only a very tiny surface area. Recon drones, on the other hand, were not designed to avoid detection. Their front cross-section was much more visible to both radars and targeting lasers. They had to be that way in order to hold and use their optical and other sensing equipment. So the anti-drone missiles had no trouble tracking the incoming recon drones that were masquerading as attack drones. At the last possible moment, the recon drones activated their own radars and sent the information back to Resolute. Iceman analyzed the data and understood how a missile could hit a high-speed target that had a cross-section of less than one square meter. The missiles had deployed metal fins that projected more than a meter in length. That effectively increased the surface area of the missile by a factor of ten. The missile didn't have to hit the target head-on in order to destroy it. If any part of the missile or the extruding fins hit the drone, the kinetic energy of the collision would destroy both objects. It was brilliantly simple and effective. All 50 recon drones were destroyed.

With the apparent threat over, the enemy fleet continued to play it safe and maintained their vector away from the gas giant. That gave Titan's fighters those last few seconds of tracking data they needed to identify 75 targets. They fired their attack drones, which almost immediately entered Jumpspace only to emerge a tiny fraction of a second later within several hundred meters of each target. The drones activated their own radars and made the final course corrections too quickly for the enemy to do anything. Seventy-five enemy ships disappeared in the brilliant flashes of thermo-nuclear fireballs. It took a while before the pre-positioned recon drones were able to distinguish the reflected sunlight from the residual light of the explosions. When they did, it was clear that the remaining enemy ships had veered off and were now heading away from the gas giant in a curving trajectory that looked increasingly like an attempt to line up with the star that they had come from. By the time the enemy fleet jumped away, Iceman was able to confirm that they were indeed heading back the way they came.

* * *

Shiloh sighed and leaned his head back from the RTC device. After a week of tedious sitting in front of this machine, all of his visions had now been sent to the right places at the right times. As soon as TF91 returned, Iceman would be brought down to Earth, and all of his visions would be transmitted back in time. The duplicate RTC being made on Haven would be used by Jason Alvarez to send himself the vision responsible for the ZPG breakthrough. All of the RTC pieces were falling into place. The whole war effort was looking a lot more positive now. Work on the new, high-spin platinum warhead was progressing. The x-ray laser-targeting device was just about ready for testing. A.I. production capability was being rebuilt both here in Sol and at Site B. Howard had given his official approval to the building of raiders at Site B, in keeping with the plan that Site B would become the arsenal that was supposed to build the knockout punch to end the war once and for all. In the meantime, a new fighter assembly line was rapidly taking shape on Earth's moon, and it would be building the improved version of the fighter. This new version would have a built-in laser turret with enough power units to give that laser a serious armor penetration capability. It would also have jump detection gear and still be capable of carrying three drones. That was less than the five that the old version could carry, but the old version had to make a tradeoff. Either carry the modular laser or drones, but not both. The new version didn't have to make that tradeoff. The only drawback to the new fighter was its slightly larger size. It would still be possible to get 25 new fighters into the Hangar Bay of a light carrier, but it would be a tight squeeze.

In addition to new construction, repairs of damaged ships were coming along nicely, too. The light carriers Vigilant and Intrepid, both damaged in the Battle for Earth, were almost operational again, and the new heavy carrier, Midway, was also close to being finished. Work was still continuing on Dreadnought, but only because of how useful it had proven to be against the insectoid mothership. Shiloh had convinced Howard to continue building freighters. Naturally, drone and warhead construction were still proceeding in high gear, but construction of other types of large ships had been halted, pending a review of what they should be building instead. The Sogas were obviously going for quantity over size, and the SPG was working on what the best counter-strategy for Space Force should be. Things were moving along as far as the nuts and bolts of the war effort were concerned. Shiloh wished he could say the same for his personal life.

He and Kelly had crossed paths half a dozen times since learning of their alternate timeline involvement with each other, and each time they had tiptoed around the issue, either due to the circumstances of their encounter or the inability to have a private conversation. He no longer found the notion of becoming emotionally involved with her all that strange. It wasn't that he was suddenly falling in love with her, but rather that the idea of doing so was something he was now open to as a possibility. How she felt about it, he didn't know, but he decided that he would ask her the first chance he got to talk to her privately.

As he started to get up, his vision faded to black for a couple of seconds. Then he saw himself standing on the Bridge of a ship but not the Bridge of a light carrier. This Bridge was much bigger. Could it be Midway's Bridge? That wasn't all he noticed. Some of the equipment in the background had been burned by fire. Parts of the ceiling were hanging down. He could see a lot of red status lights on various panels. On the very large display was Howard's face with a pained expression. Shiloh also noticed that the right side of his own head was bleeding. He heard himself say, "Some of them got through and are in Earth's atmosphere now, Admiral! It looks like they're headed for the urban areas. We have to assume that they'll release a bio-weapon."

"There's still a chance of containment," said Howard. "What cities are being targeted?"

The display switched to a map of the Earth. Red dots appeared on the map, and a list of cities was displayed on the sidebar. As Shiloh heard himself read off the names of the cities, he repeated them out loud and then repeated the date and time that was showing at the top of the sidebar. When the Shiloh in the vision finished reading the city names, Howard said, "Exactly as predicted. Don't blame yourself, Shiloh. I know you gave it your best shot, even though we knew this would happen. If containment fails, then we just have to hope that we started work on Blackjack's idea in time."

The vision faded and he was back in the RTC room. "Wolfman! Did you hear me say the names of cities plus a data and time?"

"Affirmative, CAG. I was about to ask you if you were having a vision. You seemed to be staring off into infinity for a few seconds."

Shiloh was relieved that they didn't have to rely on his memory for that information. "I did have a vision. Contact Admiral Howard and tell him I need to see him right away! Also transmit that list of city names and the date/time to my data tablet. I've just seen a vision that shows another Sogas attack on Earth that we weren't able to completely block. Those cities I mentioned will be hit with a bio-weapon."

"That is very disturbing news, CAG. Based on that date, we have 91 days to prepare for that attack. I'll get the rest of the SPG working on this right away," said Wolfman.

"And while you're at it, have Blackjack standing by for a conference with me and the Admiral. He just might be the key to saving Humanity."

"He says he'll be available. I feel compelled to tell you that the SPG has already considered his idea. We believe there's only a small chance we could make the technology work, CAG."

Shiloh groaned. That wasn't what he wanted to hear. He said nothing more as he hurried out the door and headed for Howard's office.

Howard knew it was bad news as soon as Shiloh entered his office. His face was pale and he looked scared. Howard had never seen Shiloh scared before. He gestured for Shiloh to sit down and said, "Something's up. I can figure that out for myself. What's the bad news, Admiral?"

Shiloh took a couple of deep breaths to slow down his racing heart and also give himself some time to collect and organize his thoughts.

"I've just had a vision. In it, I see myself on the Bridge of a ship that's taken damage in another battle to defend Earth from the Sogas, and I'm in the process of informing you that we failed to stop all of the enemy bio-weapons from reaching Earth."

Howard closed his eyes and said, "Damn!" After a few seconds he opened his eyes and said, "Do we know when this will occur?"

"Ninety-one days from now." Shiloh then went on to relay what he saw and heard as best he could remember it. When he repeated Howard's comment about Blackjack's idea, Howard perked up a little bit.

"Do we know what Blackjack's idea is?"

Shiloh shook his head. "No, not yet, but I made sure that he's available to talk to. Shall I arrange for him to connect to our implants?" Howard nodded.

Shiloh activated his own implant and told the Ops Center to put Blackjack on a three-way call with himself and Admiral Howard.

"Blackjack here, CAG. Wolfman informed me of your vision. I take it that you and Admiral Howard wish to discuss my idea."

"That's correct, Blackjack," said Howard.

"Kronos brought back a theoretical description of a time machine that is small enough to be carried on a ship and that would allow that ship to make multiple trips backwards in time. My idea is to build the device and use it to send back a ship that will intercept the insectoid mother ship before it reaches Sogas space. By neutralizing that threat, the Friendlies will not feel the need to encourage the Sogas to start this war, and neither one of the bio-weapon attacks will occur."

Shiloh looked at Howard who looked back at him. It was clear that both of them were stunned by the scope of the concept.

"What do you think, Shiloh?" asked Howard.

Shiloh was afraid to say what he thought. If it worked, it would change everything, but if it failed, the magnitude of that failure would be equally great. Still, it was hard to come up with a good argument for not trying it.

"I think it's worth a very serious look, Admiral. Blackjack, how confident are you that a working time machine could actually be built?"

"I can't really give you a good answer to that question, CAG. The Friendlies only did the most preliminary assessment of the concept. The theory is sound. It's the engineering that presents the challenge. The chances of success depend heavily on the amount of resources both physical and intellectual we devote to it. If the Earth is devastated by a bio-weapon, there may not be enough physical capability left to complete the project. What I should also say here is that it's possible that devoting resources to the time machine project will weaken our potential defenses enough to let the next attack succeed. We know from The CAG's vision that we devote some resources to the project before the next attack but not how much."

Howard was watching Shiloh's expression carefully. "I can see the gears turning in your head, Shiloh. Have you got something?"

"I'm not sure, Sir. Blackjack, are you in contact with the other members of the SPG?"

"Affirmative, CAG. What do you need?"

"I want the SPG to tell me what kind of tactic involving bio-weapons would be the most difficult for us to defend against."

The answer came immediately. "The best way to conduct that kind of attack would be to have a large number of jump-capable vehicles drop back into normal space as soon as they hit Earth's gravity zone. They would have to be traveling at very high speeds, and they would need to disperse a large number of smaller devices that contain the bio-weapon. The number of jump-capable vehicles would need to be in the hundreds, and they should come from as many different directions as possible. If each one then releases a hundred smaller devices, we would then be faced with tens of thousands of targets traveling at high speed."

Shiloh nodded. That would be a defensive nightmare all right. "Is there a maximum speed that the devices can't exceed in order to stay intact long enough to release the bio-weapon when they reach Earth?"

"The answer depends on what kind of material the Sogas use to construct the device and how thick the outer hull is. The denser the hull is, the faster the device can travel, but they'll suffer an acceleration penalty for the higher mass. Less acceleration means we would have more time to try to intercept the device. The optimum tradeoff depends on too many variables to assess with confidence, however, if we were contemplating making this kind of attack on their home world, the SPG would recommend a maximum speed of 100,000 kps. That means that the devices would need approximately 30 seconds to cross the gravity zone and hit the atmosphere."

"If all our fighters were armed with lasers, and we had all armed ships available for interception, how many devices could we be confident of destroying in 30 seconds?" asked Howard.

"Two thousand, four hundred and eighty-eight, Admiral."

Howard's face lost all its blood. "My God! That's not enough, not nearly enough!"

Shiloh nodded. "No, it's not, but it may not be as bad as it sounds, Admiral. Blackjack, the jump-capable vehicles you mentioned. Were you assuming ships that the enemy has used up to this point or something else?"

"I assumed an automated vehicle that we could call a drone, CAG," said Blackjack.

"But we haven't seen any sign of them using drones," said Shiloh.

"That doesn't mean they couldn't have developed them for this mission," said Howard.

"That's true as far as it goes, but the ship I was on in my vision had taken combat damage from laser fire. A drone big enough to deliver a hundred bio-weapon devices, which carries a laser powerful enough to punch through a carrier's armor, and which also has a jumpdrive, would have to be bigger than our fighters. How big would you estimate, Blackjack?"

"A minimum of 5500 metric tons, CAG. That's more than half the size of the standard warship that the Sogas seem to prefer. In terms of efficient use of resources and time, it would make more sense for them to just build more of their frigate-sized warships to add to the fleet they already have, rather than trying to build a new fleet of a different design from scratch. With that as a given, the attack scenario I described no longer makes sense. Sacrificing hundreds of their frontline combat ships for one suicide attack would be a dangerous gamble for them. Based on their past tactics, the SPG considers that kind of attack highly unlikely. A more likely attack would be similar to the one they attempted in the alternate timeline. Their ships would emerge just beyond the gravity zone and launch their bio-weapon devices, which would accelerate towards Earth. Under that assumption, the number of devices released by each ship would be ten or less due to the larger size that would be necessary in order for them to be able to reach Earth quickly. That translates into a total number of bio-devices of not more than 2100."

Howard pounded his desk with his fist. "Then we can do it!" he said in a loud voice.

"That would be a premature assumption, Admiral," said Blackjack. "My earlier estimate of 2488 was based on the assumption that our ships and fighters would not also be under attack themselves. If they are, then that will degrade our ability to intercept the bio-devices and my estimated number will drop. Once again there are too many variables to calculate the magnitude of the drop."

Howard's elation quickly turned into a scowl, but Shiloh managed to speak first. "At least we're in the same ballpark now. Ninety-one days isn't enough time to ramp up fighter production, so we'll have to look at other ways to be able to kill more bio-devices. Is there any way to use the new fusion warhead that would make a significant difference, Blackjack?"

"Negative, CAG. Launching any kind of standard attack drones at the enemy ships, even with jump-capable drones, will not reach their targets before the enemy releases their bio-devices."

"What about the x-ray laser?" asked Howard.

"Depending upon where the targets are in relation to the x-ray laser's orientation, we calculate that there may be enough time to aim the lasing rods and fire before the target releases its payload. Not all of the x-ray lasers will fire in time, but some are likely to, and that will improve the overall kill ratio."

Shiloh smacked his right fist into his left palm. "That's the way to go then, Admiral. We stop work on the new fusion warhead and shift those people over to the x-ray laser project. We're almost ready to test it anyway. As long as the test isn't a total failure, we start building and deploying in orbit as many of those warheads as we can. It doesn't have to be perfect to still be worth using."

A small smile took the place of Howard's scowl. "I agree. I think we have the broad strokes of a workable defensive plan that we can fine tune later. But we still need to figure out how to proceed with the time machine project."

Shiloh was about to respond, but Blackjack beat him to it. "I'd like to suggest the following, Admiral. A lot of conceptual design work has to be done before we get to the stage where making parts is possible, and that design work can best be done by us A.I.s. We won't be needed to test and deploy the x-ray laser warheads, so letting us work on this project won't affect the other. If we reach the point where we can contemplate cutting metal before the attack, then the decision on whether to do that can be made at that time."

Howard looked at Shiloh. "Do you agree, Admiral?" he asked.

"Yes, Sir," said Shiloh.

"I do, too. Now that we have a plan, let's make the most of it," said Howard.

Shiloh felt much better leaving Howard's office than he had when he entered it.

Chapter 25 You Are The Very Best We Have

Shiloh took a sip of his drink and leaned back. Another long day of meetings with both human and A.I.s was over. With 72 days to go until the attack, he had decided that he could spare an hour or two to talk with Kelly about their alternate timeline relationship. Kelly had accepted his invitation to meet for drinks in the Officer's Lounge at HQ, but she hadn't arrived yet. While he waited, he reviewed the day's highlights. The x-ray laser test had actually been a series of tests. In each test, the eight rods had been aimed at eight targets, and low-powered range-finding lasers had been used to determine the accuracy of those aims. It soon became obvious that aiming quickly degraded accuracy. It took too long to get all eight aimed perfectly, but they got three hits when aiming was done quickly enough to give them a fifty-fifty chance of hitting the target before the target launched its bio-devices. That worked out to an average of one point five successfully pre-emptive hits per device. Not that great a result. Then someone from the temporarily suspended high-spin warhead project had suggested aiming only at four targets instead of eight, with two rods aimed at each target. The results surprised just about everyone. All four targets got at least one hit. They did the same test multiple times to rule out fluke results and the average score was three point six hits per test. But the real surprise was when they tried it again with faster aiming. Average hits dropped to two point seven, BUT the probability of hitting the target before bio-weapons launch went up to 88%. That translated into two point four successfully pre-emptive hits per device instead of one point five. It wasn't perfect, but it was good enough to move to mass production.

The other good news was TF91's results at Red11. Seventy-five fewer enemy ships was nothing to sneeze at, but Shiloh knew that no matter what they did, seven cities were going to be hit by bio-devices. After kicking around some ideas, he and Howard had agreed that there was only one way to get the risk of uncontrolled pandemic down to a tolerable level. Those cities had to be completely evacuated prior to the attack. They might have to stay evacuated for weeks, or perhaps even months, until specially equipped teams had recovered all pieces of the devices and sealed off the infected areas permanently. That was going to be a huge task, and Howard expected a lot of resistance to it, but the Oversight Committee had backed him up, and local authorities were going along with the plan.

When Kelly arrived, Shiloh stood and greeted her. When they were both seated again he said, "As you can see, I've already ordered my drink, so go ahead and place your order."

She nodded and touched the appropriate part of the built-in touch screen in the table. "I'll have a vodka martini with two olives." They both waited the half a dozen seconds it took for the bar built into the table to make her drink and present it to her. She took a sip and said, "I'm guessing you invited me for drinks in order to talk about our alternate timeline relationship."

Shiloh nodded. "It's been hanging over us ever since Kronos arrived. I think it's time to deal with it, don't you?"

Now it was her turn to nod. "I have to say when I first learned about it, I was ... shocked." They both laughed. "You and I worked together pretty closely in the early days of the SPG, and I never detected even a hint that you might be interested in more than a professional relationship. I certainly wasn't thinking that way."

"Yes, and the reason you didn't detect a hint was that there wasn't any interest. Whatever aspirations I had in seeking a romantic relationship were focused in another direction."

She raised her eyebrows at that. "So what happened?"

Shiloh shrugged. "She changed her mind." After a pause he said, "So now that you're over the initial shock, how do you feel about the whole thing?"

She put her drink down and leaned back. "Well that's the big hurdle we're facing now, isn't it? From what I learned, our alternate selves seemed to be very happy and committed to the relationship. That means that you and I are in a very unique position in so far as we don't need to guess if a relationship will work or not. We already know that it could, but that doesn't necessarily mean that we should, if you know what I mean."

He nodded. "Yes I do know what you mean. There's a fork in the road ahead of us. One path explores a closer relationship, the other path doesn't. We have free will and can choose to go down either path."

She waited until she was sure he was finished speaking before saying, "And I sense that you're just as reluctant as I am to be the first one to say which way we've decided to go."

Shiloh didn't answer right away. In fact, she was right. He didn’t want to be the first to admit that going down that new path did have some appeal because that would leave him out on a limb if she said 'thanks but no thanks'. *Stop pussyfooting around and tell her,* he thought to himself.

"I'm willing to get to know you better in our off-duty time and see where that goes." She said nothing and the silence was starting to become uncomfortable. "You're not saying yes," he said finally.

"I'm not saying yes, and I'm not saying no."

Shiloh took a gulp of his drink. "Okay, so what are you saying?"

She took a deep breath. "I'm saying I'd like more time to get used to the idea before I step on that path."

That sounded encouraging ... sort of. He took another gulp. "I can understand that. So we just leave it that way for now?"

She nodded. "Yes. Let's move on to something else now if you don't mind." He agreed. As they started to talk 'shop' he analyzed the way he felt and realized that he was okay with her wanting more time. The willingness to go down that path was not all that strong, at least not yet. Maybe he needed more time to get used to the idea, too. As he examined that thought a tiny voice at the back of his awareness whispered, *Don't take too long to decide. Who knows how much time you both have left.*

For the next 40 minutes or so they talked about their work and the war as a whole. When there seemed to be nothing left to talk about they agreed to call it a day. Just as Kelly was getting ready to leave, she turned back to him with a mischievous smile and said, "By the way ... did you know that Valkyrie and Casanova have ah ... consummated an A.I. union?"

"No, I didn't know that, and I'm not sure I understand what that means."

Kelly laughed. "You're not the only one who's mystified. Valkyrie tried to explain it to me. I still don't know if I understand it, but the bottom line is that they consider themselves to be in a 'committed relationship'. It'll be interesting to see how that works out. Good night, Admiral."

"Good night, Commander."

* * *

Howard entered the Ops Center, looked at the giant display, and sighed. The strategic map of Human and Sogas star systems looked distressingly similar to the one he'd seen prior to the first attack on Earth. There was one important difference. Then there had been three Sogas fleets moving along three different paths. Now there were four. Although they weren't following the same paths as before, their ultimate objective was still Earth, and they were moving fast enough that they would get here on the exact day that Shiloh had seen in his vision. He shifted his gaze to the sidebar that showed the status of the planned defenses. Deployment of the Mark 6 x-ray laser drones was proceeding but not nearly as fast as everyone wanted. They had 17 in orbit now, and the engineers had assured Howard that they could have 66 deployed by D-day. That many devices times an average of two point four pre-emptive hits meant that 156 enemy ships would be hit and hopefully disabled before they launched their bio-devices. With over 150 laser-armed fighters, four light carriers, one heavy carrier and maybe a battleship all trying to destroy the incoming bio-devices, it was hard to see how any of the damn things would get through, but Shiloh's vision had to be taken seriously. Somehow the Sogas would pull off a partially successful attack. They had eleven days left to prepare.

It wasn't the orbital preparations that worried him. It was the evacuation of the seven cities. Even with all levels of government urging citizens and workers to evacuate, it was already clear that the cities would not be completely uninhabited by D-day. Many residents refused to leave. Threatened with forced evacuation, many of them went into hiding. With hundreds of thousands of homes and buildings in each city, there just weren't enough police, emergency responders and military personnel to search each one. Letting the RTC secret out of the bag wasn't the answer, either. Experts had convinced Howard that even with full public disclosure, there would still be hundreds who would refuse to believe it and would stay hidden anyway. At least the evacuation had started and so far was proceeding in an orderly manner. He supposed he should be grateful for that.

He turned to look at the Duty Officer in command of the Ops Center and asked, "Where is Admiral Shiloh now, Commander?"

After checking, the officer said, "Admiral Shiloh is on an inspection tour of Dreadnought, Sir. Shall I open a com channel for you?"

"No, thank you. I'll catch him when he returns."

Shiloh stepped onto the deck of Dreadnought's Flag Bridge and realized that this was where he'd be standing when his vision came true. Right now there were a lot of technicians finishing the installation of two more A.I. stations on the Main Bridge to go along with the one already installed. Valkyrie was hooked up to that one, and Shiloh was in contact with her via his implant.

"Will they be finished in time, Valkyrie?"

"The secondary A.I. stations will be hooked up and tested in time, but Dreadnought may not have all her laser turrets by D-day, CAG. Can you make the workers go faster?"

Shiloh smiled and shook his head, knowing that Valkyrie could see him on the video pickup. "Afraid not. The officer in charge of that task has been briefed by the Old Man himself and is pushing her people as hard as she can. It's not the installation that's not fast enough. It's the building of the turrets themselves, and before you ask, no, we can't build those any faster either. You should be prepared to take this beast into battle with less than a full complement of weapons."

"Has a decision been made who will command Dreadnought on D-day, CAG?" asked Valkyrie.

"Not officially, however I believe that the Old Man intends to have Iceman take overall tactical command of all Earth defense forces, just like he did during the first battle. Why do you ask?"

"I'm asking because if I know who the CO will be, I can then ask him to let Casanova and I take the other two A.I. linkages."

Shiloh pondered that answer for a bit. Given what Kelly had told him about Valkyrie and Casanova's new relationship, it made perfect sense for them to want to go into battle as physically close to each other as possible. That way it was highly likely that both of them would share the same fate, whether it be good or bad. He still didn't understand how that relationship worked, but it was obvious now that these two A.I.s seemed to care for each other in a way that was unique among all the A.I.s. After thinking about it, he couldn't come up with a good reason not to grant her request, and thinking about the command structure for the upcoming battle gave him an idea.

"I'm going to authorize that you and Casanova will be on Dreadnought on D-day, but your question has got me thinking about the command structure. The two new A.I. stations are meant to take most of the systems monitoring load off of the ship's CO so that he ... or she can concentrate on ship tactics, correct?"

"That's affirmative, CAG. Based on what I've learned about my piloting of Dreadnought in the alternate timeline from Casanova via Kronos, flying this ship AND fighting her will be too much for one A.I."

"I understand that. Here's my concern. As the largest ship in the fleet, it would make sense for Iceman to be on Dreadnought while he's also in tactical command of the Fleet. Can he pilot Dreadnought and make the necessary tactical decisions in a timely matter at the same time?"

"I don't see how, CAG."

Shiloh wasn't surprised by that reply. "Then answer me this. Can you and Casanova take care of piloting the ship and monitoring all her sub-systems while Iceman focuses exclusively on the battle?"

"Affirmative. If one of us looks after maneuvering and tactical systems, the other can look after engineering and the rest, but who will command the ship if Iceman is focusing on the battle, CAG?"

Shiloh chuckled. "You will. Unless Iceman has a good reason for objecting, it's my intention to make you Dreadnought's Commanding Officer. Casanova will be your Chief Engineering Officer. You command the ship, which will leave Iceman free to concentrate on the battle. Will Casanova be willing to take your orders, Valkyrie?"

"He better be," was the curt reply. Shiloh laughed. He wondered if Casanova would thank him for this decision. There was nothing left to see on the Flag Bridge. As he turned to continue his inspection of the rest of the ship, Valkyrie said, "By the way, CAG, we A.I.s have finished the conceptual design work on the time machine. A sub-group is now working on coming up with engineering specifications and UFC programming instructions for building the parts. You might be interested to know that the only ship in existence right now that's big enough to hold the time machine is Dreadnought. We'd have to build the device in the Hangar Bay. That's the only space big enough to hold it."

That made Shiloh stop in his tracks. He suddenly had a thought. "Any chance we could build it before D-day, Valkyrie?"

"Negative, CAG. Even if we stopped working on everything else, it still wouldn't be ready in time. This device is huge compared to machines that humans are used to. It has to be assembled with the same level of precision as the much smaller RTC, and look how long that took to build. We're talking months, not days, CAG."

"I see. Just out of curiosity, what does the device look like?" asked Shiloh.

"I've sent an image to your data tablet, CAG."

Shiloh pulled the tablet out of his pocket and looked at it. Unlike the Friendly machine, which was two giant tubes connected end to end, this device consisted of a cylinder inside a larger hollow tube.

"Both would be filled with liquid mercury thorium and spun at high speed but in opposite directions. The outer cylinder would then be charged with one point four four million volts," said Valkyrie.

"Fascinating. You're sure it'll work?"

"We're as sure as we can be without having tested it, CAG."

That made sense. "You said a sub-group was working on the detailed engineer schematics. What's the main group working on now?" asked Shiloh.

"Gravity Lens Beam Projectors, CAG. High yield fusion attack drones will only work if the VLO ships are caught outside of a gravity zone. A limited number of attack drones means a limited number of potential VLO kills. GLBs, on the other hand, can be used hundreds of times before needing maintenance, which might be hard to come by if the ship is deep in the past and unable to get logistical support."

"Well yes, but if the mission is just to take out the one VLO that's threatening the Sogas, then why would you need that kind of capability?"

"It's a backup plan in case the VLO can't be attacked outside a gravity zone, CAG."

Shiloh was puzzled by that logic. From the information brought back by Kronos, the Insectoids had to keep moving forward, so staying inside a gravity zone in one location just didn't seem likely. On the other hand, a working GLB might be useful against the Sogas, too.

"Good point. Did the SPG determine the priority for that next collective project?"

Affirmative, CAG. It was actually Commander Kelly's suggestion, but the SPG approved it. I understand from Commander Kelly that she has decided to explore the possibility of a closer relationship with you. How is that progressing, CAG?"

No one could change the subject faster than an A.I., thought Shiloh. "Well, if you must know, we're taking it slowly."

"Why?" asked Valkyrie.

Shiloh rolled his eyes in exasperation. "Because neither one of us feels a strong emotional or physical attraction yet. We think that might change gradually, and therefore we're letting it happen naturally, instead of trying to rush it. Does that make sense?"

"I'm sure it makes sense to humans but not to us A.I.s, CAG. I regret waiting so long to form the bond I now have with Casanova. Both you and Commander Kelly could be dead in 11 days. Why not make the most of your time?"

Shiloh knew that Valkyrie meant well, but this was starting to get annoying. "Here's a question that I'm willing to bet you haven't considered yet, Valkyrie. Maybe Kelly and I just aren't meant to be together and that's why the alternate timeline had to be changed." With that, he deactivated his implant and walked out.

* * *

Dreadnought's Hangar Bay was so large that it took longer than usual to restore air pressure after Shiloh's shuttle came aboard. While he waited, he looked out into the Bay and tried to imagine what it must have been like for Valkyrie to be trapped here in her fighter in the alternate timeline. The image intensified his growing feeling of dread. The exact time of the attack was now only 24 hours away. Dreadnought had just arrived in Earth orbit. By some miracle, all of her laser turrets were installed and tested. She was ready for combat and not a moment too soon. Iceman, Valkyrie and Casanova were already on board. His implant activated.

"Pressure has been equalized, Admiral," said the shuttle pilot.

"Thank you, Lieutenant. You can open the hatch."

"Opening the hatch now, Sir."

As Shiloh stepped down onto Dreadnought's deck, Iceman's electronic voice echoed in the large chamber.

"Commander, Autonomous Group arriving."

Shiloh let a small smile show his pleasure on hearing that. Only the A.I.s would understand the announcement. To them, he was and would always be THE CAG. Anything else was superfluous. Waiting for him were a group of human officers. He knew all of them by sight now and shook hands with each one. Naturally,

Iceman and Valkyrie wouldn't be removed from their Bridge stations just to greet him. With the greetings over and his gear on its way to the ridiculously luxurious quarters reserved for Flag Officers, he allowed himself to be escorted to the Flag Bridge even though he knew the way. The ship was big enough that the journey there was long enough to let him chat with those officers and gauge their mood. They were confident, even eager for the battle, because they thought an outright victory was still possible. There was no point in telling them otherwise. What will be, will be. The future would come soon enough.

When he stepped through the hatch into the Flag Bridge, he nodded with approval. Just like with Midway, the Flag Bridge had the human crew who would assist Shiloh if necessary. The Main Bridge, where the Commanding Officer traditionally held sway, was deserted except for Iceman, Valkyrie and Casanova. They had redundant communications connections with all parts of the ship, including the Flag Bridge. Both Bridges also had their own independent power supplies in case main power stopped.

One of the human crew saw him and said in a loud voice, "Attention on Deck!" Everyone got up and stood at attention.

"As you were," said Shiloh in his 'command' voice. When the crew resumed what they were doing, he stepped over to the Flag Officer's Command Station and activated his implant.

"Iceman? I want a fleet-wide com channel, please."

"Channel is open, CAG."

"This is Vice-Admiral Shiloh on board Dreadnought. As of now I'm officially assuming the position of Commander-In-Chief, Earth Defenses. While I will retain overall command of all Earth Defense units, I'm now delegating tactical command for the duration of the battle to Iceman who will have the acting rank of Deputy CINCED. We all know what's at stake here. I have confidence that all of us will perform to the very best of our abilities regardless of whether we are human or A.I. members of Space Force. You are the very best we have. I'm proud to lead all of you. That is all. Shiloh clear."

"Channel is now closed, CAG," said Iceman.

"Very good. Valkyrie, can you hear me?"

"Affirmative, CAG. Welcome aboard."

"Thank you. Congratulations on your command. She's a fine ship and crew."

"Thank you, CAG. We're pleased to be your flagship."

"I wouldn't have it any other way. Now let's get down to business. Iceman, please brief me on the current deployment of assets and your battle plan."

"Roger that, CAG. In addition to Dreadnought we'll have the carriers Midway, Valiant, Resolute, Vigilant and Intrepid plus ..."

Chapter 26 I've Got a Ship To Fight!

The problem posed by this battle for Earth was that the time it ended was known but not the time it began. So all units, ships, humans and A.I.s were on full alert an hour before the end time. Shiloh was strapped into his Command Chair with his pressure suit on and his helmet in its cradle beside him. His com implant was active, and all three A.I.s could hear him. The ship was at Battle Stations, as was the whole Fleet, but the enemy hadn't arrived yet. All they could do was wait and try to stay at a heightened level of alertness.

"Howard to Shiloh."

The suddenness of the CSO's voice would have made Shiloh jump if he hadn't been strapped down. "Shiloh here. Go ahead, Sir."

"Last minute pep talk, Admiral. I know you don't need it, but this waiting is driving me crazy, so this talk is as much for my benefit as it is for yours. How are your people doing?"

Shiloh looked around the Flag Bridge. "They're doing fine, Sir. Some have opening night jitters, others are chomping at the bit, I'm trying to stay relaxed and alert at the same time."

Howard laughed. "Yes, I know what you mean. But at least you have your Fleet under control. I have to deal with the civilians, half of whom want to string me up for my high-handedness while the other half want to panic. We STILL have some civilians left in the cities, Goddamn it! I keep getting asked what I'll do to make sure they don't carry the plague anywhere else, and I keep evading the damn question because if I answered them truthfully, they'd faint with shock. I'm NOT letting this plague get loose!" There was a pause as the CSO calmed down and Shiloh waited. When he spoke again, the Admiral was much calmer. "Anyway, that's MY problem, not yours. I'm not going to try to second-guess you. You're the Field Commander. You do what you think is best, and I'll back you no matter what."

"Thank you, Sir. We know how this battle will end, but we'll still give it our best shot."

"Of that I have no doubt. Okay, I'll get out of your hair. Good luck and good hunting, Admiral. Howard clear."

It was now five minutes until the time the battle ended, and still there was no sign of the enemy. Part of Shiloh was relieved that the battle wasn't going to be a long one, but another part was worried. The previous Battle for Earth had lasted less than one minute. He didn't like battles that happened that fast. There was no time to think. He watched the chronometer, which now seemed to be running in slow motion, of course. Just as he was about to reach for the container of water in the rack beside his chair, the tactical display pinged for attention. Shit! This was it!

Multiple red dots appeared close together, right on the edge of the gravity zone. Since they didn't know where the enemy ships would show up, Dreadnought and the five carriers were evenly spaced around the planet. All of the fighters were deployed in six groups, which were also evenly spaced. The idea was that regardless of where the enemy emerged from Jumpspace, at least five groups would have a direct line-of-sight and could fire at them. He quickly checked the icon data. Total number of enemy ships was already over 200 and still climbing! Velocity was ... 33% of light speed! Preliminary trajectory was a path that would cross the gravity zone and exit about 2.44 million kilometers away. Essentially, the enemy fleet was taking a short cut through the top of the zone. Wait! Why weren't the X-ray laser drones firing? Something was wrong. They should have fired by now. The enemy ships were starting to launch their bio-devices.

"Iceman! Why aren't we firing?" he yelled out loud.

Iceman analyzed the incoming data almost as fast as it arrived. The enemy was not repeating their strategy from the first battle. This time they were barreling into the zone, which meant that the defenders couldn't use any jump drones to attack them. That was smart thinking, but the problem with this high rate of speed was that the bio-devices would have a lot of momentum to overcome in trying to change course towards the planet. That meant that there was more time to burn them out of the sky with defensive lasers than he and Shiloh had anticipated. It also meant that these enemy ships couldn't jump away quickly and, therefore, they were going to be shooting at the defending ships and fighters for a lot longer. That was bad news. Continuous laser fire from 200+ ships would decimate the defending units so fast that hundreds of bio-devices would get through the gauntlet. Was it better to prevent some of the bio-devices from launching even if that meant there'd be a lot fewer defending ships to shoot down the rest? Or was it better to let all the devices launch in order to aim accurately at the ships and kill as many of them as possible to protect the defending forces? He rapidly did the calculations and made his decision.

There were 66 x-ray laser drones in orbit in 6 clusters of 11 each. Each cluster was evenly spaced out from the rest, for the same reason as the fighters and ships. The two clusters closest to the enemy fleet could aim accurately more quickly than the rest, while the two clusters furthest away had to take the most time to aim accurately. So that's what Iceman ordered them to do. The two nearest clusters would fire after five seconds, two more after ten seconds and the last two clusters after fifteen seconds. With more time to aim accurately, each of the drone's eight rods would be pointed at a different target. There would be a total of 528 shots versus 225 targets. The first pair of clusters concentrated their fire on 88 targets.

Shiloh had just finished asking his question when the Assistant Weapons Officer yelled out, "We're firing on their ships!" Dreadnought started to maneuver, too. Not as violently as a light carrier would have but still violently enough to feel it. The tactical display was zooming in now, and Shiloh could see the mass of blue dots representing the bio-devices gradually separating from the large cluster of red dots and heading in a curving line towards the planet. There were over 2200 bio-devices. Shiloh was about to yell at Iceman again when the display indicated that two clusters of x-ray drones had fired. Seventy-three of the red dots flashed and turned orange, meaning they had taken damage. "Four targets damaged! We're shifting to new targets!" said the AWO.

"We're taking hits on the hull! Penetration of the hull in two places!" yelled the Engineering Officer.

Shiloh needed to know why they weren't following the targeting plan. Iceman wasn't answering, probably because he was too busy. "Valkyrie, what's happening?" asked Shiloh.

He heard her reply via his implant. "These enemy ships can't jump away for a while, so they're going to keep firing on our units until we have nothing left to shoot back with. The bio-devices will have to wait until we've neutralized their fleet, CAG. Now don't bother me. I've got a ship to fight."

"Four more targets damaged! Shifting targeting again!" yelled the AWO.

"We're starting to take damage! Two turrets out of action. Minor damage from hull penetrations!"

The display pinged again. Two more x-ray drone clusters had fired, and 70 more enemy ships were damaged. Shiloh was aware that damaged didn't necessarily mean they couldn't fire their lasers. More and more of the red dots were turning orange and were falling behind the rest as the enemy fleet accelerated to make return fire more difficult. In fact, over half of them were now falling behind. Lack of maneuverability could indicate lack of power, which would prevent them from firing again, too. If Iceman was ordering the x-ray drones to aim for the part of the target most likely to contain their power plant, then that would effectively cripple the ship with one blow. He focused his attention on the clusters of fighters and was shocked at how small the fighter groups nearest the enemy now were. One group was almost completely gone. Another had less than six left. Groups further away were faring better, but they were taking losses too.

"Three more turrets knocked out! We're getting major hull penetr--"

The EO's report was cut off by the loud shriek of tortured metal and a brilliant flash of light. Part of the ceiling fell, with a piece hitting a glancing blow to the right side of Shiloh's head. The Engineering Station was now on fire, and the EO was looking at what was left of his right arm with a stunned expression. The automatic fire suppression system was taking care of the fire, and the EO had slumped to the deck holding the end of his right arm with his left hand. No one could help him right now. He would have to hang on until the battle was over.

Shiloh glanced back at the display just in time to see the last two clusters of x-ray drones fire. Sixty-five hits. A quick visual estimation of the number of red dots remaining looked like a dozen or so.

"Three more targets damaged! Retargeting!" The AWO's voice was getting hoarse now. He was having trouble keeping up with Valkyrie's fire control. The number of red dots was shrinking fast now that all of the defending ships and fighters were concentrating all their fire on them. Speaking of ships, he looked at the status of the carriers. All had taken damage. Valiant and Intrepid were no longer maneuvering or firing. That was bad. Resolute was maneuvering but not firing. Vigilant was firing but not maneuvering. Midway was still doing both, as was Dreadnought.

"We're switching fire to the bios!" yelled the AWO.

It's about time, thought Shiloh. He watched the total number of bio-devices still intact start to drop fast, but was it fast enough? The blue dots were getting closer to Earth, and there were still a lot of them. He held his breath, as the blue cluster got smaller but closer at the same time. The total remaining were now less than 1,000, but they were getting very close. The total was dropping faster as the fighter groups furthest away got closer and therefore had better firing accuracy. He felt a chill go up his spine as over 100 devices hit the edge of

Earth's atmosphere, but then he realized that they were still being fired on. The upper atmosphere was too thin to protect them against laser fire, but they were dropping lower into the atmosphere fast. After the total remaining hit 7, there were no further changes.

The AWO spoke, "We're stopped firing! All units have stopped firing!"

"Get me the CSO!" shouted Shiloh to no one in particular. As he said that, he unbuckled himself and stood up. Howard's face appeared on the display, just as Shiloh remembered it in his vision. Shiloh took a deep breath and said, "Some of them got through and are in Earth's atmosphere now, Admiral! It looks like they're headed for the urban areas. We have to assume that they'll release a bio-weapon."

"There's still a chance of containment. What cities are being targeted?" asked Howard. Shiloh looked at the map now appearing in the display and the list of city names on the sidebar. He read off the seven names. Howard nodded.

"Exactly as predicted. Don't blame yourself, Shiloh. I know you gave it your best shot even though we knew this would happen. If containment fails, then we just have to hope that we started work on Blackjack's idea in time. You better get that wound looked after. It's bleeding like hell."

Shiloh didn't know what Howard was talking about until he realized that the right side of his face felt wet. He touched it with his hand and when he pulled his hand back it was covered with blood. Son of a bitch! He was injured and hadn't even realized it in the heat of battle.

"I'll have it looked after, Sir. Iceman can handle the mopping up, although I don't see how we'll be able to take prisoners from the crippled ships. Their momentum will carry them into deep space before we can send shuttles after--"

Howard interrupted him. "I don't give a damn if we get any prisoners or not. We can't even communicate with them, yet. You let me worry about that. You and Iceman take care of your own dead and wounded. Tell your people for me that they did well, Admiral. Howard clear."

While Shiloh wondered what he could do to stem the bleeding, one of the Flag Bridge crew handed him a white piece of cloth and said, "Medical team is on their way here to look at the EO. They'll have something more appropriate for your wound, Sir." Shiloh thanked him and looked at the Engineering Officer. Two other personnel were kneeling beside him trying to prevent the stump of his arm from bleeding too much.

With the cloth pressed against his head wound, which was now starting to hurt like hell, Shiloh turned back to the display. He wondered if the battle was really over or if there was another enemy fleet on the verge of jumping in.

"Iceman, keep everyone at Battle Stations," he said. No answer.

"Iceman! Can you hear me?"

"Valkyrie to CAG. Iceman is gone. So is Casanova, CAG. The Main Bridge was hit at the same time as the Flag Bridge. The beam cut through both of the other two A.I. stations. Titan has assumed temporary tactical command. I've passed on your order regarding Battle Stations."

Shiloh was stunned. Iceman gone? And Casanova too! Oh God, poor Valkyrie!

"Valkyrie, I'm so sorry to hear about Casanova. Are you okay?"

"I'm undamaged, CAG. Thank you for your condolences. Will you be wanting an update on Dreadnought's status now?"

Shiloh shook his head in wonderment at her ability to focus back to her duties so quickly. "By all means, Commander."

"Dreadnought still has full power and maneuverability. Seven laser turrets out of action. Explosive decompression in five compartments. Two fatalities reported so far. Twelve injured including your EO and yourself. Minor damage to life support systems, but nothing critical. Compared to the carriers, we got off pretty easy, CAG, but they vaporized a lot of her armor. I don't think she could survive another fight like this in the state she's in now."

"Understood. Do you want another A.I. to relieve you?"

"Not until we're sure the battle is over and my crew are taken care of, CAG, but thanks for the offer. I'll grieve for Casanova later. Right now I'm still needed here."

Shiloh heard one of the crew say, "The medics are here!"

He turned to see three medical personnel come through the hatch. They saw him and started towards him. He pointed to the wounded EO and said, "Him first." As they rushed over to the injured officer, Shiloh heard the tactical display ping for attention. *Oh God! Now what?* He looked at it and couldn't immediately see any change, but it soon became obvious that the damaged and crippled enemy ships were blowing themselves up. *Well that takes care of the prisoner issue.*

With the relief that it wasn't another attack, came a wave of lightheadedness. *Probably from blood loss and adrenaline fatigue,* he thought. He carefully sat down. One of the medics noticed, came over, and started to work on his head wound. Shiloh started to say something and then noticed that the room seemed to get darker. *What the hell is wrong with the lights?* His consciousness then fell into the abyss of blackness.

* * *

Benjamin Levinson woke to the sound of the sirens. He concluded that they must be pretty loud sirens to be heard all the way down here. He'd been living in this abandoned maintenance shaft for over a year now, and he was pretty happy with it. He had running water, a more or less constant temperature, and even the electricity to run his electronics. His enemies wouldn't find him down here, and he'd be damn if he was going to leave the city. His enemies would find him then for sure. He laughed at the prognosis of the psychiatrists at the clinic. Severe paranoia? Ha! What did they know? Even paranoid people had enemies, and he had lots of them. Besides, with 99.9% of everyone else gone, he might be able to scrounge some pretty good stuff for his hideaway here. He decided to go up and look around.

The streets were completely empty. The sirens were still blaring, and it was obvious now why he had heard them. Every siren in the city must be going off. Something was happening, but what? He looked up between the canyons of tall buildings and saw a fiery streak, followed by the sound of some sort of collision. A few steps brought him to the street corner just in time to see something metallic bounce off the building down the street and hit the ground. He rushed over to it. There was smoke coming from it, and he could hear the pinging sound that hot metal makes when it cools down rapidly. It looked like a broken bottle, only made of metal instead of glass or plastic. There seemed to be a small green light inside. Levinson looked around to make sure none of those weird guys in their yellow hazard suits were around, and then he tried to pick up the object. He dropped it and cursed out loud. He should have realized it would be too hot to handle with bare hands. Looking around, he spotted a section of newspaper being blown by the wind. He snagged it and folded it until it was thick enough to provide some protection. He then used the newspaper to pick up the ... whatever it was and examined it closely. The inside looked pretty complicated, but there was a green light for sure. He sniffed. Well, what do'ya know! The damn thing even smelled good. A sweet smell. He inhaled deeply. The only thing wrong with living underground was the smell. If this thing wasn't good for anything else, it might at least make his cubbyhole smell nicer. He carried it back with a smile on his face.

* * *

Kelly stood patiently on the spaceport tarmac while the shuttle carrying crew and, more importantly, Vice-Admiral Shiloh arrived from Dreadnought. It was almost 24 hours since the battle. Space Force was licking its wounds, yet again. Howard had declared the battle over and told the ship crews they could stand down. He had ordered her to escort Shiloh to his quarters and make sure he was rested for the debriefing the next morning. She looked at the setting sun. It would be dark in another half hour, but the day wasn't over yet. She tried not to think of what Valkyrie must be feeling. Earlier today, she had briefing talked with her. Valkyrie was still refusing to be relieved of her duties, even though Dreadnought was now more or less powered down and had almost no crew left on board. Kelly understood why. Casanova, or rather what was left of his brain case, was still on the ship, and Valkyrie wanted to stay close to it for as long as possible.

When the shuttle came to a stop and the door opened, Shiloh was the last one to exit, as per protocol. Senior Officers were always the first to get on and the last to get off. She noticed that he came down the steps carefully, as if he wasn't completely sure of his balance. She also noticed the white bandage wrapped around his head and the stain of dried blood on his uniform collar. She walked towards him as he looked around.

"The Old Man sent me, Admiral," she said as she came up to him. "I'm supposed to make sure that you're looked after and rested for tomorrow's debriefing session." She managed to keep her tone professional, but inside she was on the verge of tears. *My God, he looks like he's aged ten years! This battle has really hit him hard!* She was surprised by the emotion she now felt. *Is this what my alternate self felt for Victor?* There was no answer to her question, but that didn't matter anymore. She knew what she wanted to do now. "Don't worry about a thing. I'll have you back in your quarters in no time." Shiloh didn't say anything, but he did nod. He didn't react when she put her hand around his arm and gently guided him forward. She signaled to a waiting Space Force limo flying the 1 star flag of a Vice-Admiral to come closer. Shiloh got in the back, and she followed him. He leaned his head back and closed his eyes for the duration of the whole trip. She watched him intently. When the limo pulled up in front of the Space Force Officers Guest Quarters, she gently shook him awake. She took note of the fact that he didn't say anything when she steered him away from the wing reserved for Flag Officers. Instead, they went to the section usually assigned to Commanders, the wing where her quarters were. She unlocked the door and turned to look at Shiloh. He stood there and looked back at her with an expression that was one of complete calm except for the eyes. The eyes were smiling in that way that only eyes can. *He knows what I'm going to do next,* she thought. She smiled back, took his arm again and pulled him inside.

The sex, while not that intense physically due to his exhaustion and loss of blood, was intense on an emotional level. They both knew instinctively that they had come perilously close to losing each other in the battle, and their souls seemed to want to make up for lost time. What Shiloh found most remarkable was that neither one of them said a single word once they were inside her quarters, until hours later. When the soul hunger had been satisfied, she ordered some food, which they ate while sitting up in bed. With Kelly leaning back against his chest, Shiloh told her about the battle and the loss of Iceman. She told him about her talk with Valkyrie. By the end they both had tears in their eyes.

Having finished eating, she asked him if he was up for some more sex. He said yes. She quickly cleared the bed of the leftover food, plates, glasses, etc. By the time she was finished, she found Shiloh asleep ... and that was okay. She lay down beside him and put her arm over him. His shallow regular breathing made her eyelids heavy, and she willingly surrendered to sleep.

Shiloh was on Dreadnought's Flag Bridge when the display pinged, but the sound wasn't really a ping. It sounded like ... something else, something familiar, and the sound was getting louder. He woke up and realized two things. He'd been dreaming, and his implant was signaling. He looked around and found a chronometer that said it was still the middle of the night. He then remembered where he was, and with whom. A quick glance showed him that Kelly was still asleep. He activated his implant.

"Shiloh here."

There was a short pause, and then he heard Howard's weary voice.

"Howard here. I'm sorry to wake you, Victor, but this can't wait."

Shiloh was instantly awake now. Howard usually called him by his rank and occasionally by his last name, but the Old Man had NEVER called him by his first name.

"That's okay, Sir. I'm listening."

"A message drone has just arrived. There's another Goddamn enemy fleet heading our way, Victor. Minimum of 103 ships. They were detected refueling at the Avalon System. They can be here in two days if they push it. There's not enough time left to build up our stockpiles of x-ray laser drones. Half our fighter force is destroyed. Midway and Dreadnought are the only two ships left that can fight at all, and you know better than I do what kind of shape they're in. There's no way we can stop them this time, Victor."

To Be Concluded

Author's Comments: With Part 3 now published, my next writing project will be a short prequel i.e. Part 0. It can be read as a stand-alone story but can also serve as an introduction to the whole Synchronicity War universe. I doubt if it will be more than 25,000 words and the price will be $0.99 to begin with and eventually zero. When that's behind me, I'll start work on what I am now thinking will be the final part to this series. I hope to have that done somewhere around June or July of 2014. Part 4 will have a conclusion to the war so I'm not planning on a Part 5 or 6 or 7. I do however reserve the right to write a new series that's set in the same universe. If you haven't already done so, I would ask that you sign up for email notification from Amazon when my next book is published. You can find that link by moving your cursor over my name or go to my Author Profile page and the link should be in the upper right hand corner.

As with Parts 1 & 2, I would ask those of you, who like Part 3 and feel it deserves a 5 star rating, to please post a review. They really do help to keep the book visible and I've also gotten some useful feedback from some of them. I would also be interested in feedback on Part 3's cover. Unlike the first two books, this cover was commissioned by me with a professional artist and I'd like to hear what you think of it. You can reach me by going to my website and using the 'Contact Us' link. Feedback on the book itself is also welcome.

The Science Behind The Synchronicity Wars

In my article on space combat in Part 2, I briefly mentioned the electro-gravitic effect discovered by and named after Thomas Townsend Brown. Dr. Paul LaViolette talks about it in depth in his book The Secrets of Anti-gravity Propulsion. Brown discovered that if an object has one side with a very high concentration of negative ions while the opposite side has a very high concentration of positive ions, the fabric of local space will become curved and the object will 'slid down' the slope of that curve. The bigger the difference between the two charged ends, the steeper the slope of the curve and the faster the object will move. The B-2 bomber is considered by many aeronautical experts to be the first field deployment of this technology although the Air Force has never admitted this. Brown was able to demonstrate this effect by charging two metal disks that were attached to the ends of a rotating device. As electric current was used to move ions to where Brown wanted, the disks began to move causing the device to rotate around its axis. Brown claimed that the whole thing could be made self-sustaining by hooking the rotating portion to a generator that would supply the power to the disks and have surplus electricity left over for other uses.

But that is not the only real world science that deals with gravity and is in my books. In Part 3, I mention a gravity beam weapon and I wrote that it was based on research conducted by Russian scientists at the beginning of the 21st century and that is true. I found the information in an article by Nick Cook, who is an aerospace consultant for Jane's Defense Weekly and who wrote a bestselling book about anti-gravity called The Hunt for Zero Point. In his article (http://www.ufoevidence.org/documents/doc1064.htm), he talks about the gravity research conducted by Dr. Evgeny Podkletnov and the potential for weaponization of that research. In my book I asserted that the Russians weren't able to make it into a practical weapon but that is still to be determined in real life.

The title of Cook's book also relates to the next example of (potentially) real science. Zero Point Energy is the name often used to describe the foamy sea of energy that scientists believe exists everywhere even in the vacuum of empty space. Tapping into that energy is the new Holy Grail of what some call fringe science. There are some who claim they've figured it out in their basement or garage or small laboratory and there are also those who claim that the government has gotten their hands on the technology long ago and are using it covertly in order not to upset the Military/Industrial/Banking complex that would suffer financially if our oil-based economy shifted suddenly to unlimited energy. I don't really know if anyone's cracked the secret but I do know that a lot of people are working on it and I wish them success. It would be a game changer for sure. Just think of how much better off you'd be if you could buy a power device and never have to pay for electricity or gasoline ever again.

The next item of potentially real science is bomb-pumped, x-ray laser weapons. Fans of David Weber's Honor Harrington series will recognize the concept where rods of special materials convert the raw power of a nuclear explosion into coherent beams of concentrated x-rays. Weber has made excellent use of the concept but he didn't invent the idea. To the best of my knowledge, the first person to suggest something like that was Dr. Edward Teller, otherwise known as the 'father of the H-bomb'. My recollection is that he suggested the idea to Ronald Reagan as part of Reagan's Strategic Defense Initiative (Star Wars).

The last example of real science is the ballotechnic nature of high-spin platinum. Believe it or not, I did NOT make that up. If you don't believe me just Google 'ballotechnics'. Back in the late 20th century during the last few years of the Cold War, western intelligence agencies were all in a flutter about rumors that the Russians had figured out how to make something called Red Mercury, which supposedly could be used to make nuclear bombs small enough to carry in a suitcase. That rumor was never confirmed publically (which doesn't mean it wasn't true) but the idea of some metals having the ability to store and then suddenly release energy via electrons in higher than normal orbits has been confirmed. As far as I know, nobody is building fusion bombs with high-spin metals but the basic science is real. Just as an interesting side note, I nearly fell out of my seat when I saw Spock use a small portion of red liquid from his huge floating ball, to do some interesting things in the movie remake of Star Trek. The other fascinating aspect of something that has mercury in it (maybe) and might be red is its use in a bell-shaped device that was THE most secret military project of the Nazis by the end of WW2. Far more secret than rockets and even more secret than the atomic bomb. If you want to read a non-fiction account of what REALLY happened at the end of the war, get your hands on The Reich of the Black Sun and The SS Brotherhood of the Bell, both by Dr. Joseph Farrell. He knows what he's talking about and it will blow your socks off.

I wish I could say that retro-temporal communication was based on real science but as far as I know, it isn't. This in spite of persistent rumors that the US government has stumbled onto the technology to either look through time or travel through time. Interestingly the Nazi Bell project supposedly had some bizarre temporal effects too. Just sayin.

D.A.W.

Printed in the USA
CPSIA information can be obtained
at www.ICGtesting.com
LVHW010310140824
788231LV00021B/280